'Tough little thing, aren't you?' Katie said, delivering another hard smack across the seat of Paige's now red bottom cheeks. 'Let's see if you're so tough when I use my crop, shall we?'

The response was a soft whimper, but Paige made no move to stop her as Katie retrieved her riding crop from where she'd hung it on a broken branch. Paige was looking back, her big eyes wide with fright, her flesh trembling, but still she stayed in position, even as Katie lifted the crop. It felt good, delightfully cruel, to have her friend so obedient and so eager to accept pain.

'This is going to hurt,' Katie warned, but Paige merely nodded.

Katie brought the crop down, slashing it hard across the full fat width of Paige's bottom, to wring a scream from her friend's lips and leave a long white line across the reddened flesh that quickly coloured up to a rich purple. Paige was whimpering badly and shaking her head, obviously in pain, which filled Katie with sadistic glee.

'Another?' she asked. 'Come on, ask for it.'

Paige let out a single bitter sob before speaking. 'Whip me, Katie . . . if you want to . . . whip me.'

'Do you want it?' Katie demanded.

'Yes,' Paige sobbed, and Katie brought the crop down a second time, harder than before.

MOST BUXOM

Aishling Morgan

nexus

First published in 2007 by
Nexus
Thames Wharf Studios
Rainville Rd
London W6 9HA

A catalogue record for this book is available from the
British Library.

www.nexus-books.com

Typeset by TW Typesetting, Plymouth, Devon

Penguin Random House is committed to a sustainable future for
our business, our readers and our planet. This book is made from
Forest Stewardship Council® certified paper.

MIX
Paper | Supporting
responsible forestry
FSC® C018179

Printed and bound in Great Britain by Clays Ltd, Elcograf S.p.A.

ISBN 978 0 352 34121 1

The Voyeur

Her bra came loose and her breasts came free, as round and plump and bouncy as those Daniel was used to seeing in his more fevered dreams. Each one was a fat cream-coloured ball of girl flesh, so big he could barely have cupped it in two hands, and topped with a large slightly puffy nipple. She was pretty too, and young, which made her exposure all the more thrilling, but the true ecstasy came from his knowledge that she had no idea whatsoever that he was watching her.

She stepped out of view and Daniel moved back from the telescope, closing his eyes so he could once again picture her abundant beauty. His cock was hard in his pants and his muscles ached from holding the same position so long, but it had been worth it, *well* worth it, just for that fleeting glimpse of mammary magnificence. For weeks he'd been hoping she'd take her bra off, and for weeks she'd gone through the same ritual of removing her blouse, washing her hands and splashing a little water on to her face before applying a towel, putting her blouse back on and returning to the office. Even that had been too much for him, so that no amount of masturbation could get her out of his head, but to see her bare breasts was pure heaven, leaving him dizzy with excitement as he once more pressed his eye to the telescope.

His hand had started to shake, making the image shimmer in the hot air between her office block and his rooftop vantage. She was still invisible, but her blouse and bra hung on the back of the door, so he knew she hadn't left the tiny bathroom. That could only mean she was in the cubicle, and as he continued to watch his mind swam with images of her seated on the toilet, her lovely big breasts bare, her smart office skirt rucked up, her panties around her ankles as she did her business. He wondered what sort of panties she'd have on, perhaps black and lacy like her bra. Yes, she looked like the sort of girl who'd wear matching bra and panties, always neat and tidy.

Daniel reached for one of his sandwiches and put it to his mouth, never once removing his eye from the telescope. She was taking rather a long time, while it seemed odd to have taken her bra off just to go to the loo. He wondered if she'd done it on purpose, not just because the day was so hot, as he'd supposed, but because she wanted to be bare. Perhaps she wasn't using the loo for its proper purpose at all. Perhaps she'd gone into the cubicle to masturbate, panties down and legs open while she rubbed her pussy and played with her nipples.

As she came back, he crammed the last of his sandwich into his mouth and gave his full attention to the window, now with his heart hammering in his chest. Her breasts were fully visible, pushing out round and proud from her chest as she looked into the mirror, then lolling forwards as she bent to the sink. Daniel swallowed hard and fought the temptation to take out his cock and finish himself off then and there. But, as she cupped a hand to splash water into her cleavage, it became too much. One tug and his fly was down, a second and his cock was free, thrusting up from his pants as he began to tug furiously at his shaft.

The girl was washing her breasts, holding each up in turn to dab water beneath, making them jiggle and bringing her nipples to full erection as she touched them. It was turning her on too, he was sure, as she closed her eyes and took one chubby globe in each hand, her fingers spread to hold them, excess flesh still spilling over the top. She stopped after just a moment, her eyes open once more and her painted mouth moving briefly into a sweet naughty smile at her own behaviour, but she was still bare, still flaunting her magnificent chest, only now on tiptoe, admiring herself in the mirror with a critical eye as she held her breasts up for inspection.

Daniel came in his hand, unable to stop himself any more than he could fight down the overwhelming guilt that hit him the instant he finished. As he cleaned up with frantic haste, he was telling himself he'd never do it again, and in his head he was apologising over and over to the unsuspecting girl he'd violated with his eyes. His shame was almost unbearable, an emotion as strong as his lust as he'd watched her undress and masturbated as she washed her breasts.

The sense of danger was no longer a thrill either. The little nook among the leaded roofs seemed horribly exposed and as he put his things away he was sure that somebody would come out and catch him. Nobody did, and he quickly concealed his telescope and stand in the false bottom of his briefcase, leaving him once more just another office worker taking his lunch in the sunshine of the London rooftops.

He finished his sandwich, all the while telling himself it would be the last time, and that he'd never peep at a girl again, but he knew it was a lie, and he still found it impossible not to throw the occasional glance at the big office block where she worked. It was hard to see much without the telescope, but he saw that she'd left the washroom and returned to her desk a few windows away, in an office where she and two other young women spent their time at computers and talking on their telephones. He'd never been able to figure out what she actually did, but it was probably not so very different from his own job docketing parking-fine disputes.

Back at his desk, he found it impossible to keep his mind on his work, his thoughts shuttling back and forth between his ecstasy at having seen the girl's bare breasts and his guilt at having peeped at her. Part of him wanted to make amends, although he knew full well that he lacked the courage to confess his sin to her, or to anyone else, while he knew he would be back on the roof soon enough. Briefly he considered sending her a present, anonymously of course, maybe some flowers with a little note of apology on a card, only to dismiss the idea as impractical. He didn't know her name, or which company she worked for, and he could hardly address it to 'the girl with the gorgeous tits'.

By three o'clock, he had decided that in an attempt at atonement he would file a case relating to a woman called Lola Balabanova as appeal accepted. He had no idea whether Lola Balabanova had large breasts or not, but she sounded as if she did. By four o'clock he'd decided to file Mollie Ryan's case as accepted too, just to be on the safe side. By five o'clock, he'd been called into the line manager's office and given a formal written warning.

The Rider

Katie smiled at the piece of paper in her hand. West Hants might not be Oxford or Cambridge, but it *was* a university, and in some of the best riding country in England. Just as long as Daddy was decent about finding stabling for Achilles, she could look forward to three idyllic years, while French and Philosophy was sure to be a breeze. West Hants was big enough to ensure she met the right sort of people too; not that people really mattered, so long as she had Achilles.

Tossing the acceptance slip down on her dressing table, she bounced on to her bed, where she lay back, imagining what life would be like. It would certainly be very different from school. Rather than the endless, tedious lessons at Roegate, she would be able to attend lectures when she pleased, visit the library when she pleased, work as late as she pleased and get up as late as she pleased. There would be no compulsory hockey either, or athletics, or swimming, or any of the other irritating sports activities she'd always tried so hard to avoid but always ended up getting dragged into. Of course, there'd be no Tia either.

Her smile faded to a little frown of vexation at the thought. Now that Tia's parents had gone back to Trinidad, it would be a very long time until they saw each other again, and she had no illusions about their relationship, which would never be the same again. How could it be, when they were longer at Roegate, and yet it was a shame. Unable to stop herself, she let her mind wander back to the beginning of the summer, with their A levels over and done with and nothing to do but be together, at school and in the countryside around.

She closed her eyes, thinking back to the moment when she'd finally plucked up enough courage to touch Tia's cheek as they lay together, drinking a stolen bottle of wine in the long grass of the river meadow. Her heart was hammering, her fear of rejection like a physical plug in her throat. There was no rejection: Tia's response was immediate, and electric.

Katie sighed as she remembered the excitement of the encounter, and the wonderful details; how good Tia's mouth tasted as they kissed, the feel of her friend's full firm breasts, the giggling delight when she had her own still bigger chest pulled out from her blouse. That had only been the start, the urgent, clumsy fumbling as they opened each other's clothes, each eager to explore, and hurried guilty orgasms beneath each other's fingers.

The later encounters had been better, so much better: long, loving kisses stolen at every opportunity; hands down each other's knickers in the changing rooms one sultry afternoon; the sweet ecstatic moment when she'd found the courage to put her mouth to her friend's sex; and, last, that perfect moment, drunk and dirty in her study while the rest of the school were in church, when she held her bottom wide for Tia to pucker up and kiss her anus.

A shiver passed through Katie's body at the memory. She closed her eyes, no longer in her bedroom at all, but back at school in Tia's arms, a moment now lost for ever, and, even as her hand pushed down the front of her panties to masturbate, the tears began to well up in her eyes.

The Domina

Olivia slid her foot into the boot, encasing her leg in soft black leather all the way up to the top of her thigh. The sensation was even better than she had imagined, and went far beyond the physical. She felt empowered, stronger and taller, far more confident. If was as if she had put on armour, to become at once protected and a frank expression of the person she was inside, free and openly, unashamedly erotic.

'How much are they?' she asked.

'Two hundred and forty,' the assistant replied.

Olivia's heart sank. It was far, far more than she could possibly afford, but she struggled to keep her disappointment from showing as she pulled the second boot on. Even if she wasn't going to buy them, she had to be in them, just for a moment.

'You look good,' the assistant assured her. 'Let me do the laces up and you'll look great.'

Unable to resist the offer, Olivia extended one leather-clad leg. It was a position she had imagined herself in so often, seated comfortably while a man knelt at her feet, or a woman for that matter. Maybe he was only trying to sell her the boots, but it still felt good, as if she was being served, and as he pulled the cross-lacing into the hooks it was easy to let her imagination run. He would be at her feet for real, begging for her lightest touch or even a word of approval. He would be completely in thrall to her, her slightest whim the law, her needs his most earnest desires. He would worship her, counting it a privilege to lace her boots, to put the slender metal heel in his mouth, to kiss the ground on which she walked. He would spend his life at her feet, his body constantly at her disposal, to serve her and to please her, and perhaps, if he was very, very good, she might even

7

allow him the supreme privilege of applying his tongue to her sex.

'How does that feel?' he asked, shattering her erotic reverie.

'Great,' she admitted, and stood up.

It was a little difficult to balance on the four-inch spike heels, which were much higher than she was used to, but she did her best to strike a pose in the mirror, extending one leg forwards and lifting her chin. The strappy top and yellow summer skirt didn't really work, but her legs looked great, in fact, perfect. She had to have the boots, even if it meant living on stale bread and water for the whole of her first term at West Hants. Anyway, what use was a student loan if you didn't spend it?

'I'll take them,' she said, struggling to sound casual.

'Black or red?' he asked.

'Black,' she said firmly.

Ten minutes later, she left the shop with the precious boots in a bag and an uncomfortably large hole in her bank balance. Nor was that the only problem. If her parents found out she'd bought a pair of thigh-high leather boots, they'd lose the plot. Worse, they'd want to know why, and, while she could pretend it was only a fashion statement, she was pretty sure that her mum at least would see through her.

She would have to hide them, carefully, and once she was at uni she could dress up in them and imagine herself as the object of worship for some grovelling male slave. Maybe she could even make fantasy reality, either with a boyfriend or, perhaps better still, with an older man, somebody who really understood where she was coming from and who would want to buy her more gear. In fact, that was essential, because she had nothing to go with the boots, except perhaps lacy black underwear, which wouldn't allow her to express her true dominance.

What she needed was a pair of leather shorts, so small and tight they fitted her hips like a second skin and made her bottom a fitting object of worship for her slave. She'd have a matching top as well, which would have to be tailor made, as otherwise it would be impossible to find anything to display her breasts properly. That was the trouble with being big on top, she could rarely find bras to hold herself in, let alone to fit snugly around her back at the same time.

She was smiling as she thought of how she'd look, and how her hypothetical lover would grovel at her feet. All she needed was to find the right man.

The Clown

The man's eyes looked as if they were about to pop out of his head as Holly hooked her thumbs into her bra cups. She stopped dancing, looking down at him, her mouth curved into a deliberately mocking smile.

He reached up, stuffing a pair of damp badly creased ten-pound notes into her garter belt as he spoke, his voice little more than a lust-filled croak. 'Go on, love, get 'em out. You've got the best ... you've got the biggest ...'

'I know,' Holly answered, and turned her back on him as she began to dance once more, walking away across the stage with a taunting sway of her hips.

On the far side, two men were staring up at her, their eyes fixed on the tiny triangle of blue cloth which covered her pussy, while a third appeared disinterested, sipping his drink as he talked to his

companions. He was no more or less attractive than
the others, a typical punter, middle-aged and well
dressed, although he had no money in his hand, or on
the bar in front of him. Holly moved close, strutting
forwards step by step until she stood directly in front
of him. He finally seemed to notice her, looking up
just in time to receive the full weight of her tits in his
face as she flopped them from her bra.

Holly jumped back, laughing, as he made a grab
for her, and when the manager gave her a warning
look from across the room she merely stuck her
tongue out. Keeping her back firmly to the man who
was so desperate to see her topless, she quickly
adjusted her bra, once more covering her nipples
before turning and shaking her chest at him.

He immediately thrust out two more ten-pound
notes, but kept hold of them as she came close,
speaking once more. 'You want your money, love,
you get 'em out. Come on, stop being a tease, I want
to see them. You showed *him*, and he didn't even pay
you!'

The man next to him reached up, slipping a
five-pound note into Holly's garter. She turned to
him, smiling, and cupped her breasts in her hands,
pushing the fat chocolate-coloured globes out to
within an inch of his face. He blew his breath out, his
eyes wide in admiration as she gave him a jiggle,
allowing the little bump where one nipple pushed up
the material of her bra to rub ever so briefly against
his nose.

'You fucking prick tease!' the other man growled.
'Come on, get them out. I want to see those tits,
darling, right now. Here's fifty.'

Holly gave him an arch look and once more turned
away, strutting back across the stage to collect
another note from a young Japanese man, who she

treated to a wiggle of both bottom and boobs before turning away.

The first man now looked angry, thrusting two fifty-pound notes towards her as she moved close, and his voice now a rasp as he spoke. 'Stop fucking teasing me!' he demanded.

He pushed the notes at her, but Holly stayed as she was, swaying her hips to the rhythm of the music.

'I can buy you,' he hissed, adding a third note to the other two, 'any time I want to.'

'I don't think so,' Holly teased, and leant forwards, cupping her breasts in her hands to show off how big they were.

'Come on,' he urged, 'out with them, right now.'

'Say please,' Holly taunted, squatting down to bounce her breasts within a few inches of his face.

'Fuck that,' he answered. 'I'm buying you, and you do as you're told. Now get them out like you're paid to.'

He'd added another note to his bundle, but Holly merely bounced to her feet and walked away once more. The young Japanese man was now watching as one of the waitresses served a customer, with the back of her knickers and a good deal of bare bottom cheek showing beneath the hem of her tiny skirt as she bent down. Holly moved close and squatted down to jiggle her breasts against the side of his face and quickly step back before he could react. He reacted with a grin and pushed another note into her garter.

'Get over here, you black tart!' the first man called, thrusting out his money.

Holly turned, smiled, swung herself around the pole and came down on one knee directly in front of him. He was red in the face, sweating profusely, the notes in his hand damp with perspiration.

'Two hundred pounds,' he drawled, holding up the money. 'Now fucking get 'em out.'

'OK,' Holly said sweetly, took the money, tucked it into her garter and threw the full contents of his drink into his face.

The manager and one of the doormen were already coming towards her. They didn't look best pleased, but it didn't matter any more. Within three weeks, she would be at West Hants University, and after working all summer at the strip bar she had enough money in the bank to see her through her first year.

The Innocent

Paige glanced back across the heads of the crowd towards the stage. The roadies had gone, leaving it empty, and if she didn't hurry she was going to miss the opening. To judge by the queue of girls in front of her, she'd not only miss the opening, but also spend half the concert watching from the toilet queue. She was also beginning to feel distinctly uncomfortable, her thighs pressed tight together and her toes wiggling in her sandals as she fought against the ever increasing pressure in her bladder. The hedge behind the row of chemical toilets was beginning to look inviting.

If she used it, she'd have to squat down to pee in front of maybe three thousand people, but, then again, they weren't looking at her, they were looking at the stage. Besides, why would anybody want to watch her pee? It was ridiculous to feel embarrassed. Nobody would mind, not the sort of people who went to outdoor festivals. They'd be much too cool. They probably wouldn't even notice.

They'd certainly notice if she wet herself, which was what was going to happen if she waited much longer, and, as she was wearing pale tight jeans, she knew the stain would show just as badly as it possibly could. No, the only sensible thing to do was to go in the hedge.

She was still blushing as she left the queue and scampered quickly in behind the line of toilets. A lot of people could still see her, women and men too, but it was now a question of whether they watched her pee in the grass or wet her jeans. There was no shelter either, the hedge thick and thorny, with a long row of nettles growing beneath, into which she had no intention of sticking her bare bottom.

There only remained the choice of whether to show them her bum or her fanny. Her bum was best. Who would worry about seeing a bare bum, and who could be dirty enough to want to watch a girl pee anyway? Still she hesitated, but as her bladder tightened in pain she was wrestling with the buckle of her belt, and treading her feet in her desperation as she fought to get her jeans and knickers down all at once.

Her blush had grown hotter still as her bottom came bare, but there was no stopping herself. Sinking into a squat, she grabbed her jeans and knickers to stop them getting wet and let go with a long sigh of relief as the pee squirted from her fanny. Even as it began to come out, she heard the first laugh, then a man calling to his friends to watch. Her face flared crimson, but there was nothing she could do, her pee gushing out in a powerful stream, leaving her no option but to hold her pose until she was done.

'Couldn't hold it?' A girl laughed, followed by a male voice, much louder.

'Do it tits out, babe, I've got my camera!'

Paige jerked around, mouth open in shock, just in time to hear the click of the man's digital camera pointed right at her bare bum. At the same instant, she lost her balance, and rolled backwards, sending a fountain of pee high in the air and showing off her open fanny as the man took a second picture.

There was nothing she could do, save lie there and let the rest of her pee come out, before struggling back into her knickers as fast as she possibly could. The man was still taking pictures as she wriggled her bottom into her jeans, and she knew that her face was the colour of beetroot. There were one or two sympathetic voices, but most of her audience seemed to think what had happened to her was funny, and as soon as she was covered up she ran.

Quite a few of the men in the crowd seemed to think that what she'd done was sexually provocative, more than one of them making lewd remarks, generally about the size of her breasts or the way they bounced as she ran. One man even propositioned her, asking if she liked her cleavage fucked, which set her face alight with embarrassment and made her run all the faster in her desperation to escape their attention.

Only when she was deep in the crowd did she stop, sure that none of the people around her could have witnessed her humiliation. She was still blushing, and it was impossible to get the image of how she must have looked out of her head, rolled on her back like an overturned beetle with the pee gushing from her open fanny in full view of at least a hundred onlookers. She hadn't expected them to be so rude either, but as the concert started she was consoling herself with the thought that in a few weeks she'd be at West Hants University, in the company of sensible intelligent people rather than a bunch of perverts.

Daniel

Daniel put his biro down. The numbers added up – just. If he sold his flat and moved to a cheaper area, he would have enough money left over to live on the interest and whatever he could get in rent at his new place. That meant no more work, no more endless forms, no more management, no more feeling bad because he was helping squeeze money out of some stressed-out mother who'd parked for thirty seconds longer than she was allowed to while trying to control three children and a dog.

It was feasible, and he had to do it.

There was another reason too. The day before he had taken his usual rooftop lunch, and set up his folding telescope in the hope of catching the girl from across the road as she washed. But it had gone badly wrong. Just before lunchtime one of his colleagues had stopped by his desk to ask a question and he'd been late out on to the roof. As he climbed into his usual hiding place, he saw his busty beauty was already in the bathroom, and by ill luck she was looking out of the window. He realised too late, and he was sure she'd seen him. The afternoon had been spent in guilty terror, sure she would come over to make a complaint and imagining hideously embarrassing scenes in which his telescope was discovered and he was exposed as a Peeping Tom in front of the entire office.

It had to stop, but he knew full well he lacked the willpower. She was too tempting, her breasts, now glimpsed, too glorious to be ignored, unless he took himself well away from temptation. That was only possible by resigning his job and putting his scheme into operation. It was what he wanted to do, what he'd been thinking about for years, but he had never plucked up the courage to act.

Now he was determined, but he knew that, if he didn't do it immediately, he never would. Doubts were already beginning to grow in his mind as he typed out his letter of resignation, but he forced himself to go on, to write the envelope, place the stamp on it and post it on his way to the estate agent's. It was a hot day, the best of August weather, and the high street was full of scantily clad girls, drawing his eyes to well-filled trouser seats and bulging T-shirts, tiny skirts that hinted at the possibility of a flash of panties, the enticing little bumps made by stiff nipples beneath thin cotton.

By the time he got to the estate agent's, his cock was hard in his pants and he was in an agony of embarrassment, yet still his eyes followed the sweetly rotating rump of a young mother as she pushed her pram, her cheeks clearly outlined beneath lightweight white casuals, apparently pantiless, or at most in a thong. To make matters worse, all three of the staff in the estate agent's were women, dressed in crisp white blouses, their top buttons undone against the heat, providing teasing glimpses of soft pink cleavage as they went about their work.

Daniel very nearly left, but one of the girls asked to help him before his courage could fail him completely and he found himself trapped. She was smart, brisk and had quite a full chest for her petite figure, the sort of woman who could overawe him completely without even being aware she was doing it. From the moment she began to speak, he was in thrall, stammering out his explanations and agreeing with everything she said.

Once he'd begun, he could no more have backed out than he could have made the raging erection in his pants go soft. She took the specifications of his flat and put him on the firm's books. She contacted several other branches and had details of the sort of property she felt he might want faxed through. She discussed mortgages and insurance and a dozen other things, all the while with Daniel goggling like a goldfish and trying desperately to keep his eyes off the creamy slices of breast flesh that showed between the edges of her blouse every time she moved.

By the time he left, he had already put his signature on several documents and made an offer on a house in Silbury.

Two weeks later, Daniel had moved. The new house, Number 47 Myrtle Road, was pretty much as he had imagined it, a plain red-brick suburban semi in a long street of others much the same. There was enough parking for two cars at the front and a small garden at the rear, backing on to open farmland. No other houses were visible from the back, to his mingled relief and disappointment, as he knew full well he would have been unable to resist the opportunity for spying on any female neighbours there might have been.

A young lime tree in the street obscured what view there might have been from the front, making him feel positively virtuous, but he selected the back room as his own, it being the largest in the house. The previous owner had also taken lodgers, and very little work needed to be done. There were three other rooms on the first floor, all much the same size, a bathroom newly tiled in black and white check and a tiny loo. Downstairs was the kitchen, one large room and one smaller, which he decided to use as a community room and a fourth bedroom respectively. There was also a large clean loft, ideal for storage.

After a frantic week of internet shopping, DIY stores and flat-pack construction, he had all the furnishings he needed. After walking into town, he placed adverts in several shop windows and on the appropriate notice board at the university. It was another hot day, and as always his eyes were drawn to the girls, an impressive feast of breasts and bottoms. By the time he got back, he was so stiff that there was nothing for it but to log on to his favourite internet site for sneaky peeks and upskirt pictures.

Five minutes after the first picture came up, he had come in his hand and was telling himself he would be sure to select four of the ugliest, shyest men he could find as lodgers. That way he could keep the temptations of female flesh to an absolute minimum.

The next day, he had to shop, and took the opportunity to explore Silbury, which proved to be a typical market town, with an ancient centre surrounded by a belt of suburban sprawl built up over the previous hundred years. A pretty river ran through a belt of parkland with a fine large church on a low rise to one side, a view somewhat spoilt by the stark orange-tiled roofs and garish signs of the town supermarket beyond. The park's other views were rather better, as the bright sunshine seemed to have brought out an extraordinary number of girls, presumably students, and many of them seemed either unaware of or unconcerned by what they were showing.

A brief stroll by the river while he ate a lunchtime sandwich provided him with the vista of one girl sunbathing in a blue bikini so brief and so tight it displayed almost the full glory of her well-shaped bottom; another with no bra to hold in a pair of round, heavy breasts beneath her red and white striped top; a third cycling in a pair of jeans shorts so snug it seemed her pert little bum cheeks must burst free at any instant; and a pair of delightful little poppets in skirts so brief and so light it would only have taken the slightest breeze to have them providing a free panty show for him and every other male in the park.

By the time he reached the far side, he had an erection that felt fit to burst, and he was forced to stand outside a newsagent and read the headlines in the *Guardian* until he once more went limp. Only then did he continue on his way, peering idly into the shop windows and trying to ignore the display of feminine delights all around him. It wasn't easy, but, when he reached a shop specialising in camera equipment, it became impossible.

Most of the display was given over to the latest ranges of digital cameras, but the side of one window showed a selection of sports cameras, although the sports they were designed for were not those that came to Daniel's mind. Some were too hi-tech and too expensive for him, but some of the simpler and cheaper ones were tempting in the extreme. One in particular caught his eye, an optical pick-up housed in a tube no larger than a wine cork and attached to a compact digital recording unit by a thin wire. It was all too easy to see how the Microcam, as it was called, could be used or, rather, abused, because there was no question in his mind that the whole thing was wrong. Nevertheless, he told himself, there was no real harm in speculating. It would be easy to convert a briefcase to hold the system, with the lens almost invisible among the folds of leather and pointed upwards and at an angle. That way, he would be able to take upskirt pictures as good as any on the net and with next to no risk.

Had he had the device ready, his recent stroll through the park would have been not merely titillating, but actually thrilling. He had passed within a foot of the two little poppets in miniskirts, and they hadn't seemed to notice his existence, much less regard him as suspicious. With the briefcase he could have taken a whole series of pictures, looking right up their skirts and they would have been none the wiser.

The results could hardly have failed to be exquisite, two sweet young bottoms straining in cotton panties, or maybe little camel-toe cunts where the material had pulled up into their slits. Maybe they'd have been in sports knickers, bottle green or navy blue, encased chubby young bottom cheeks, so firm and juicy it made him feel faint just to think about it. More likely they'd have been wearing thongs, leaving their luscious little bottoms to all intents and purposes bare, with every detail of their beautiful kissable cheeks on display. Just possibly they'd have had no knickers on at all, delighting in the knowledge that their cheeky little bottoms and sweetly turned pussies were naked, never once suspecting that they'd given a man an eyeful. Yes, that was best, no knickers at all, and with any luck he might manage a snap of perfectly formed little cunt lips, maybe even shaved, or better still, dirtier still, more intrusive still, their tight little rosebud bumholes.

His cock felt like a iron bar within his pants, but he told himself firmly that he was not going to buy the camera, or any of the others that held out similar possibilities for spying on unsuspecting girls. Instead, he would continue down the road to the supermarket, where he would buy his dinner, some groceries and a few of the things he would need for the house. Forcing himself away from the window, he managed to follow his plan, distracted only by a particularly busty black girl who quite obviously wasn't wearing a bra under a top at least two sizes too small for her massive breasts, and had a pair of extraordinarily prominent nipples.

It was no better in the supermarket. The place seemed to be entirely full of women and, while he knew, rationally, that they were simply going about their daily business, both their clothes and their postures seemed deliberately provocative. One little popsy at the fruit display was bending forwards in such a way that her bottom was pushed out into the seat of her bright-red trousers to make a ball just the same shape as one of the apples she was selecting. Another had her midriff bare and a top so tight it seemed as if her well-formed breasts had been painted blue. Even the pretty young Indian girl at the checkout had her blouse far enough undone to afford him an enticing glimpse of honey-coloured cleavage, and he left the store feeling painfully aroused.

Only his heavy shopping bags and a major effort of will prevented him from going into the camera shop, but there was nothing he could do to keep the dirty pictures out of his brain. Going back across the park only made it worse. The girl sunbathing was as before, her pert bottom still uppermost, but she had undone the strap of her bikini bra and was propped up on her elbows so that she could read a book. As he passed, he caught the briefest of glimpses of one breast, in profile, hanging down with a small pink nipple just visible at the tip.

His cock hadn't gone down, and as he reached the narrow path between the churchyard and the river the urge to simply whip it out and jerk himself off then and there was close to overwhelming, held down only by his embarrassment and fear of authority. The streets beyond were relatively empty, at least of pretty girls showing off their bodies, and he reached Myrtle

Road without further incident and with his cock at least partially deflated.

As he started up the road, a brilliant-red BMW Mini passed him, a cabriolet model driven by a young girl in a red summer dress, looking impossibly cool in a pair of reflective shades as her long honey-blonde hair moved to the breeze. She was driving slowly, and he caught only the briefest impression of a well-endowed chest before he looked away, fearful she might notice his attention. If she did, she gave no sign of it, apparently intent on scanning the house numbers, and stopped directly outside Number 47.

Daniel was still well down the road, but his mouth had come open in surprise and alarm as he saw her pull up outside the house, parked diagonally so that her car took up the entire space. She climbed out and he swallowed involuntarily. Her chest was every bit as impressive as he had suspected, and the light dress clung to her contours, showing off the shape of full firm breasts, a lean waist and elegant hips, while it was so short that almost the full length of her bare legs showed, long and exquisitely shapely.

'Not a girl like that,' he mumbled to himself as he approached, 'not as a lodger, please. I couldn't stop myself.'

She had gone to ring the bell, and when there was no immediate response her expression shifted to disapproval, as if it was unthinkable that nobody was there to greet her. Again she rang, then gave a little shrug of annoyance for a world that evidently failed to meet her standards.

Daniel was now close and managed a weak smile, wondering what he could say to put her off if she did turn out to be looking for accommodation. She ignored him completely.

'Er . . . hi,' he managed. 'Were you looking for me?'

The glance she turned on him suggested that she'd rather be looking for slugs, but as he stepped around her Mini she gave a carefree laugh, implying such utter contempt he found himself blushing, then she spoke. 'Oh, you're the landlord. I thought you were some horrid little man trying to make a pass.'

Daniel felt himself shrink inside, metaphorically, and in the case of his cock, literally. Her accent was pure county, exactly the sort which had always made him feel so desperately inferior, and he found himself blushing and stammering as he replied.

'I – I'm the landlord, yes ... that is, I own the house, er –'

'Well, open the door then,' she interrupted him.

'Yes – yes, of course,' he answered, hurrying to obey.

As he put down the shopping, one of the bags spilt its contents on to the ground. She paid no attention at all, and yet Daniel found himself blushing redder still, convinced that she now thought of him not only as a 'horrid little man', but also a clumsy fool. The key didn't want to turn either, and he could feel the back of his neck prickling at her icy disdain as he struggled to open the door. When it finally opened he found himself holding it for her, and there was no mistaking the tone of her 'thank you' as she stepped inside. He might have been the owner, but as far as she was concerned he was nothing more than a servant.

Daniel went back out to retrieve his shopping, before returning just in time to follow her down the corridor into the community room. Her dress was loose and lightweight cotton, so that as she walked it clung to the contours of her well-fleshed and apparently muscular bottom. She didn't seem to have any panties on either, or she was in the most minuscule of thongs, a thought that left him weak as he followed.

'Aren't you going to put your shopping away?' she asked as he came in behind her.

It was a dismissal, and Daniel accepted it as such, disappearing into the kitchen. He already knew he lacked the willpower to turn her down if she decided to take a room, also the courage to answer her back. She represented everything that made him feel inferior, her very existence a taunt to both him as a person and to his masculinity. Obviously, she didn't want him around either, and he began to make himself a coffee, only to stop as he realised it would be rude not to offer her one.

'Aren't you going to show me around then?' she asked from directly behind him.

Daniel started so violently he spilt the sugar he'd been spooning into his cup, leaving him too tongue tied to do more than mumble incoherently as he tried to reply. She waited, with what seemed to him more contempt than patience, until he finally managed to speak.

'Yes – yes, of course. Do you want a coffee?'

'No thank you,' she answered.

Daniel felt himself wither at the rejection. 'I – er, I won't have one either then,' he found himself saying. 'I'll, er – I'll show you the upstairs, shall I?'

He could not resist gesturing that she should go first, despite the guilt raging in his head at why he wanted her to. The stairs were steep, her dress was very short indeed and he really, really wanted to know if she had panties on or not. He was sure she would guess his intentions too, but she went ahead, apparently as oblivious to his gaze as if he'd been a dog, which was exactly how he felt.

His heart was thumping in his chest as she mounted the steep narrow staircase, and he followed, red faced with guilt and lust and embarrassment as he stole a sneaky upwards glance, to find himself staring directly up her dress. He could see more than he had possibly hoped for, the full glorious length of her legs, smooth and shapely and perfectly feminine, and the tuck of two firm athletic bottom cheeks between which he caught the faintest hint of white thong panties.

He looked quickly away, sure she would notice and dreading what she would say, no doubt some caustic little put-down that would leave him feeling not so much like a dog as like a worm. If she'd realised what she was showing, or that he'd looked, she gave no sign whatsoever, as she trotted quickly up the stairs.

Daniel hung back as she inspected the rooms, without comment until she came to the big one at the back, his own.

'That one's mine, I'm afraid,' he managed, but she took no notice, walking across to the window, where she stopped, staring out over the fields.

'This one will do,' she said.

'But it's –' Daniel began.

'What are you asking?' she cut in.

'Three hundred,' he said, 'a month, but –'

'Hold on,' she said, and Daniel went quiet.

She had taken a mobile phone from the small red clasp bag she was holding, and turned her body half away from him as she pushed a number into it and lifted it to her mouth. Daniel found himself staring at the shape of her discreetly painted lips as she spoke into the phone and looked quickly away, telling himself he'd insist she chose another room as soon as she'd finished her call.

'Daddy?' she said after a moment. 'Oh never mind your silly meeting. I've found myself a room. Yes, a shared house . . . only three hundred a month, and it's only five minutes away from Greymartens. I can see the chimneys from my window. OK, I will. OK . . . Oh, just some man. I think he wants this room himself though, so can I go up a bit? Three-twenty? OK. I love you, kiss, kiss.'

She closed her phone and put it away before turning back to Daniel.

'I'll take it for three hundred and twenty,' she said. 'Be a lamb and bring my things up, would you?'

'Um,' Daniel began, but as she finished speaking she smiled, and his entire body seemed to melt and he found himself hurrying to do her bidding.

As he left the room, he was apologising for the mess in which he'd left his things, and on the way downstairs he was telling himself that the extra twenty pounds a month was well worth giving up his room for, although deep down he knew he was being pathetic. That didn't stop him carrying her things up for her, or moving his own into the room at the front.

He had left his telescope out, and he was convinced she'd realise what it implied, but once again she said nothing. Not that she needed to, with his imagination working overtime to flesh out her scorn and disgust at him for being a Peeping Tom. When he was done, she rewarded him with another casual 'thank you' and closed the door firmly behind him, leaving him standing in the passage. She hadn't even troubled to introduce herself, or ask his name.

Katie

Finally allowing her exhaustion to get the better of her, Katie kicked her shoes off and flopped down on the bed. It had been a long day, first the seventy-mile drive, then registration and all the social and bureaucratic business at the university, then choosing a suitable stable for Achilles, before finally sorting out her accommodation. Now it was done, and she could relax, or at least she would be able to once she'd had a shower and put on a fresh pair of knickers.

She got up again, stretching in the warm afternoon sunlight now streaming in through the window before peeling her dress off. Her bra was getting uncomfortable so she took that off too, leaving herself naked but for her panties as she dug her robe and sponge bag out of her luggage, along with shampoo, conditioner and soap. As she pushed down her panties to go fully nude, it briefly occurred to her that she should have made sure the landlord had provided proper facilities for laundry, but it seemed ridiculous to assume there wouldn't be at least the basics.

After pulling on her robe, she bundled her bra and panties together and headed for the bathroom. One advantage of her room was that it was at the far end of the passage, so she wouldn't be disturbed by other people showering or using the loo. It was a decent bathroom too. A large bath ran right across one end with a shower unit above it, all apparently quite new and decorated with black and white tiles. There was plenty of cupboard space too, although the mirror on the unit above the sink was rather small and there was no laundry basket. Frowning slightly, she poked her head out of the bathroom, from where she could see into the landlord's room. He was setting up a computer at his desk, but turned as soon as he saw her.

'What do we do about laundry?' she asked, holding out her bra and panties.

He seemed to suffer from some sort of minor speech impediment, but she waited patiently and he finally managed to get the words out. 'I don't know,' he said. 'I suppose there must be a laundrette somewhere. I only moved in two days ago myself.'

'A laundrette?' Katie asked. 'Don't you have a washing machine?'

'Well . . . no,' he admitted.

'A laundry basket?' she queried, wondering if he was actually mentally deficient.

'Um, no. I . . . er . . . I'll go and buy one.'

'Good idea.'

'Yes, of course. I'm, er . . . Daniel, by the way.'

'Thank you, Daniel.'

'Er, may I ask your name too?'

'Katie Shalstone. Now, if you could put these in a bag or something.'

She handed him her bra and knickers, which he took as if she'd just passed him something dangerous. As she closed the bathroom door on him, she was smiling to herself. He was pretty well completely clueless, but seemed happy to do as he was told, which was really ideal. One of her worries about university life had been that there wouldn't be any servants, and it would be very useful indeed if he would make up for the deficiency, at least in part. Otherwise, things like laundry, refuse and housework were likely to be a nuisance.

As she shrugged her robe from her shoulders, she put the landlord out of her mind. The air in the bathroom was pleasantly warm, making her feel drowsy as she stepped into the shower. It felt good to be naked too, and better still with the cool water cascading down over her body. She began to soap herself, enjoying the slippery sensation on her skin and the hardness of the soap bar on her flesh.

Being in the shower brought back memories too, of holding back after games so that she and Tia would be last into the changing rooms, and last out. It had always been risky, but that had been half the fun, and more than once they had allowed their hands to stray to each other's body while some of the other girls were still getting changed, out of sight but just yards away. Not that it really mattered, when half the school knew what was going on, or at least suspected, but it was one thing to have people whispering about them and quite another to be caught soaping each other's breasts in the changing-room showers.

She began to rub the bar of soap over her own, remembering how it had felt to let Tia take her breasts in hand, at once such a delightful sensation and so naughty. Tia had a little trick of gently pulling out Katie's nipples until they were achingly hard and then flicking the tight little buds with her fingernails. It had stung, a delicious tingling pain, but was easily bearable because it had turned her on so much. But it wasn't as if Tia had been bullying her, because they'd always taken turns; and, if Tia had sometimes liked to be a little rough, she had also wanted to kiss Katie's bottom hole, and done it.

The memory sent a powerful shiver through her, and she began to masturbate, closing her eyes as her fingers moved over her wet skin, stimulating her neck and breasts, her belly and bottom, all the while imagining it was Tia doing it, and fighting down her sense of regret and loss even as she began to caress her sex. Not that she was going to let her sadness stop her. The memories of Tia were the best she had, and turned her on far more than anything else.

Katie adjusted the shower a little and sat down in the bath, cocking one leg over the side to spread her pussy to the water, so that it was splashing down on her breasts and belly and thighs, which brought back the memory of what Tia had suggested just before

29

they parted. It had never happened, partly because, it would have been so risky they'd never had the chance, and partly because while the idea turned both of them on, it had been too naughty to actually go through with. Tia had wanted them to pee on each other.

Now masturbating with hurried dabbing motions to her puffy slippery sex, Katie shut her eyes. She could feel the hot droplets of water spattering her naked body, and it was easy to imagine Tia standing over her, giggling in delight as she let go her pee. It would have surely felt much the same, hot and wet on her bare breasts and the swell of her belly, trickling down between her cheeks to form a pool under her bottom, splashing beneath her busy fingers as she brought herself to orgasm at their exquisite outrageous behaviour.

Katie came with a long deep sigh, her back arched to the water from the shower and her finger busy between her pussy lips as wave after wave of pleasure swept over her. Only with the last did her sense of regret well up once more, and as she let her body go slowly limp she was promising herself that, if there was a next time, she would do what she wanted to do without holding back.

Olivia

As she scanned the advertisements for student accommodation, Olivia was feeling increasingly desperate. She'd been right to decide against living in a hall, with the rent at ninety pounds per week, but she'd been wrong in assuming she could pick up some cheap rooms in the town. As it was, even if she took the cheapest room available, she would be in financial difficulty long before the end of term.

For a brief moment she even regretted purchasing the assortment of electronic gadgets, clothes and implements she'd fallen for, even her thigh boots, the tight black leather shorts and top set that fitted her like a second skin, her spiked collar, her whip. The spending spree had left her with rather less than half the money she would otherwise have had, which would probably mean she had to find work.

From what she'd learnt, there seemed to be fabulous sums available, just for dressing up in black leather and laying a whip across some old fart's scrawny backside. What she needed was somebody to beat, preferably the local MP. She'd have preferred to lay her whip across some young stud's muscular backside, but an old fart would do so long as he made a decent sugar daddy and didn't expect anything intimate from her. Unfortunately, she had no idea how to go about it.

London would have been a different matter, or any other decent-sized city. Silbury looked far too small to offer anything more than the most basic line in sugar daddies. It also seemed all too likely that she'd get caught, and while the authorities at West Hants had a liberal reputation she was fairly sure they'd draw the line at students thrashing dirty old men for money, or not for money for that matter. In any case, she could hardly hope to find a suitable man in the course of the afternoon, and she needed accommodation more or less immediately.

Feeling somewhat lost, she went back to studying the board, but re-reading the advertisements didn't make the rooms they advertised any cheaper. She began to think about ringing her parents, only to immediately dismiss the idea. They'd only try to help, and she knew that they could no more afford it than she could. She would just have to find somewhere, and pray she could either find herself a job or a man who enjoyed a good thrashing before she got in trouble with the bank.

She moved a little to one side to let another girl get closer to the board, a black girl with her hair in canary-yellow beads and an expression of casual confidence and strength. They exchanged sympathetic smiles and Olivia went back to reading the notices. Most of the landlords seemed to want deposits, sometimes as much as three months' rent paid in advance, which was another thorn in the side. Of those who didn't mention deposits, the cheapest wanted three hundred pounds a month. As she began to copy the details down, the black girl spoke to her.

'D'you reckon that one?'

'It seems cheap,' Olivia replied. 'Cheaper than most anyway, and he doesn't mention a deposit.'

The black girl nodded and began to copy the details down. Olivia wrote a little faster. The other girl laughed and Olivia found herself grinning.

'I spent all my money on gear,' she explained. 'I need that room!'

'You get first choice, OK?' the black girl offered. 'How about we go up together?'

'Great, thanks. What course are you on?'

'Architecture. OK, so where's Myrtle Road? I'm Holly, by the way.'

'Olivia.'

Daniel

Sitting on his bed at 47 Myrtle Road, Daniel was desperately trying to tell himself that he was not going to masturbate in Katie Shalstone's underwear. It was not easy, despite having hastily thrust both bra and panties into a plastic bag. He'd held them, tiny white thong panties which had carried a hint of girl sweat and ripe pussy and a bra ample enough to cup her firm well-grown breasts. The urge to wrap the panties around his cock and jerk off into the bra cups was so strong it had his cock hard, his balls aching and his skin prickling with need. Only the thought of her disgust and contempt held him back, and yet even that was beginning to seem erotic.

It was all too easy to imagine himself doing it in front of her, kneeling nude on the floor at her feet as he tugged furiously at his dirty little cock, with her looking down at him, sneering. She'd be in the little white bathrobe she'd been wearing, so short it almost showed her bottom, and he knew she'd been nude underneath. Maybe she'd even take pity on him and open it, allowing him a glimpse of her perfect golden body as he spunked up in his own hand like the pathetic grovelling little worm he was.

Daniel's hand was reaching for the plastic bag when the doorbell went. He hurried to answer it, his hands shaking so badly he was fumbling at the door knob for several seconds before he could get it open. As it swung wide, he was praying he'd find a male student standing outside, some spotty computer type whose presence would allow him to keep a little pride, but as he saw his visitor his heart sank. It was a girl, perhaps not exactly the sort of girl who populated his fantasies, but close enough.

Her face was soft and sweet, with large hazel eyes looking out from beneath a fringe of glossy brown hair. An upturned nose and a small firm mouth added to her look, sweet and innocent yet also resolute, while a pair of large round glasses added an intellectual touch, creating just the sort of face he liked to imagine sticking his cock into during his rare moments of sexual aggression. Her body didn't help either, plump yet firm, an abundance of ultra-feminine flesh set off artlessly by tight low-cut jeans and a top that had never been designed to hold her outsize breasts.

'Er . . . hello?' she said, as Daniel realised he had been gaping like a fish. 'I came about your advertisement, for student rooms.'

'Oh, er . . . yes,' Daniel stammered, trying to will himself to tell her he was already full but failing. 'Come on in.'

He held the door for her, his eyes following her movement, his still-hard cock twitching as he caught a delicate floral scent, and again as she started down the passage. She had the most magnificent bottom, and his eyes were glued to the sway of her hips and the soft jiggle of her cheeks as she walked, so that he had to remind himself to close the door before he followed.

She had sat down, and was looking around wide-eyed, as if the completely ordinary community room was somehow extraordinary. Daniel struggled to think of a good reason for rejecting her as he too sat down. Otherwise, with Katie already installed in the house, he could look forward to a future of guilty sneaky peeks and yet guiltier masturbation.

'Um . . . didn't you get a place in hall then?' he asked.

'I'm really just looking for somewhere quiet,' she said. 'The halls are so noisy, and this guy in the second year was desperate for a room, so I said he could have mine.'

'Oh. That was kind of you.'

'I don't mind. I'm Paige, by the way.'

'Daniel. Don't you mind being so far away from the university then?'

'It's not far at all. I've got a bicycle anyway.'

'Oh, right,' Daniel answered, trying not to imagine how her bottom would look balanced on a bicycle seat . . . and failing. 'The rent is three hundred per month. I hope that's not too much.'

'It seems a bit less than most people are asking,' she said, 'and, of course, there's no deposit, which helps. There isn't a deposit, is there?'

'Deposit?' Daniel queried, and was about to invent one when Katie's plummy aristocratic voice spoke from behind him.

'Hi, I'm Katie. You're going to take the room, aren't you?'

Neither Paige nor Daniel managed to speak again before Katie continued.

'The rent is fair, and there's a wonderful view. Daniel here needs a little domestication, but otherwise it's great. Do you ride?'

'Occasionally,' Paige said. 'I used to belong to a pony club . . .'

'Wonderful!' Katie cut in. 'There's a stable just up the road, Greymartens, where my Achilles is boarding. They've plenty of other horses.'

'I'm not sure I can afford –' Paige began, only to be interrupted once more.

'You'll put your fees on my account, silly. Daddy won't mind. He's always saying I should go with somebody else. He's so protective.' Katie laughed.

Paige responded with a shy smile, and Daniel knew he had lost. He also felt as if he wasn't there, with the two girls entirely absorbed in their conversation. Katie offered to show Paige around the house and he was left on his own in the community room, feeling sorry for himself, although at least his erection had gone down, which always seemed to happen in Katie's presence.

Olivia and Holly

'This is it,' Holly said as they reached Number 47. 'I wonder who's got the Mini?'

'The landlord, I suppose,' Olivia replied. 'I don't suppose a student could afford it.'

Holly shrugged and rang the bell. A moment later it was opened by a blonde girl no older than herself, who spoke immediately.

'Hi, are you looking for rooms?'

'Yeah,' Holly said. 'Is it your house?'

'Oh no,' the girl answered. 'I'm a student, Katie. Come on in.'

'Is the landlord around?' Olivia asked.

'I think he's gone to find a laundrette or something,' Katie said, 'but don't worry about him. The rooms are three hundred a month, and there's no deposit. Go for it, and we'll make it an all-girls house, shall we?'

Holly followed Olivia into the house. Katie seemed to be just the sort of girl Holly had always hated, and envied, rich and spoilt; yet it was impossible not to respond to friendliness, and as they began to look around the house it took a conscious effort to hold her own instead of instantly accepting what the blonde girl evidently considered the natural order of things. A shared glance with Olivia showed that her new friend felt much the same, but there was no denying that the house was just what she'd been hoping for. Ten minutes after arriving, they'd decided to take the two remaining rooms and accepted Katie's offer of a lift in her Mini to fetch their things.

Daniel

As he lay on his bed, staring at the ceiling, Daniel was wondering if he could survive the year, or at least if he could keep out of prison for that long. The presence of the four girls in his house had driven him to a state of guilty erotic turmoil unsurpassed in a lifetime full of the same. Each one was a torment in her own way, and during his frequent and fevered sessions of masturbation over the previous two days his main difficulty had been deciding which girl to come over.

Katie spoke directly to his sense of social inferiority. Her effortless confidence, her easy condescension, the way she so obviously barely even noticed the money she spent – everything about her made him feel small and unimportant, even without taking her exquisite body into account. Full, golden skinned and golden haired, she was as he had always imagined the goddess Aphrodite, or possibly Athena. She was not only unimaginably beautiful, but also aloof and unapproachable. She treated him as if he was a servant, and to his immense chagrin he found himself not only obeying her, but actually being grateful for the opportunity.

Olivia was very nearly as bad, because, while she treated him with a haughty superiority, she did at least seem to be aware of his existence as a human being. She had even flirted with him, after a fashion, suggesting that he'd look good naked but for a pinny when he'd taken the bins out the night before. Her looks were also enticing – long dark hair and creamy skin, with shapely legs and breasts that might very well have come out of some erotic cartoon – while, if her poise seemed a little contrived next to Katie's, it still made him want to grovel.

Holly just made him want to run away, although she turned him on every bit as much as the others did. She was always laughing and full of life, but she seemed to consider the entire male sex a rather bad joke, himself very obviously included. He found her bold unabashed manner intimidating, just as he did her dark skin and full proud face, and the way her breasts thrust out from her chest was enough to make him weak at the knees. She was also the only one who didn't defer to Katie, which made her more awesome still.

Last was Paige, who was quiet, shy and always deferred to everybody, himself included. Despite that, he found both her voluptuous body and her intellect intimidating. They had played chess and she had beaten him with ease, much to the amusement of the other girls, while she seemed to consider Balzac and Proust to come under the heading of light reading.

All four filled him with so much lust and guilt that he lived in a constant state of sexual frustration and agonising shame, which was getting worse by the day. Led by Katie and Olivia, all four girls were now in the habit of giving him their dirty clothes to be taken to the laundrette, including their underwear, which they seemed to get through at an extraordinary rate. Each evening he had been to the laundrette, exchanging the frustration of their company for the equally poignant agonies of watching their panties and bras go round and round in the wash.

He already knew their preferences in underwear. Katie wore only designer labels, thong panties from the best-known names and bras handmade to fit from some company in Knightsbridge. Olivia liked black, especially satin, and preferred full-cut panties and bras that provided plenty of support for her breasts. Holly seemed to have matching sets of everything, all of them brightly coloured, and she wore her panties so that the back showed above the hem of her jeans. Paige had simple tastes, sensible bras and full-cut plain white panties, which to Daniel's fevered imagination seemed like school knickers.

There would have to be another trip to the launderette that evening as well, the large wicker basket he had purchased for their clothes already close to overflowing. He had a fairly good idea what was in it too, including the jodhpurs Katie and Paige had worn to go riding early that morning and the brilliant-green thong panties which had been peeping provocatively over the back of Holly's jeans the day before. Only the fact that the basket was in the bathroom and at least one of the girls had been in the house all the previous day had allowed him to prevent himself from selecting some item of girlish underwear to masturbate with.

He'd even dreamt about them, imagining himself peeping on Paige as she sunbathed in the garden and getting caught, which had caused him to wake covered in sweat, so embarrassed his face seemed to be on fire, and with a raging erection. It wouldn't go down either, and he knew it would show underneath his dressing gown if he went out to the loo. Katie was still in the house and sure to come upstairs at exactly the wrong moment, so with a last frustrated sob he took himself in hand and began to imagine her undressing after her ride.

She'd been in her jodhpurs, and as soon as she'd come in she'd gone straight up to the bathroom. He'd watched from the corner of his eye as she mounted the stairs, her full bottom encased in tan-coloured corduroy, so tight she might as well have been bare. Better still, she'd bent briefly, allowing him a glimpse of the enticing bulge where her jodhpurs covered her pussy, so tight the outline was clearly visible, and all the more so for a harp-shaped mark where her sweat had soaked through ... and perhaps something more.

The thought of his goddess juicing with excitement as she rode was almost too much, at once an exquisite thrill and so inappropriate for him to think about that he paused for a moment before starting to masturbate again. He could imagine her in the bathroom all too easily. First, she'd have locked the door to be sure of keeping out his prying male eyes, before removing her black leather riding boots. Then she'd have stripped, stark naked, her thumbs in the waistband of her jodhpurs and panties, pushing them down to display her glorious bottom, full and nude. As she bent to pull it all off her feet, she'd have been showing the rear view of her cunt, an angle Daniel had always enjoyed, and she'd have been naked from the waist down as she began to unbutton her blouse, with her bottom cheeks peeping out from beneath the hem, another of his favourite poses for a woman.

He began to writhe on the bed as he imagined her undoing her blouse, one button at a time, exposing her deep pink cleavage, the lace of her bra where the cups joined, the gentle swell of her belly. Off it would come and she'd be in just her bra, which she'd undo, unclipping it, then lifting her cups from her heavy breasts to expose both beautiful globes to his eager gaze, fat and round and glistening with sweat, her big puffy nipples sticking up hard and suckable.

The thought of Katie's nipples was too much, and Daniel came with a groan of mingled ecstasy and guilt.

Katie

Daniel would have been surprised at how shallow Katie's air of nonchalance was as she swung her legs into her car. Despite her best efforts, life at university was not going as she had hoped. All had seemed to be going well, until she found herself sharing a house with a girl who looked, and acted, in a way painfully similar to Tia.

Holly Williams was so like Tia they might have stepped from the same mould, with the same smooth chocolate-brown skin, the same bold assertive face and the same half-playful, half-mocking manner. Their figures were similar as well, and if anything Holly was rather fuller and more womanly. Only one major difference existed, in that, while Tia had been the daughter of a senior diplomat, Holly appeared to come from a housing estate in some ghastly suburb of Birmingham.

As she drove in towards the university, she was trying to fight down her own reactions, which were deeply humiliating. It was quite obvious that Holly disliked her, or at the very least was antagonistic towards her because they came from such different backgrounds. Yet, instead of dismissing the little oik, Katie found herself wanting to make it up, to be friends, even if it meant subordinating herself. And why not? After all, she and Tia had hated each other for over three years before finally giving in to their true feelings. Perhaps it would be the same with

Holly. Perhaps one day they'd be friends, or even more than friends. Maybe she would be permitted to get down on her knees and lick Holly to ecstasy, or pucker up as Holly's full dark bottom was pushed out into her face for that exquisite gesture of intimacy and submission, a kiss on another girl's anus.

Katie slammed the brakes on and parked, absolutely furious with herself for allowing her thoughts to stray in that direction. It was all very well with Tia, but to think of doing such a thing with some common little brat was truly appalling. Yet it was impossible to entirely deny her need, and she found herself both grateful and sad that the black girl's tastes undoubtedly ran to muscular young thugs of her own social class rather than other girls.

Paige

The lecturer's words were a drone, his explanation of Derrida and deconstructionism long familiar. Still Paige struggled to make herself concentrate, partly from a sense of duty, but mainly because she did not want to think about her feelings. It just wasn't fair that she should suffer the same impulses which had troubled her at sixth-form college, but there seemed to be nothing she could do about it. She had a crush on Katie Shalstone.

It was a part of her she had always found embarrassing, and which she had time and again told herself she would soon grow out of; yet the moment she met a woman of a certain type she found herself with that same sense of longing and worship, even though she knew it was entirely irrational. It had been the same with Laura Brown and Alice Maxted, both girls with the confidence and physical prowess Paige found so lacking in herself; fortunately, both girls had barely been aware of her existence.

Unfortunately, the same could not be said of Katie Shalstone, who not only lived in the room next door to her but also seemed determined they should be friends. Already Paige felt beholden, after riding that morning, during which Katie had simply put everything on her father's account. It had been fun too, there was no denying that, but long before they got back she'd begun to feel those all-too-familiar feelings.

She wasn't sure exactly what she wanted to do, except that it involved subjugating herself to Katie, physically, and perhaps even sexually. Already she had done most of the work with the horses after they returned, and volunteered to polish Katie's riding boots. As she knelt on a piece of newspaper and rubbed away at the smooth black leather, she told herself it was only fair after Katie had treated her to everything, but she knew it was a lie. She was polishing Katie's boots because she *wanted* to polish Katie's boots.

Daniel

As he stood in the aisle of Electromart, Daniel considered the various makes of washing machines on display. They didn't seem all that expensive, and the only way he could see of not disgracing himself, while the idea of actually being caught masturbating into the girls' panties and bras didn't bear thinking about.

He had more or less decided which one to have, but needed to ask several questions about installation before making his purchase. All the assistants seemed to be busy, and his half-hearted attempts to catch their attention had failed utterly. Telling himself he would wait until one of them was free, be began to wander around the store, first looking at the toasters, then the televisions, and then the computers, none of which he intended to buy.

Before long, he found himself in the camera department, looking at an identical display to the one in the shop in town, only with everything marked down by twenty per cent. Sure that anybody who caught him looking would know exactly what was going through his mind, he stepped away, only to freeze as a silky voice spoke directly behind him.

'May I help you at all, sir? The range is reduced for this week only.'

Daniel turned to find the only female assistant in the shop, a tiny Indian girl with her hair in braids. She was looking at him with a bright smile as he struggled to find an excuse for his behaviour.

'I, um . . . I own a student house,' he stammered, 'a house where students stay, and I was thinking of some sort of camera, to prevent burglars, naturally, not to – to look at –'

'A wise decision,' she broke in. 'I was always leaving windows open when I was a student. I recommend this dummy unit, placed in a conspicuous location at the front of the house as a deterrent, and then this all-functions compact system, which comes with two miniature cameras, twenty metres of wire, a dual DVD capable of storing . . .'

She went on, describing the benefits of the system as Daniel desperately tried to think of a reason *not* to purchase the awful thing, which was perfectly designed for snooping on girls.

Half-an-hour later, he left Electromart, having purchased both the dummy camera and the surveillance system, a washing machine and a tumble dryer, complete with comprehensive five-year insurance for all the items, which were due to be delivered the following day.

Olivia

Moving her pen slowly down the paper, Olivia considered her finances. Just as long as there were no disasters, she could manage for a month, which hopefully gave her enough time to sort out an alternative source of income. Not that she intended to flip burgers on the minimum wage, not when she knew she could earn ten or even a hundred times more doing what she yearned for anyway.

The problem was getting off the ground and, once she had done so, keeping it secret. Obviously, she wouldn't be able to bring her clients back to the house. Not that her housemates weren't OK, especially Holly, who had worked as a stripper and been sacked from half the men's clubs in Birmingham. Holly was cool, and would understand, but the others were a different matter. They were nice enough, but Olivia could easily imagine Katie's sneering response to any suggestion of sex work, while Paige would undoubtedly be shocked, perhaps so shocked she'd go to the university authorities.

Everything had to be strictly private, which meant making her contacts on the net under an assumed name, and with luck she could find some clients in Silbury, or near by. Meanwhile, there was always practice. She was smiling as she rose from the bed and locked the door. None of the others had come back yet, which was ideal.

Burrowing into the space below the lowest level of her chest of drawers, she pulled out her thigh boots, shorts and top, which she laid out on the bed. Her fingers were trembling as she began to undress, the twin thrills of the illicit and the erotic already rising within her as she thought of the transformation she was about to undergo. Naked but for socks and knickers, first she pulled on her shorts, encasing her bottom and belly and hips in soft tight black leather. Her top followed, providing the same delightful feeling for her breasts, which felt fuller and more sensitive. Last came her boots, tugged up her thighs one after the other to leave her four inches taller and feeling wonderfully strong and sexual.

She took out her whip and arranged her pillows on the bed, smiling at her own behaviour as she struck a pose and began to flick at the smooth white surfaces. Even that felt satisfying, even though she knew it would be the merest shadow of how it would be to give a man's buttocks the same cruel treatment. She began to strike harder, leaving lines across the pillows with each blow, and to strut back and forth across the room, all the while admiring herself in the mirror and imagining what she would say to her victim.

It was fun, but she felt a little silly and stopped after a while, wishing she had a real man to beat. Even the landlord would do. In fact, he would do quite well, because while he was fairly good looking he was also a wimp, and no doubt just the sort who'd benefit from a well-welted backside. It was only a pity that he was sure to run screaming to the university authorities at the first sign of kinky behaviour, otherwise she might have had an excellent way to reduce her rent, or perhaps abolish it altogether.

She pushed the thought away, knowing it was far too risky, and instead turned to admire herself in the mirror. There was no doubt that she looked the part, as good as any of the dominas she'd seen in magazines, and better than most. She definitely had the figure for it, womanly yet elegant, the way dominant women were drawn in cartoons. And, as the cartoons were drawn by submissive men, that was presumably the ideal – most cartoons, anyway, because she had recently seen some on the net that showed women with tiny waists but enormous yet perfectly formed bottoms and breasts, like Holly or Paige, only more so.

In most of the pictures, the women had been sitting on the faces of small scrawny men, which was presumably how the artist liked to see himself. One or two had been ruder still, and more fascinating, with the man being whipped, or dressed up in a ridiculous frilly parody of female clothing. It was easy to imagine herself in a similar situation, with the man naked on the floor, his buttocks whipped, his cock hard with excitement as she sat her leather-clad bottom into his face.

Naturally, she would keep her shorts on, because to do it nude would be far too intimate, far too great a privilege for him. As it was, it would probably make him come. And, while she liked the magnificently excessive anatomy of the girls in the cartoons, it was satisfying to know that if she did it at least there wouldn't be a risk of breaking the poor sod's neck.

She turned away from the mirror, feeling rather pleased with herself but also horny and frustrated. The restrictions of society annoyed her, and yet she was very much aware of them, including the potential for hypocrisy among the sort of men she hoped to get as clients, who she imagined as the sort who would preach family values in public while indulging their perversions in private. That made it all the more fun to whip them. They deserved it.

As she sat down on the bed, Olivia already knew she was going to masturbate. She felt no guilt, and no more than a twinge of concern for her housemates. Her body was hers to do with as she pleased; and Holly at least, she suspected, would be more likely to ask to borrow her vibrator than anything.

The little silver device was in her bedside drawer, handy for the slow climax she liked to take when she went to bed, and also for sudden emergencies. She took it out and propped a pillow against the wall, lying back with her legs splayed wide, perhaps not the most dignified of positions, but one she enjoyed. It made her feel open, even with her shorts on, and it would have been ideal if she'd had a man to kneel at her feet.

She closed her eyes as she pressed the vibrator to where the seam of her leather shorts was pulled tight between her sex lips. It felt good, not too strong, but it was important for her to have her clothes on when she came, both because it helped with her fantasies of domination and because it made her take longer. As she began to masturbate, she was imagining a man at her feet, kneeling as he watched.

He wouldn't be allowed to touch, let alone do what was uppermost in his mind and apply his tongue to her pussy. That would be far too great a privilege. No, he would be in restraint, his hands tied tight behind his back to stop him playing with his cock and his collar attached to the radiator behind him so that all he could do was watch in helpless worship as she toyed with herself.

She knew from the magazines and the internet that a lot of men were obsessed with shoes and boots, and in this case just the sight of her outstretched legs encased in soft black leather and ending in elegantly pointed toes and sharp stiletto heels would be enough to get him hard and keep him hard. Or maybe he'd be a leg man, drooling helplessly over her calves and thighs, admiring their length and shape, wishing he could touch, even lick.

Possibly, if she was in a generous mood, she might allow him to lick the soles of her boots clean and suck on her heels, but that would be as far as it went. After all, she certainly didn't want his disgusting tongue soiling the leather, let alone on her bare skin. Yes, he could lick the soles of her boots clean, leaving his mouth full of the taste of dirt as he watched her play with herself.

He'd be naked, his little cock sticking up from between his thighs like a flagpole, his welted buttocks smarting from the whip cuts she'd applied. She would be clothed, in boots and shorts and bra top, the body he worshipped concealed beneath black leather as she took her pleasure, but not in him save as a sex toy, a slave for her to amuse herself with, a mere aid to masturbation, which he'd know was all he was good for, as all other men were.

Olivia had come, her head thrown back and her back arched in ecstasy, the vibrator pressed hard to the leather of her shorts so that the seam was against her clit, providing a long tight orgasm that left her completely satisfied, her face set in a sleepy happy smile, as she allowed her body to go slowly limp.

Holly

'We're going to have to sort some kind of rota,' Holly said. 'Believe me, it's the only way to stop arguments.'

'How do you mean?' Katie asked.

'We take it in turns to do things,' Holly explained, 'like wash up, and cleaning and that.'

'Is that necessary?' Katie rejoined. 'I really feel it would be more sensible if each of us was to be responsible for her own concerns.'

'That doesn't work with hoovering, or keeping this room tidy, or anything communal,' Olivia pointed out. 'I think Holly's right.'

'Couldn't we have a cleaner come in?' Katie suggested.

'If you can pay, girl,' Holly answered.

'I hardly think that's fair,' Katie objected.

'Then best do it my way,' Holly responded. 'Let's take a vote, yeah? Who's in favour of having a rota for household duties?'

Olivia immediately raised her hand, with Paige following after a moment of hesitation.

'Oh, very well,' Katie said, 'if only for the sake of peace, but I don't know anything about this sort of thing, so one of you will have to work it all out, and make sure it's fair.'

'I don't mind doing it,' Paige volunteered.

'You do that,' Holly agreed, pleased with her little victory over Katie.

'Shall we cook together?' Paige suggested. 'It would save time, and money.'

'I'm up for that,' Olivia responded.

'Me too,' Holly agreed, 'if Katie can cook?'

'I cook very well, thank you,' Katie answered, 'but I really don't think this is a good idea. I wouldn't want to come back to find myself presented with a plate of boiled tripe and onions, or anything equally foul, while I absolutely draw the line at ready meals.'

'I am vegetarian,' Paige pointed out quietly.

'There we are, you see,' Katie said. 'While I respect

50

Paige's principles, I can hardly be expected to make nut cutlets or cook tofu, let alone eat it. I suggest we look after our own food, and, as democracy seems to be the order of the day, I suggest we vote. Paige?'

'Maybe it would be better to look after ourselves,' Paige agreed.

'We should do it communally,' Holly responded.

'How about Daniel?' Paige asked.

'The landlord?' Katie queried. 'What does he have to do with it?'

'Well, he does live here,' Holly pointed out, 'and I don't see why he shouldn't do his share.'

'Certainly he should do his share,' Katie responded as both Olivia and Paige nodded their heads. 'Indeed, I really don't see why he shouldn't keep house in general. After all, he has nothing better to do with his time, and we're studying.'

'Do you think he would agree?' Paige put in.

'He does the laundry, and the refuse,' Katie pointed out. 'I wouldn't trust him to cook, but he can certainly clean the house. After all, we are paying him.'

'I don't think it usually works like that,' Paige said doubtfully.

'Then it should,' Katie responded, again to general agreement, 'and then we needn't worry about this silly rota, which will only cause arguments.'

'That's true enough,' Holly agreed, 'but what if he kicks?'

'Katie can whip his arse with her crop!' Olivia joked.

'It's a riding whip,' Katie pointed out, 'a crop is quite different. Where is he anyway?'

Daniel

Despite the outward appearance of a man eating curry with no particular concern, Daniel was suffering from extreme guilt as he sat in the Taj Mahal. He ate mechanically, the flavour of his chicken tikka masala barely registering on his taste buds as he dwelt on what he had done, and what he wanted to do. There was no question in his mind as to how the camera system he had purchased could be put to best use, for spying on the girls, and the only question mark over whether he would go through with it was whether he had the courage.

The need to see them naked was overwhelming, and as he ate his mind hatched excuse after excuse for doing so. Perhaps, he told himself, if he saw them in the nude it would break the spell they held over him, but he knew it was a lie. He wanted to see them nude, and wank his dirty little cock until he was sore. Next he tried to persuade himself that it was a reasonable thing to do because they teased him, because girls shouldn't taunt men with their half-clothed bodies, and they deserved to have their bras taken off and their knickers pulled down to make a proper show of what they had. Unfortunately, he knew it was a double lie. Girls had every right to dress as they pleased without male interference, and they weren't teasing him anyway.

But he still wanted to see them nude – and more. The thoughts of what he might see if he planted the cameras had kept his cock so stiff he hadn't dared to return home, sure that they would notice and react with either disgust or laughter, possibly both. Instead, he'd gone to the Taj Mahal, and even there the look the head waiter had given him as he came in had been distinctly odd. Yet it was impossible to get the thoughts out of his head.

Most of all, he wanted to see Katie, preferably stripping, and ideally doing something both rude and intimate, which would make her seem less inaccessible. Holly came next on his list of desire, then Olivia and finally Paige, although their bodies appealed in more or less reverse order, and it seemed a great shame to miss out on any of the potentially magnificent displays of female flesh. So the best thing to do was put one of the cameras in the bathroom, which was not only next door to his own room, but also meant that he would be able to spy on all four of them, in the bath and in the shower, undressing and washing at the sink, or whatever other private, secret, intimate things girls might do when they thought they were safe from prying male eyes.

That left the second camera, which was a more difficult choice. He could install it in one of the bedrooms, but that might be risky, and it would be hard to choose. If he did, then he might be rewarded with yet more intimate peeks, certainly undressing, perhaps girls going about their business in the nude, many even more. He wasn't sure if real girls masturbated, as opposed to girls in porn films, but it might not be too much to hope for, especially with Holly and Olivia, who were definitely what his mother had called 'bad girls'.

There would also be boyfriends, which might mean anything, even seeing the girls suck cock, or have their pussies licked, perhaps even getting titty fucked. The thought of watching a man work his cock between Holly's gigantic black breasts made him almost choke on his curry and he immediately put her at the top of his list to have her room bugged. But sadly she was sure to choose some big athletic black man as a boyfriend, and he knew watching them would make him feel inferior.

So would watching *any* of them with a boyfriend, he considered, even Paige, although she was possibly still a virgin. Then again, all girls had to lose their virginity sooner or later, and perhaps now she was at university Paige would let herself go. Briefly, he wondered if he himself might not be the lucky man, only to dismiss the idea almost instantly. She would never choose him. Rather her boyfriend would be some intense young intellectual, the sort of student who would end up as a university lecturer.

The successful man would be sensitive and thoughtful, but firm, coaxing Paige slowly out of her clothes and into bed over a matter of weeks, until one evening of perfect intimacy. There would be a candle-lit supper at some expensive restaurant, a trip to the opera or something equally highbrow, a bottle of fine wine shared in the supposed privacy of Paige's room, and finally, late at night, the insertion of his cock into her virgin pussy, leaving her sheets stained with her surrender.

The thought was almost enough to make Daniel come then and there, save for the annoying certainty that such a man would take Paige's virginity with the lights out, robbing him of the pleasure of sharing the moment on camera. Besides, Paige was the least likely to get up to anything.

Olivia was better, openly sexual, but, judging from one or two comments he'd heard her make to Holly, in favour of older men. That was not to his taste, as he knew it would make him more jealous still if the man who came to enjoy her favours was as old or older than him, and when watching porn he always preferred the male participants to be good looking.

No, it would have to be Katie. Katie might not be a bad girl like Holly and Olivia, but she had taste, and would choose a fine man to take to bed. Watching Katie and her man would be a pleasure and, as Daniel had no doubt whatsoever about his social status compared to her, it wouldn't feel so bad watching another man have her. In fact, it wouldn't feel bad at all; it would both add to his fantasy and make the feeling of intrusion that made peeping so exciting all the stronger. Yes, it *had* to be Katie.

But there was another option. He could bug the loo and actually watch the girls pee . . . but no, that was too intimate, too intrusive, even though the thought had set him trembling and made him come in his pants.

The next instant, he was berating himself for his dirty thoughts and swearing he would send the camera system back to Electromart as soon as it arrived.

Holly

The project was simple enough, Holly considered, but there had to be some way of doing better than the other students on her course. She was also sure the lecturer had set it as a test to give him an idea of which students were genuinely interested in architecture and which were just along for the ride. That left her with a number of options for her model cathedral, but it was clear she needed to put a lot of thought into it. All in all, a modern design loaded with Christian symbolism seemed best, and she had begun to draw a tentative plan on her sketch pad when the bell rang.

She ignored it, reasoning that it was unlikely to be any of the friends she'd made over the last few days, and anyway it was the landlord's job to answer the bell. After the four girls had spoken to him, he was officially allocated the job of answering the bell, along with dealing with the rubbish and basic maintenance, although he had finally found the guts to put his foot down at Katie's suggestion that he do all the washing-up and cleaning. He had also promised to install a washing machine and tumble dryer, and as the bell went for a second time she realised that it might be the delivery man.

She put her work down with a mild curse and made her way downstairs. Sure enough, there was a van outside and a man with a trolley and several large boxes. He was quite a man too, big and fairly dark, maybe Spanish or Greek, just the sort she liked. There was another behind him, younger and less attractive but not entirely hopeless. She struck a pose, more or less by instinct, and looked them up and down.

'I hope you don't think *I*'m going to carry all that?' she said.

'Don't worry, love,' he answered her. 'We'll do all that, and install it too. Where do you want it?'

'In the kitchen, I suppose. You need to speak to the landlord, really, but I don't think he's about. Come in anyway.'

The men came in, bringing the boxes with them, and Holly settled down to watch them work, telling herself that she'd get on with her project when there weren't two young men about. Ever since she'd been dancing, she'd liked the idea of simply sitting back while men performed for her, and, if there was nothing openly erotic about installing a washing machine and tumble dryer, at least there was no doubt that it was hot sweaty work. It also gave her the opportunity to torment them, deliberately bending to show off her bum as she indicated the fuse box then standing in a pose that set her breasts off to advantage, secure in the knowledge that, while one might make a move on her, they were unlikely to do so together.

An hour later, she was rather wishing the young one would go away so that she could be alone with his older colleague. His smell was intensely masculine, as was his body, while the glances he'd been throwing at her body showed open admiration. He'd been flirting too, until Daniel came back and started making an arse of himself, getting under the workmen's feet and asking an endless stream of stupid questions. For some bizarre reason, Daniel also seemed deeply embarrassed about the security cameras he'd ordered.

Once the younger workman had gone off with Daniel to fit the dummy camera to the front of the house, she was finally left alone with the big Greek. She knew the others would be back in minutes, and the best part of a year stripping for men had eroded what little natural modesty she'd had to almost nothing.

'So,' she addressed him, 'you going to ask me for a fuck, or what?'

Daniel

Daniel was so flustered he nearly dropped the camera box as he ran upstairs. It had not gone to plan at all. He had specifically asked for the delivery to be made in the afternoon, and it had not only come in the morning instead, but also while he was out shopping. Holly had taken it in and signed for it, so she could hardly have failed to notice the camera system, or to guess his intent. The only possible solution was to have it installed outside the house, at the back and rear as he had been advised, and for its proper purpose.

A vast weight of guilt had been lifted from his shoulders as he watched the workman fix the two little cameras into place, but he was also conscious of his disappointment, which was bitter and promised to be lasting. The DVD recorder and control system would still be in his room, but, instead of pretty girls doing the sort of things pretty girls only did when they were alone, the view would be of an empty passage and the back garden.

He tried to tell himself that it was for the best, but as he listened to the workman explain how the system worked, his chagrin was growing ever stronger. The cameras produced an impressively detailed image, in colour, which was completely and utterly wasted on the almost featureless side passage and the distinctly uninteresting garden. He still sat playing with the apparatus for the best part of an hour after the men had gone, which was when he discovered that the DVD recorder had another four USB ports, each presumably capable of taking another camera.

A brief investigation of the software showed that it was indeed the case, and that there were a variety of record settings, as well as an option to view the input from each camera in a separate window. That meant he could install up to four more cameras of any compatible type, something he was telling himself he would resist even as he checked online whether he had enough in his current account to pay for the new devices.

Olivia

Spitting swearwords under her breath, Olivia closed down the window she had been working in. Not only did the university system require her personal number to log in, which was going to leave a trail a mile wide, but it also barred access to the sort of website she needed. The town library was worse, with the single bank of computers positioned so that whatever nosy old cow was sitting at the desk could see straight over the users' shoulders. She definitely couldn't afford her own PC, let alone internet access, which left her with the option of using internet cafés and yet more expense. Unless, of course, she could somehow convince Daniel to let her use his computer when he wasn't around.

It was certainly a possibility. She'd need her own login, but he didn't seem to be particularly knowledgeable about computers, or the sort who would want to pry into what she was doing anyway. If anything, he seemed rather straight-laced and dull, but he was certainly easy to influence unless pushed too far, as they'd discovered when he'd come in during their discussion on how to run the house. Most landlords, she was sure, would have put their foot down at sharing any housework whatsoever with their tenants, but he'd quickly accepted that it was reasonable so long as he wasn't expected to do more than his fair share.

She pushed her chair back and glanced at her watch. It was another three hours until Professor Deakin's lecture on social changes brought about by the Black Death, which meant she could easily get home and back. She packed her books away and set off, wondering how best to charm Daniel into doing what she wanted. As she walked towards the park, she found the man himself in the high street, staring into a shop window. He jumped like a startled frog when she addressed him.

'Window shopping?' Olivia asked conversationally.

'No, er . . . yes,' he answered, blushing. 'That is, I was – I was just thinking how much cheaper the security cameras I installed were at the store I got them instead of here.'

'Oh,' Olivia said. 'It's very nice of you to install them for us, anyway, not that we've got much worth nicking.'

'It pays to be careful, I find.'

'I'm sure it does,' she agreed. 'Look, Daniel, I was wondering if I could ask you a favour. Do you think I could use your PC sometimes?'

'Well, I – er . . .'

'I wouldn't make a pain of myself, I promise. I just need my own login so that I can tidy up my essays and that sort of thing without having to come in to uni. Please?'

She gave him her brightest smile and he seemed to wilt under her gaze.

'I suppose so,' he said.

'Thanks,' she answered before he could impose any conditions. 'You won't know I'm there.'

She kissed him. It was a mere peck on the cheek, but it left him blushing pink, making her wonder just how innocent he was. Certainly, he seemed to have real difficulty relating to women, which was a pity, but it made it even more unlikely that he'd want to exchange an occasional thrashing for a reduction in her rent.

Daniel

Daniel could feel his heart beating as he watched Olivia walk away down the high street. Just watching her bottom move in her tight blue jeans was almost too much for him, and yet he knew she was completely and utterly untouchable, at least to him. Maybe she flirted, but he was growing increasingly sure it was only so she could get her own way. After all, how could she possibly be interested in him?

He had given in to her request, though, without even putting up a fight, and once she was using his computer the other girls were sure to expect the same privilege. That meant being extra careful about the porn sites he visited and his collection of dirty pictures, as the thought of their reaction if he was discovered was unbearable.

And their reaction if they caught him spying on them would be ten times worse, but that didn't stop him going into the shop as soon as Olivia was out of sight. After all, it was only fair that if they expected to use his things and have him doing half the work around the house he should get something in return. Ideally, they could have paid off some of their rent in blow-jobs, a thought that made his cock start to harden even though he knew it was nothing but an idle and impossible fantasy.

On the other hand, showing their naked bodies to him seemed reasonable enough. In fact, it was little enough to ask, considering how easy it would be for them and how much pleasure it would give him. Unfortunately, girls didn't see things quite that way, but tended to place an unrealistically high value on their naked beauty, which made it all the more fun when he managed to catch a sneaky peek.

Now determined and frantically justifying his actions to himself, he managed to purchase four of the smallest cameras that could provide colour images. They weren't even all that expensive, and certainly looked as if they'd do the job, as the salesman demonstrated a clear view of the high street.

Installing them was going to be another matter; it wasn't technically difficult, but he needed peace and quiet, and to be absolutely sure they were properly hidden. Carrying the precious boxes in supermarket bags, he hurried home. Nobody was in, to his immense relief, but even as he began to consider where best to plant the cameras he found himself constantly imagining the sound of keys in the front door and stopping to listen or peer from the front window to make sure the street was clear.

Only slowly did he grow bolder, and, as he investigated the girls' rooms for possible camera hiding places, his fevered imagination began to work overtime. Holly had casually discarded a pair of bright-red thong panties on her bed, and it was all too easy to imagine her slipping them down over the gloriously full dark mounds of her bottom cheeks, and probably topless at the time as well – a full strip he could so easily have caught on camera.

Her room looked easy to bug too. For one thing it was messy, which made it unlikely that she would notice any minor changes. Her window frame rose to within a half-inch of the ceiling, which provided a long thin gap ideal for the concealment of a camera lens. Better still, a quick visit to the attic revealed that he would be able to plant the camera in the narrow angle between the roof and the beams, where he could guarantee it would never be found by accident. But still he held back, terrified of discovery and determined to consider the problem from every possible angle before starting work, including investigating all the girls' rooms.

Unlike Holly's, Paige's room was immaculate, with everything in its proper place and the floor newly hoovered. Yet it was the twin to the other, with the same narrow gap above the window, and a brief experiment with a stuffed olive positioned where the camera lens would be showed that it would be almost impossible to see. She had placed her bed in a good location too, not directly under the window as Holly had done, but against one wall, so that he would be guaranteed a perfect view. Already he could imagine her shyly undressing, perhaps even putting her nightie on before pulling her knickers off underneath, which would make any display of flesh she did give all the more exciting.

The thought of bugging Katie's room was even more daunting than the others, but of all of them she was the one he most wanted to see nude. Not that it was going to be so easy, because her windows opened into the end wall of the house, and like Holly she had positioned her bed directly underneath them. The end wall was completely blank at the top, with no opportunities for concealment, leaving only the door, the top of which provided a long slim crack similar to those above Holly and Paige's windows, but which was below the open attic. A second trip up the ladder revealed that the wire could be concealed beneath the insulation and run alongside a beam to join the others.

That left three options: the downstairs bedroom, which was Olivia's, the bathroom or the loo. He badly wanted to watch Olivia strip, but if the loo could be eliminated on the grounds of it being impossible to get a decent view of anybody sitting on it, then the bathroom offered some extremely interesting possibilities. Alternatively, he could do without one of the other girls, but it was impossible to choose which. Each was enticing in her own way: Holly for her voluptuous black body; Paige for her innocence; Katie for her air of effortless superiority. Yet one had to go, unless of course he took one of the real cameras in from outside and replaced it with a fake; then he could bug all four rooms and the bathroom as well. It was too good an option to resist.

There was still no sign of anybody, the September afternoon drowsy and oddly still, which to Daniel made it seem sinister, although he was the one up to no good. He knew it too, his guilt constantly at the back of his mind as he set to work, slowly and carefully, first laying out the wires in the attic and double-checking they were properly concealed, before leading them down to his DVD system.

He now realised that being made to install the security cameras was a blessing. Without them, one of the girls might have wondered why he needed so much electronic equipment in his room, but now he had the perfect excuse, their own welfare. There was still the problem of having six wires leading into the back of the recorder when there were only supposed to be two cameras, but he solved that by cutting a long slit where the thick old wallpaper curved around in the corner of his room and concealing the extra ones beneath; he then positioned the recorder and his computer so that considerable physical effort would be required to get at the back.

The cameras were now ready for installation, but he was growing increasingly nervous about the return of the girls, a concern tempered by the thought of watching them undress for bed that very evening. At last he decided to start with the bathroom, only to hear the sound of Katie's Mini while he was poking a hole in the plasterwork above the window. He climbed down from the chair he'd been standing on and hastily tidied up. He went downstairs to find her making herself a coffee. As usual, she took no notice of him beyond the briefest nod of recognition.

Holly

'Come on in,' Holly offered, crooking an inviting finger to Andros.

He grinned and steered her through the front door with his hand placed firmly on one buttock. She turned him an arch glance and took his hand, leading him quickly to the stairs. As they passed the door to the community room, she caught a glimpse of Paige, looking up from her book in surprise and a little shock, while Daniel was just coming out of the bathroom, already in his dressing gown and slippers. Holly prepared to defend her right to bring men back to the house, but he said nothing, merely standing gaping as she pulled Andros into the room behind her.

Both Paige and Daniel were going to know, perhaps the others too, if they'd been in the community room but out of sight, which added to her sense of mischief. She pushed Andros down on the bed and sank to her knees, intent on getting his cock in her mouth without delay. He let her lead, as he had done all evening, too confident in his masculinity to worry, and he was grinning happily as she tugged down his fly.

'I'm going to suck your cock,' she told him, relishing every word through the haze of wine and brandy in her head. 'I'm going to suck your cock until you're nice and hard, but you're not to spunk. I want you in me.'

He responded with a casual gesture of one hand and lay back against the wall, watching. Holly licked her lips in anticipation as she burrowed her hand in to his fly. He'd already told her he didn't wear underpants, and his cock was bare beneath the denim of his jeans, thick and already half stiff from their kissing and fumbling on the way back from the restaurant. She gave a little purr as she freed him into her mouth, taking in as much as she could and sucking eagerly.

He gave a pleased grunt, then spoke. 'Get those tits out, love. I like it that way.'

Holly nodded around her mouthful of cock and began to lift her top as she worked on him, never letting his rapidly growing shaft leave her mouth as she undid her bra and hauled it high to spill out her breasts. They felt sensitive, and for once their size and weight was a pleasure instead of a nuisance as she began to stroke them, pushing them forward to show off and tweaking her nipples to erection for her own pleasure.

Andros watched, clearly enjoying not only the sight of her pretty mouth wide around his now rigid erection and the way she was playing with her big black breasts, but also having her on her knees between his thighs. Holly didn't mind, more than happy to indulge his machismo so long as it meant she was treated to a full portion of the thick dun-coloured penis in her mouth. He was big too, every bit as big as she'd hoped he would be, with a long gnarled shaft and a large glossy head, now wet with spit as she let it slip from her mouth and began to lick and kiss his balls.

'That's right,' he groaned. 'You're a good little

cock sucker, so fucking good. Now your tits, let me fuck those big fat tits.'

'Pig!' Holly laughed, but she had already knelt up, allowing her breasts to loll forwards so that she could fold them around his erection.

He began to fuck in her cleavage, grunting as his cock moved in the slippery, spit-wet groove she'd made for him. Holly began to jiggle her breasts on his cock and rub her stiff nipples on the coarse fabric of his shirt. She was ready, her pussy warm and eager, her knickers moist with juice. His grunting was getting all too excited as well, and she pulled quickly back before he could waste his spunk between her breasts.

'Oh no you don't,' she breathed. 'I said I want you in me.'

Andros merely nodded and reached forwards, picking Holly up under her arms and hauling her on to his lap. She gave a squeak of surprise at his strength, then a long sigh as her panties were pulled aside and her body lowered on to his erection. He began to bounce her up and down, his hands now on her breasts, but only gently, letting then move to the motion of her fucking. She'd lifted her skirt as her pussy hole filled with erection, deliberately showing off to him, and now tucked it up so he could watch it go in and out as they fucked.

'You are one dirty bitch!' he laughed.

'Yeah, and you love it,' Holly answered, taking her breasts from his hands into her own so that she could caress them as his cock worked in her hole.

She closed her eyes, lost to the pleasure of the first good honest fucking she'd had in ages. Working the strip clubs had made men seem so sleazy that by the time she'd finally quit she'd preferred to play with her fellow strippers, and had become more familiar with having a tongue applied to her sex – and giving the same favour in return – than with cock.

Andros was different, all man, and as he pumped into her it seemed he was just about all cock too. She was ready to come anyway, and slid one hand down her belly, rubbing herself in full view of him as her body bounced on his erection. The bed had begun to squeak, but she didn't care, too high to worry, or even to think about her housemates any more. She was going to come, her clit burning under her finger, and as the orgasm burst in her head she screamed out loud, unable to hold back from the full expression of her pleasure.

He'd been calling her a dirty bitch and worse as she masturbated, which had only served to heighten her pleasure, while his voice had been growing steadily more hoarse with his own passion. The moment she'd finished, he lifted her bodily off his cock and dumped her on the floor as he began to masturbate in turn, tugging his slippery juice-smeared shaft right at her face.

'In your mouth,' he demanded. 'I want to spunk in your mouth, bitch, and all over those fat . . . black . . . titties . . .'

Andros came on the last word, full into Holly's mouth, which she had opened obligingly. The next shot went higher, into her face and hair, before he pushed his cock low to spurt out gout after gout of sticky white spunk all over her top and bra as well as the heavy chocolate-coloured globes of her breasts, which she was now holding up for coating.

'Fucking gorgeous!' he swore as he finally slumped back on to the bed.

'You are a dirty bastard, Andros.' Holly giggled, and leant forwards once more to suck his cock clean for him.

Paige

Paige cast a worried look at Katie as Holly's scream died away. It was quite obvious what was going on, and she'd been feeling increasingly uncomfortable. Olivia just seemed to think it was funny, but Katie at least was an ally.

'What a slut,' the blonde girl remarked. 'Do you know, I think that was the man who installed the washing machine. Still, like with like, I suppose.'

Olivia was going to say something, but stopped as Daniel entered the room. He obviously knew what had been going on, and looked as if he disapproved, but Paige couldn't find it in herself to bring the subject up. There was no denying the physical response of her own body either, which made her embarrassment even worse. Her sex ached and her nipples were so stiff that they showed through her top.

Sure that Daniel would notice, she hastily excused herself and ran upstairs, locking her door behind her. She could hear Holly talking to her new man through the wall, although not clearly enough to make out the words, and laughing too. It seemed outrageous that they could do something so rude so casually, and yet there was considerably more to her own feelings than the distaste she knew was the proper reaction or the helpless excitement of her bodily response.

She was jealous for one thing, not so much of the physical act, but of Holly's confidence in picking up a man and taking him to bed on their first date, as if it was a perfectly natural thing to do. Then there was a strong feeling of resentment for her own arousal, and in turn guilt because that effectively meant she'd allowed herself to be turned on by another woman, because the pictures running though her mind were as

69

much of Holly as of the hairy, testosterone-soaked muscle man she'd taken to bed.

It was bad enough having to cope with a crush on Katie, never mind Holly as well, and as Paige began to undress she was alternately pouting and biting her lip as she struggled for control over her own emotions. As always, she stripped to her panties and put her bathrobe on to wash, then got into her nightie and bed, and as always she left her bedside light on and picked up her book, hoping that a few chapters of Jane Austen's *Emma* would soothe her tattered feelings and help her get to sleep.

Austen did no good at all. Usually she could lose herself in a book immediately, especially an old favourite like *Emma*, but now it was impossible, the elegant sentences and dry wit entirely lost on her, the words with no more significance than had they been in a telephone directory. The sensations of her body wouldn't go away either, with her sex still aching and the cleft of her bottom irritatingly sticky with her own juices.

She knew what she wanted to do, but she also knew it was something utterly improper and frankly silly, her guilty little secret she had never revealed to anybody. Katie would never do it, she was sure, nor Olivia, nor even Holly. She wanted to masturbate, but she was determined not to. It was just too dirty, a filthy little game that was frankly unnecessary, or should have been, yet which she still played all too often.

Telling herself that only dirty old men went in for that sort of behaviour, she rolled over and once again tried to concentrate on her book. She immediately found herself wondering if Emma would have masturbated and, if she had, if she'd have felt any more guilty. Annoyed at herself for spoiling the book, she

70

put it to one side and turned the light off, telling herself that she would soon be asleep and that all the dirty thoughts and needs crowding her head would be gone by the morning.

It didn't work. She tried counting sheep, but each one turned into a ram as it jumped the stile, complete with an improbably large bright-red penis dangling from its belly. She tried working on the arguments for and against Derrida's theories, but even he managed to obtrude himself into her mind, complete with a towering erection thrusting up from his open fly. She tried working out cube roots, but even the numbers came complete with little cocks and balls, and were trying to fuck her.

Finally she gave in, pulled up her nightie, slid her hand between her thighs, eased her fingers down her panties, and began to masturbate. The moment she touched the wet swollen flesh of her sex she was lost. It was just too sensitive, even the plump furry mound above her slit. Stroking her lips had her shivering with pleasure and the hot little point between felt so good she had to bite her lip to stop herself crying out.

At that, she realised that she had no right to criticise Holly. She was no better herself, no more able to restrain her physical needs; the only difference was that Holly was honest about it and had the courage to admit it and bring a man home, a big rough man, a man who'd undoubtedly put his cock in the black girl's hole – and maybe even ruder things.

Just to think the words sent shivers of pleasure through Paige's body as she stroked herself, but, try as she might to focus on what might have happened between Holly and the man, it was impossible to stop her mind slipping to the person she really wanted to masturbate over . . . Katie. Before long, she'd given up, chiding herself for her weakness even as she pushed the bedclothes down.

Her panties came off, her thighs spread to the cool evening air, her nightie came up all the way over her breasts and she was masturbating openly, rubbing at her sex and teasing one nipple. Her eyes were lightly closed and her teeth pressed on to her lip as she let her imagination go, involving Katie in her favourite and most shameful fantasy. They were going riding the next morning, and it would happen then. As before, they would enjoy their outing, making their way up to the open downs where the horses could be urged to a full gallop.

Afterwards, she'd rub the horses down, as usual, and when they came back she'd do Katie's boots. Only this time, it would be in Katie's room, with the door locked. Katie would start to tease, saying that Paige would make a good maid for her, and get quickly worse. Soon Paige would be told to do her work in just her bra and panties, then naked. She'd have boot polish smeared in her face, then on her breasts, and on her bottom, as she knelt on the floor at Katie's feet, in the nude, bum up and open, her sex and anus showing as the laughing girl smeared on the boot polish.

Paige was on the edge, her teeth pressed hard to her lip, her fingers busy in the wet slit between her thighs, her other hand squeezing at her breasts. They felt huge, as they always did when she masturbated, huge and fat, like two great big melons, huge and fat and impossible to hide, yet they felt good too, for all her shame. She took them in her hands, squeezing and jiggling them, imagining Katie's laughter as she soiled the fat white globes with boot polish, and the biting shame as she was told to get on her knees and show off her bottom.

Unable to resist, she flipped herself over into the rude position she was imagining, biting into her pillow as she lifted her bottom into the air and set her knees apart. Her hand went to her sex once more, rubbing in her slit as she thought of holding the same rude pose as Katie slapped on the boot polish, rubbing it in and smacking at Paige's cheeks, smearing it along her bottom crease before pushing one slippery finger in up Paige's anus. Katie would see Paige was virgin, holding her sex lips spread to inspect the tight red plug that shut off the hole, laughing as she smeared boot polish on that too. Paige would be made to masturbate, as she was, only with her body soiled and dirty, her filthy bottom stuck in the air as her cheeks were spanked, maybe with something stuck in her anus to further humiliate her, and all the while with Katie laughing and laughing and laughing . . .

Paige came with a muffled sob of shame-filled ecstasy, biting at her pillow and rubbing at her slit as the thought of Katie's derisive laughter ran through her head. It was too much; there were tears in her eyes before she'd finished and, even as she slumped over on to her side, she was telling herself that as a punishment for being such a slut she should sleep without her panties.

Daniel

A full week passed before Daniel managed to get his camera system installed and operational. It was a highly frustrating time, even alarming. One or another of the girls always seemed to be around, and even when they weren't he never knew when one of them might come back. Katie, in particular, seemed to do very little work, at least not at the university, while Holly also spent a lot of time in her room. Only Paige had any sort of routine at all, and even she could not be relied upon to stay out all day.

The result was that he had to work with extreme care, never allowing himself to get into a situation in which he would give himself away if one of the girls returned. Even then he was almost caught twice, once when Katie came back while he was in the attic installing the bathroom camera, and once when he was drilling the hole above Holly's window only to have her return with her boyfriend. Fortunately, he managed to pretend he'd been adjusting the ball-cock on the first occasion, and on the second he succeeded in escaping the room in time and she was too eager to get to grips with Andros to notice the telltale plaster dust on her bedroom floor.

Andros had proved a nuisance in other ways too; he was arrogant, aggressive and confrontational. He was always nice to the girls, but clearly despised Daniel, and obviously enjoyed having noisy sex with Holly, to the point where it began to seem deliberately provocative. Daniel ignored the situation as best he could, telling himself he had no right to interfere in Holly's private life, and, secretly, that he would have his revenge when he could spy on them having sex.

The situation had grown worse in other ways too. Katie continued to treat him like a servant and Olivia continued to flirt, both adding to his growing frustration. Even Paige managed to make him feel small, although he knew full well that her air of cool intellectual aloofness was entirely natural and didn't reflect on him in any way. He still yearned to see her with her breasts bare and her big white bottom out of her panties, and now it looked as if he would be able to do so.

He finished the work on a Friday afternoon, made a careful double check to ensure than all five cameras were invisible and began to run his final tests on the system. It worked perfectly, allowing him to bring up six different windows on his monitor screen at once, and in such a way that a single click of his mouse would place the harmless view of the back garden on top. Two minor problems remained: there was no longer a view of the side passage and the telltale information boxes at the bottom of the screen showed that the other cameras were in operation. He put both down as acceptable risks, given that the only person who ever came into his room was Olivia to use the computer, and it was easy to ensure that the system was off then. Nor did she show any interest in the surveillance equipment.

All six cameras gave clear pictures, and, if the one in Holly's room gave a less than perfect view of her bed, then that was probably just as well. After all, who wanted to see a sweaty hairy Greek backside pumping up and down? With any luck, all the cute action would take place where he could see it, and it was all too easy to imagine Holly treating Andros to stripteases, lap-dancing and yet ruder shows, all of which Daniel could now enjoy, and record.

He could hardly wait for the girls to get home, although he still felt a good deal of apprehension. Despite all his careful arrangements, he was sure that they would notice immediately, in which case he could no doubt expect to be hauled down to the local police station and denounced as a pervert. The thought made him cringe, and yet it was more than compensated for by the prospect of ripe young bottoms and breasts for his eyes to feast on.

They didn't notice, all four of them coming back as usual and going about their business. Daniel kept to his room, sure that if he went downstairs his nerves would give him away, and constantly fiddling with the apparatus as the mixture of guilt and fear and lust built to an unbearable peak.

By half-past eight, he'd already locked his door and was pretending he'd gone to bed, but the girls showed no inclination to hurry. All four of them were in the community room, drinking wine and talking, which made him wish he'd placed a camera there too, or at least a microphone, so that he could listen in on what they had to say. He knew they tended to change their topics of conversation when he was around, and was sure there would be some juicy titbits to hear, maybe confessions of what they'd done or what they liked.

It was ten o'clock before anything happened. He heard footsteps on the stairs and guessed it was Paige. Sure enough, as he switched to her camera, there she was, just coming in at her door. His guilt was agonising as he watched, but his eyes remained fixed firmly to the screen. She was in pale-blue jeans, beautifully tight on her well-rounded bottom, and a loose red and white striped top that clung to the shape of her breasts as she moved.

He'd got his cock out, ready for the supreme moment, but she didn't seem to be in any hurry. Rather than start to undress, she sat down in her armchair and began to read a book. Daniel bit his lip in frustration. It was not how he'd pictured girls at bedtime, but, then again, Paige was hardly the sort to practise striptease, nor any of the other things his fevered imagination had managed to invent.

Yet she would have to undress, that much seemed certain, and he kept his attention on her until the creak of the stairs once more alerted him to another girl coming up. It was Katie, a much more enticing prospect, and she was already in her room by the time he managed to find the right screen. Like Paige, she was in jeans, only dark, obviously new and one of the top designer brands. They hugged her bottom and thighs so sweetly that Daniel had taken his cock in hand again even as she was moving around the room. Her breasts looked good too, pushing out a loose white blouse, with a little cleavage already showing where she'd undone a button, and a hint of lacy white bra.

He watched enthralled, nursing his gradually thickening cock as he waited for her to undress. She was going to do it too, unfastening another button of her blouse, and a third, only with her back to the camera. Daniel was praying she would turn around, either that or take down her jeans with her bottom towards the camera, but she did neither, instead she walked to the window, opened it, then drew the curtains. Her blouse was now undone to her tummy, providing him with an enticing glimpse of a well-filled white bra perfectly fitted to her heavy breasts and a generous slice of baby-pink cleavage.

His cock was now hard, rearing up from the opening of his pyjama trousers, and painfully sensitive. He began to wank slowly, but struggling to hold back. A quick check on Paige showed that she was still reading, but Katie had begun to do exercises, touching her toes to make her breasts loll and swing under her chest, then a series of what seemed to be dance steps, but once more with her back to him as she watched herself in the long mirror on her wardrobe.

Daniel cursed himself for not realising that she would spend a lot of time looking in her mirror, and yet the situation offered interesting possibilities for the display of her bottom. She began to undo her trousers. Daniel swallowed, thanking every god he had ever heard of as Katie opened the front of her jeans and stuck her thumbs into the waistband, pushing them down to expose the top of a pair of tight white panties, and more, as a rap sounded on his door, so sudden and unexpected that he felt his heart jump and his chest tighten, leaving him unable to answer as Olivia's voice sounded from the passage.

'Are you awake, Daniel?'

He managed a strangled noise in response as he frantically closed down the windows on his monitor. His cock was as hard as ever, blatantly obvious even as he fought to untangle his dressing-gown cord from the chair he was sitting on.

'Are you having a wank or something?' Olivia laughed and Daniel's face flared crimson.

'Just coming,' he panted. 'I mean . . . that is, I was – I was just undressing. One minute.'

He'd managed to close his dressing gown, hiding his erection, but his entire body was trembling and his skin was prickling with sweat, while he was sure she would smell both his fear and his cock. Quickly he opened his curtains and pushed the window up, just as she spoke again.

'Are you going to let me in, or not?'

'Yes, fine . . . right away,' Daniel stammered, and pulled back the catch.

Olivia stepped into the room, immediately throwing him what he was sure was an accusing look. 'I just wanted to check my emails,' she said. 'Sorry. I didn't realise you'd gone to bed so early.'

'I – I'm not feeling quite right,' Daniel explained.

'Well, don't give me anything,' she answered as she seated herself at the computer. 'Do you mind not looking?'

'Um, no ... yes,' Daniel replied, and quickly turned away, pretending to look out of the window as she typed in her password.

He watched her reflection as she worked, his heart still hammering in his chest, but unable not to admire her and think how it might be to watch her strip down later on. She was in calf-length suede boots, a green and yellow summer skirt and a bright-yellow top, light, almost girlish clothes that went some small way to eroding the awe he felt in her presence. He began to imagine how it would be if she was his girlfriend, only to quickly push away the thought. She was unobtainable, far too young for him, far too attractive for him. All he could hope for was to peep at her naked body as he hammered on his engorged cock to take himself to a desperate, frustrated orgasm.

Olivia

A glance towards Daniel showed that he was being a good boy and minding his own business, and Olivia clicked on the symbol that would show if there were any responses to the ad she'd placed on a website. There seemed to be an awful lot of women offering domination services on the net, but not in Silbury, while the prices some of them were asking struck her as outrageous. She had asked roughly half what seemed to be the average London price, confident that if she was successful then an hour's work a week would cover her rent and leave a bit over. It didn't seem too much to ask, but so far there had been no responses.

But tonight there was a response. The annoying little zero that had been winking at her for the previous three days had changed to a one. Once more she glanced at Daniel, but he appeared to be contemplating something out in the road, and she clicked on the message bar. It came up immediately, addressed to Mistress Black, the screen name she had chosen for herself, but the first thing she noticed was that the 'Mistress' had been omitted in the actual message. It read:

Black,
   It is not enough merely to declare yourself a Mistress. The title must be earned, and it can only be earned at the feet of another. If you are serious, you may come to Me and I will teach you what you need to know, but, until then, do not presume to offer what you do not know how to give. Do not trouble to reply unless you wish to be My pupil and are willing to approach Me with suitable humility.
   Mistress Anastasia

Olivia read the message once, and then a second time, hardly able to take in the woman's sheer arrogance. Yet it was there, quite clear.

'The fucking bitch!' she hissed under her breath.

She closed the window down and sat back, still staring at the screen. It really was an unbelievable piece of arrogance, on so many levels, and yet it was also clear that her own message must have given her away as a novice, which just possibly explained why she hadn't had any replies. Maybe it would be best to accept, and to train for a while, especially as that would presumably mean a share of Mistress Anastasia's business? No, her pride would not admit the idea. 'Earned at the feet of another' indeed!

Again, she leant forwards to the computer, determined to compose a reply so scathing that it would inflict the same humiliation she was now feeling on Mistress Anastasia. Perhaps she should make the same offer in return, or suggest that the Mistress would benefit from a taste of the whip or, better still, a bare-bottom hand spanking across Olivia's knee, as if the conceited bitch was still in the nursery.

She'd begun to type her reply when she hesitated. To insult Mistress Anastasia might wreck her chances, both on the net and in the real world, and it made sense to at least make some enquiries first. She began to search, pulling up results immediately, and the more she read the more her heart sank. Mistress Anastasia had her own website, a slick professionally produced one that demonstrated a cool certain knowledge of the art of dominating men. She was beautiful too, a tall elegant woman in her mid-thirties with a fine assertive face and a lean yet powerful figure.

There also seemed to be an endless supply of accolades from grateful men, all of whom seemed to regard Mistress Anastasia as something close to a goddess, exactly the attitude Olivia herself would have liked for herself. It was infuriating, and also extremely disheartening. True, the woman was in nearby Winchester rather than Silbury, but her clients – or, rather, slaves, as she liked to see them – came from as far afield as London, Birmingham and Exeter.

It was clearly a bad move to start a flame war against the woman, and Olivia deleted what she'd written with an inner sigh. Evidently, it was going to be a lot harder than she'd imagined, but she was not going to subjugate herself to some stuck-up bitch. Instead, she would adjust her advert to emphasise her advantages, particularly her age and the size of her bust, both areas in which Mistress Anastasia could not possibly compete.

'Right, you bitch,' she muttered as she began to make the changes.

'Are you OK, Olivia?' Daniel asked from the window.

'Just someone's pissed me off,' she told him.

'Oh, sorry.'

'Don't worry, I'm nearly done, then you can get back to your wank.'

She smiled to herself at his instant embarrassment, which made her feel a little better. He was so easy to manipulate, eager to please for the mere hint of anything sexual, and blushing scarlet at a word. It was really quite funny, and again she wondered how far he could be pushed, only to dismiss the idea as too risky.

'That's it,' she said as she hit the Enter key. 'Thanks.'

'No problem,' Daniel answered as she got up.

Daniel

As Daniel turned the key in the lock behind Olivia he was feeling more guilt ridden than ever. It was bad enough to peep at girls he didn't know, worse when he did know them, and worse still when he'd just had a friendly if embarrassing conversation with one and now intended spying on her as she stripped for bed. That didn't stop him going straight back to the monitor, but he told himself he'd look at one of the others instead of Olivia.

He clicked on Katie's window, but the room was dark. So was Paige's. Holly's was dimly illuminated because her door was open and the passage light shone in, but she wasn't there. Daniel gave a sigh of resignation and clicked on Olivia's window, just in time to see her come into her room and lock the door firmly behind her. His cock was now limp, and he was so full of self-recrimination he wasn't sure if he'd be able to get an erection again, but, as she bent to unzip her boots, showing off the full length of her legs from behind, he felt an all-too-familiar twinge in his crotch.

Her boots off, she padded over to her chest of drawers and bent once more, making Daniel wish the camera was lower to get what must have been a prime view up her skirt. She opened the lowest drawer and, to his surprise, pulled it right out. His surprise grew as she reached into the space underneath, to pull out two thigh-length leather boots with sharp heels and elaborate laces.

'She's kinky!' he whispered to himself, his mouth and his eyes wide in astonishment. 'Oh yes, she's kinky!'

He watched in fascination, too drawn in even to think of playing with his cock, as Olivia pulled the boots on, slowly and with obvious relish. The result was a little odd, with her colourful summer skirt above kinky black boots, but it didn't stay that way for long. Her hands went behind her, and, as she eased down the zip on her skirt, Daniel's breathing grew long and hard. He sighed as she took the skirt down, exposing little black panties pulled taut between full creamy bottom cheeks, and now his hand was on his cock.

She was divine, her bottom as cheeky and round and feminine in panties as he had ever imagined when seeing her clothed, and it was going to get better. Her hands had gone to her top, lifting it off to bare her back and the strap of her bra, then more as she unclipped the bra, let it fall from her breasts, tossed it casually on to the bed, and turned around. Daniel gave a sob of desire as Olivia's breasts came on show to the camera. They were full and round and extraordinarily firm, with big puffy nipples. She seemed pleased with them too, making a brief inspection in the mirror, with one fat tit in either hand to show off how big she was. He heard her mutter something in a cross voice, which seemed at odds with admiring her breasts, but he wasn't bothered. Olivia was in nothing but kinky boots and black panties while he was spying on her, and nothing else mattered.

He was hammering on his now stiff cock, and was determined to come while she was showing off so beautifully. The same thoughts were going through his head again and again to the rhythm of his wanking; kinky boots, bare bum, bare tits ... kinky boots, bare bum, bare tits ... kinky boots, bare bum, bare tits ... and she was giving him quite a show, adjusting her panties, lifting her tits in her hands again, admiring them from the side, before finally bending low to once more get to the compartment under her wardrobe.

Daniel gasped. Her big tits were dangling down, a fine view, but her bottom was almost directly towards him, showing twin slices of pale soft thigh top above her boots, full bare bottom cheeks spilling out to either side of her knickers, and her sex, in rear view, the pouty little cunt lips encased in black stain, the gusset ever so slightly moist where she'd juiced in them, and that was too much. Fountain after fountain of spunk erupted from Daniel's cock, all over his hand, all over his pyjamas and dressing gown, all over the monitor screen, but he didn't care, hammering at his aching erection with his eyes fixed on Olivia's satin-clad cunt lips until he'd milked himself

dry and the inevitable wave of guilt had swamped his
arousal.

Olivia

As she took her shorts and top from beneath the
chest of drawers, Olivia had lost none of her
determination. She didn't need to be taught how to
dominate men by some wrinkly old bitch. Dominance
was part of her nature, while her body was far
superior to Mistress Anastasia's, at least fifteen years
younger for one thing, with some decent curves,
making her a far more suitable object of worship. In
fact, the only reason Mistress Anastasia could have
for making her offer was jealousy. The bitch knew
full well she'd lose out in the long run, so was trying
to get Olivia under her control from the start. It
wasn't going to work.

Leaving the drawer as it was, Olivia pushed her
booted feet cautiously into her shorts and pulled
them up, wriggling her bottom into the seat and
breathing in deeply to do the button up. A check in
the mirror showed how big her bottom looked, a
good deal of plump white flesh bulging out from
around the leg holes, but she remembered the cartoons of the fat girls sitting on men's faces and
reassured herself that a full feminine bottom was
what was wanted, even if it made her feel rather
self-conscious.

Having no top on didn't help either, her bare
breasts helping to keep her look rude and smutty
rather than dominant. She quickly pulled her top on,
adjusted it to hold her breasts properly and then
inspected herself in the mirror once more. Before, she

had seemed the perfect image of the dominant woman. Now, she seemed something of a parody, a girl dressed up so that she could be ridiculed for attempting to ape a true domina, like Mistress Anastasia.

'Bitch!' Olivia spat, and reached in under the chest of drawers for her whip.

Just to hold it was immensely satisfying, bringing out her aggression and making her feel a good deal less silly. Telling herself it was just practice, she put a cushion on her bed and sprinkled it lightly with talcum powder, to allow her to see how the strokes landed as she began to apply the whip. It was practice, but she was no longer thinking of the cushion as a man, but as Mistress Anastasia, tied naked to Olivia's bed as her oh-so-perfect little backside was whipped up to a mess of scarlet lines.

It was a satisfying thought, and, although she knew she'd never have the nerve to do it, it didn't stop the fantasy evolving in her mind. Mistress Anastasia would be naked, after being made to strip – no, to do a striptease, a lewd smutty little striptease, shaking her tits and sticking her bottom out as she took down her knickers, and all of it in front of her pathetic male slaves. Then she'd be made to grovel at Olivia's feet, naked, begging to be let off her whipping.

Olivia was lashing at the cushion, no longer even bothering to aim, and sending up a cloud of talcum powder with every stroke. She imagined how Mistress Anastasia would look at her feet, kneeling, naked, face streaked with tears of humiliation, her slaves standing back in awe at Olivia's sheer power. However much she begged, the Mistress would get her whipping, tied face down to the bed as a dozen whip welts were applied to her oh-so-elegant little arse – no, two dozen, and she'd be made to count them, and to thank Olivia for every one, utterly humiliating herself.

Nor would it finish there. Once Mistress Anastasia was well whipped, Olivia would sit on the bitch's face, just like the fat girls in the cartoons, to have her pussy licked, to have her arsehole kissed, and licked. After a last furious cut at the cushion, Olivia threw herself down on the bed. She was shocked at her own aggression even as the thoughts ran through her head, but her hand was already between her thighs, rubbing the soft leather of her shorts against her pussy.

She closed her eyes as she masturbated, imagining the scene, with her bare bottom poised on Mistress Anastasia's face, just high enough to let the men see that their supposed goddess was licking another woman's anus, and enjoying it. Maybe one of them would even take pictures, close-ups, clearly showing the contact between tongue tip and bumhole, so that Mistress Anastasia could be reminded of what she'd done. And that would not be all. Once she'd come in the bitch's face, Olivia would have Mistress Anastasia crawl to each of the men in turn, naked, with her well-whipped bottom on show, to suck them off and swallow their spunk, or take it all over her perfect arrogant face.

Olivia came, her back arched in ecstasy, one hand busy between her thighs and the other clutching at one leather-clad breast. It was a good orgasm, full of anger and triumph as well as arousal, hot and long and tight, enough to leave her with a delicious sense of satisfaction and a wicked smile on her face as she came slowly down.

Daniel

Lying in bed with his body telling him that to move would be more effort than it was worth, Daniel felt grateful he had nothing to get up for. It had been quite a night, and the cameras were successful beyond his wildest dreams, his sole regret that he had taken his first orgasm so quickly. Yet he could never have imagined Olivia would be so dirty, not merely showing her gorgeous young body in the mirror, but dressing up in leather to masturbate. He'd managed to come a second time as he watched her, and a third, much later, as he lay in bed playing over in his mind what he had seen.

Once she'd come, she had stripped naked, giving him wonderful views of her bare bottom and pussy, although not in the full intimate detail he would have liked. She had also gone up to the bathroom to wash and clean her shorts, allowing him to linger over her curves as she soaped herself in the shower and stood naked at the sink. She also slept in just her panties, and he was still staring at the monitor screen when she'd finally turned her light out. By then, Holly was also in bed and asleep, but Daniel had been forced to masturbate again, leaving his cock sore and his excitement still so high it had been nearly two in the morning before he finally got to sleep himself.

He now felt exhausted, happy, thoroughly smug at what he'd done, but also guilty and scared. It was all too easy to imagine Olivia applying the vicious whip she'd used on the cushion to his buttocks, and he wasn't entirely sure that she hadn't been thinking of exactly that while she did it. He was unable to imagine how much it would hurt, but he knew it would be a great deal, and also that, if she caught him peeping and demanded that he accept a whipping, he would have no choice but to comply.

The thought was both terrifying and arousing, because after what he'd seen there was no question in his mind that Olivia was a genuine sadist, and would not only enjoy beating him but would grow aroused by it as well. What she might do to him afterwards he could only guess at, but it seemed not completely impossible that she'd want her pussy licked, a thought so desirable it made him ache and sent his hand questing for his cock once more.

A single touch and he decided against it. He needed a break, or he'd be too sore to enjoy himself that evening, when there would be another opportunity for spying on the girls.

Holly

Very little of the lecture had managed to penetrate Holly's brain, although she'd done her best to concentrate and take notes. Most of the time she'd been thinking of Andros, and his rough primitive masculinity. They were meeting for lunch, and she knew full well there would be sex for afters. He always seemed to be ready, and he had a wonderful indifference to other people, once taking her up against the wall of an alley simply because he lacked the patience to get her back home before he fucked her. Another time he'd made her go down on him among some bushes in the park, at night, but close enough to a light to make it a thrill every time somebody went past.

Just thinking about him made her wet, and to hold him filled her with an irrepressible excitement she thought she'd lost through too much exposure to the men in the strip clubs. Now it was back, with a vengeance, and she intended to make the best of it. She went straight from the lecture theatre to the loos, where she adjusted her makeup, put on a fresh pair of panties and applied a few dabs of perfume to her wrists and neck. Now feeling ready for anything, she made for the pub where they'd agreed to meet.

Andros was already there, a pint of lager in his hand and an empty glass beside it. She kissed him as she reached the table, and was immediately pulled in, one big hand finding her bottom as he mashed his mouth to hers, forcing her to open it and return the kiss. A wonderful sense of excitement filled her at being made to kiss in public, although she knew the emotion was faintly ridiculous when she had stripped so many times for so many men. Now it was different. She was in an ordinary pub, and it was Andros making her show her sexuality.

She was giggling as she finally broke away, and her body was already thrilling to his touch. He gave her a long knowing look, as if he knew exactly the reaction he'd inspired in her, before he stood and went to the bar. Holly knew he'd buy her a vodka mixer, which he seemed to assume was what girls drank, but she didn't protest. She knew his overwhelming masculinity might eventually grow tiresome, but for the moment she was more than prepared to make sacrifices in order to enjoy the feelings he gave her. The mixer was cold and refreshing in any case, so she put the glass to her lips and swallowed most of it down in one.

'Use the glass, huh?' Andros chided, but he was grinning.

'Sure,' Holly promised, and poured out what remained of her drink.

Andros sat back, his eyes feasting on her with undisguised relish. A sizeable bulge showed in the crotch of his jeans, making Holly suddenly urgent to get what was concealed into her mouth.

'So,' she said, 'are we going to sit here drinking all afternoon, or are you going to take me somewhere private and make me blow you?'

'Hey, I thought we were having lunch?' he answered. 'But OK.'

He stood up, extending his hand. Holly took it, uncertain as to exactly what he was doing, until he made directly for the loos. She found herself blushing, for the first time in years, sure that every other customer would know exactly what was going on. One or two did cast her appraising looks, before she had been led through the door to where both female and male loos were hidden.

'Check if anyone's about,' Andros ordered, jerking his thumb towards the Ladies.

Holly nodded and swallowed, feeling deliciously nervous as she pushed into the Ladies. Nobody else was there, and she quickly called for Andros to join her, both of them immediately nipping into a cubicle and locking the door. There was no question of how it was going to be done. Andros had already seated himself on the toilet, giving Holly no option but to kneel on the floor between his thighs. She went down, her excitement rising quickly as she caught the smell of his cock, and higher still as he freed it straight into her mouth.

'That's my pet,' he sighed, 'my dirty little cock sucker.'

With his erection already growing in her mouth, Holly could only nod agreement. There was no denying it, after all. She loved to suck cock, and had never been able to see why some people depicted it as a degrading act. It felt good, and it made her want to touch herself, which was all that mattered.

She quickly extracted his scrotum and took the full mass into her mouth, gaping wide as she sucked his balls and tugged at the now stiff cock rearing above her face. He was soon fully erect, his shaft thick and hot and hard in her hand, making her eager to have him inside her. She tried to rise, meaning to sit on him for a fuck, but he placed a hand on her head, keeping her firmly in place.

'In your mouth,' he instructed. 'I want to see you swallow.'

Holly felt no more than a twinge of resentment as she obeyed his order, once more taking his erection in her mouth, now as deep as it would go, to give him the pleasure of feeling her throat squeeze on his helmet as she gagged. He gasped as he felt the first contraction, and tried to force himself deeper still, making Holly's eyes pop before she could get him out. She was gasping for breath, with her mouth wide open and a thick streamer of spittle connecting her lower lip to his cock head.

'Do it,' he demanded, and pushed her head back on to his cock.

She began to gag again immediately, the muscles of her throat in urgent painful spasm on his cock head as he held it deep, until her eyes were watering and her stomach began to lurch in her desperate need to be sick. He sighed, calling her his darling and a bitch, pulled back just long enough to allow her to gulp in a desperately needed lungful of air and once more jammed himself deep, triggering Holly's gag reflex for the third and last time. She felt him erupt in her throat, her muscles tightened uncontrollably as a great mass of spunk and mucus exploded from her nose, all over the base of his cock, balls and the front of his trousers.

'Ah, fucking great!' he swore, his hands locked tight in Holly's hair as he held her in place to milk the last of his spunk down her throat. 'You give a great bj, Holly, the best.'

Holly came up the instant her hair was released, coughing and retching on to the floor before she could recover herself enough to swallow what remained in her mouth and force a smile. 'Yeah, I know,' she told him. 'Now my turn.'

Andros didn't seem to have heard.

'Look what a fucking mess you've made!' he said, looking down at his slime-smeared jeans and filthy cock. 'You're going to clean that up, now.'

'Sure,' Holly offered, reaching for some loo roll, 'and then you're going to lick me out, aren't you?'

'Do what?' Andros demanded.

'Lick me out,' Holly repeated. 'Come on, Andros. I need it, and I did you.'

'It doesn't work like that, doll,' he answered, his voice full of disgust.

'Oh come on!' Holly urged. 'I need it badly, and it's no big deal, is it? I mean, it's not like you have to gag on me like I did for you.'

'I'm a man,' Andros pointed out. 'Giving head's for women . . . and poofs.'

Holly laughed. 'I'm not asking you to suck cock, Andros! Just give me a lick, yeah? You like pussy, don't you?'

'It doesn't work that way,' he said again, now defensive. 'No man goes down on a woman, not a real man, only a poof.'

'So if a man licks a girl it makes him gay?' Holly demanded.

Andros shrugged. 'No, not gay gay, but like, in prison, if you get a poof to suck you off, it don't make you gay.'

'Er,' Holly began, trying to understand his reasoning and then abandoning the attempt. 'You're a pig, Andros, you know that?'

Olivia

Seated at Daniel's computer, Olivia mused on Mistress Anastasia. It was impossible to get the woman out of her head, and she knew that one way or another she would have to respond to the message. Her fantasy of the night before was sadly impractical, and even if her new advert drew some responses she had still been made to feel small, which wouldn't do. The question was: what to say?

She sat back in the chair, sucking on the tip of a pencil in an absent-minded manner. An aggressive response was tempting, but clearly pointless. At best she would make herself look like a brat, which was hardly going to help her efforts to be accepted as a dominant. Accepting the awful woman's offer was out of the question . . . or was it?

Olivia began to consider the situation. Mistress Anastasia's message oozed arrogance, and to judge by her website that was a genuine reflection of her character. Therefore, if Olivia sent a humble response, asking to be trained, it would probably be accepted at face value. Then, once she was safely installed as Mistress Anastasia's pupil, Olivia could do as she pleased, including poaching the better clients, who she would also be able to evaluate before making her move, and they were sure to want to come. After all, what man would prefer a scrawny middle-aged harridan to herself?

Now with a wicked smile on her face she leant close to the keyboard once more, bringing up Mistress

Anastasia's message and typing out a carefully worded reply, with what she hoped was the balance of egotism, natural dominance and naive enthusiasm the other woman would expect:

> Mistress Anastasia,
>   I am so happy to get your message. I am serious, please believe me, and I could want nothing more than to learn from you, only I had not realised that sort of thing was possible. As you know, I am in Silbury, but I can travel to Winchester at the weekends, and would love to meet up. Please reply soon.
>   Yours respectfully in dominance,
>   Black

Having finished, Olivia sat back once more, considering what she'd written and whether it expressed the sentiments Mistress Anastasia would expect. After making two changes and in both cases reverting to the original, she decided it was best as it stood, and after a last moment of hesitation she clicked on Send. The message vanished and reappeared as the screen refreshed. Now she only needed to wait.

Daniel

All day Daniel had been in a state of nervous excitement. He'd found it impossible to keep still, or to concentrate on anything other than his camera system. For once all four girls had been out for most of the day, and until Olivia had come back he'd been testing and retesting the system, over and over again, despite the fact that it was working perfectly. He'd even spent some time observing the girls' empty rooms on the monitor, even though he could have visited any of them for himself.

With Olivia in the house, he'd finally managed to pull himself together sufficiently to go out and shop for food, but even the delightful sights available in the supermarket and in the park seemed to pale in comparison to what he'd witnessed the night before and his anticipation of what he might see in the future. One little brunette poppet on skates even provided him with a brief flash of pink panty seat, which would normally have had him rushing home for a bout of guilty masturbation. Now it seemed merely a pleasing moment, a sweet foretaste of the far sweeter delights yet to come, not just panties, but bare rounded flesh. There would be panties, certainly, on full show, and more – bellies and bums and tits and cunts, all nude, all his to masturbate over, a feast that promised to provide more than he could possibly consume, that night and every night.

Not that there was anything wrong with a foretaste, especially when a full meal could be guaranteed. The girl on skates had certainly been cute, with her long brown hair caught up in a loose ponytail and her muscular little thighs pumping as she picked up speed on the path. From the moment he saw her, he'd know that with the light summer breeze and the way she was moving there was a fair chance her skirt would come up enough to show her panties, and sure enough, it had, affording a teasing glimpse of smooth pink cotton hugging a neatly rounded little bottom.

He kept the image in his head all the way home, and as he began to prepare the evening meal. The communal cooking idea had never worked out, mainly due to Katie's expensive tastes and Paige's fussy ones, but he knew that if he cooked a half-decent pasta with sauce both Holly and Olivia would eat it. That always made him feel pleased with himself, as he liked to imagine that he had then contributed something to their magnificent figures, so that by the end of term each might have an extra inch of boob and bum that was all his doing.

All four girls were in, chatting in the community room while he cooked, and by serving the pasta separately and offering a jar of organic black pesto he even managed to persuade Paige to have some too. Only Katie declined, taking a little York ham, quail in aspic and a salad from the continental delicatessen in town instead. One or two comments were passed, good natured enough, but leaving Daniel keener than ever to see the rich girl stripped down.

As usual, they sat around and talked once dinner was finished, and as usual Daniel felt somewhat left out, but his exclusion now served only to enhance his excitement at the thought of watching them undress, and somewhat lessen his guilt. Paige was the first to go up, but only to write her essay, so Daniel lingered, hoping that with the bottle of wine Katie had opened to loosen their tongues their conversation might grow intimate.

Only when Holly and Katie had started a heated debate about the pros and cons of private and public education did he give up and go to bed. Evidently none of the girls was in the mood for sexy conversation, or at least – so he suspected – not in front of him. In the privacy of his bedroom, he locked the door and turned on the camera monitor, activating the cameras one by one to take a brief glance into each bedroom. As he knew perfectly well, only Paige was there, seated at her desk with a pile of reference books beside her and another open in her hands.

He sat back, conscious of a certain quiet elation. Maybe there was nothing to watch, yet, but he was in control, his cameras ready to capture whatever might be on show. A well-timed push sent his chair across the carpet to his computer desk and he settled down to surf, avoiding porn sites for once so as not to excite himself too early and casting optimistically frequent glances to the other monitor screen.

Nearly an hour had passed before there was any movement other than Paige's studious assault on her essay. Holly appeared, presumably having grown tired of arguing with Katie, and threw herself down on her bed with a magazine. Daniel watched for a while, admiring the full swells of her well-packed jeans and the soft curves of brown flesh where her midriff showed, but she didn't seem in any hurry to undress and he soon lost interest.

Olivia was next to retire, not upstairs, to Daniel's relief, but to her own room. Like Holly, she flopped down on the bed but, unlike Holly, she seemed intent on her body, if only her feet. Ten minutes later, he had grown bored of watching her pedicure routine and switched back to Holly, who was still reading, and Paige, who was still writing.

'Come on, get dirty!' he urged under his breath. 'Let's have those knickers down, ladies, or at least let's have my rich bitch come up.'

As if in response to his plea, the stairs creaked to the sound of Katie's footstep. Daniel quickly clicked on her window, in time to see her enter the room. She looked tired and a little drunk, yawning and steadying herself on the door handle before going to the bed. Daniel licked his lips, hoping she wouldn't stay up, and, sure enough, her hands had already gone to the button of her jeans.

'Oh yes!' he sighed. 'Down they come, Katie, down they come . . .'

His voice broke to a whimper of pleasure as she obliged, hooking her thumbs into the waistband of her perfectly fitted jeans and pushing them swiftly down over a pair of lacy, white silk panties. A quick adjustment and his cock was out of his fly and in his hand, already growing as he watched Katie first push her jeans down and then off before she began to walk around the room with her panties and the tuck of her bum cheeks on show beneath the hem of her blouse.

'That's good,' he breathed. 'Now pull them down, darling, let's have some bare bum.'

This time Katie failed to oblige, instead putting on a robe and making for the bathroom. Daniel quickly switched cameras, watching as she entered the room and shrugged off the robe, once more providing him with a view of sweetly turned cheeks encased in white lace as she washed and brushed her teeth. His cock was now hard, and stayed that way, but he was only squeezing gently, sure that there would be more to see and determined not to waste his orgasm.

She seemed to be taking forever, and Daniel made a quick check of the other girls in case anything fruity was going on, only to find them much as before. Switching back to the bathroom just in time, he caught Katie as she was undoing the last button of her blouse. Both his heart rate and the speed of his wanking picked up, his eyes glued to the monitor as she let the blouse fall from her shoulders and tossed it casually into the laundry basket.

His view was less than perfect, with the full globe of Katie's panty-clad bum on show but only a portion of her ample chest reflected in the mirror. It made little difference. She was Katie, and she was about to go nude, or at least down to panties, her hands already behind her back, her fingers on the catch of her bra. Daniel nearly came as her bra snipped open, allowing her breasts to loll forwards under their weight, and to his utter joy she was turning sideways, towards the wash basket as she eased her cups free to expose two of the plumpest, most suckable, most fuckable breasts he had ever seen.

The spunk was dribbling down his hand as he stared open mouthed at the monitor, still drinking in the sight of Katie's naked chest despite the guilt and self-loathing now filling his head. She was just too beautiful to miss, too perfect, too desirable. Her breasts were heavenly, each full pink globe tipped by a medium-sized somewhat protuberant nipple, reminding him irresistibly of puppy dog's noses. Even in his post-orgasmic agony, he wanted to suck them, to bury his face between them, to rub his slippery cock in her cleavage.

He also wanted to grovel at her feet, apologising for daring to peep at her, for daring to aspire to her body in any way at all, and for her to punish him, maybe kick him or slap his face. Yes, that was what she should do, slap his face, hard, as he grovelled at her feet in the nude, his pathetic little cock dribbling spunk down his hand as she towered over him in just her panties, her magnificent breasts naked and proud.

Daniel gave a little whimper as he shut his eyes, unable to cope with his emotions any more. Katie, blissfully unaware of his prying gaze, had continued to wash, lifting each heavy breast in turn to wipe a flannel beneath, a sight far too engaging for Daniel to ignore for long. Soon his eyes were open again, feasting on her naked flesh as she continued to wash, while his cock, although somewhat deflated, had not shrivelled to its normal limp size.

There was no doubt at all in his mind that what Katie was now doing was erotic, the idea of any woman touching her breasts without turning herself on being completely alien to him. He began to wonder if she was going to masturbate, and hoping she'd be really dirty about it if she did. She was so aloof, so untouchable, and yet he had heard what posh girls were like and her superior attitude made the idea of watching her get really filthy with herself infinitely more desirable.

No doubt, he considered, she'd put her fingers up her pussy, perhaps suck them to taste her own juice. Maybe she'd show off to herself in the mirror, playing with her breasts and pussy, perhaps her bottom too, spreading her glorious cheeks to admire her bottom hole, perhaps even tickling her ring or putting a finger in. A shiver ran through his body at the thoughts and he began to pull at his cock again.

Katie was drying her breasts, which had made her nipples fully erect, each stiff pink teat now sticking up like a small raspberry, and much the same colour. Daniel gave a soft moan at the sight, and another as she abruptly pushed her panties down and kicked them off, bending just far enough to afford him a brief teasing glimpse of the shadowy secrets between her bottom cheeks. Now she was nude, and as she dropped her discarded panties into the wash basket Daniel was staring in awe.

Her body was as good as any of his favourite porno models, better in fact. She was real, all woman, and all curves, her heavy breasts and full bottom cheeks brought to perfection by her long perfectly formed legs and narrow waist. No girl on the net or in a magazine had ever looked so good, not even when showing far more, because this was Katie, haughty, beautiful Katie. She wasn't being paid to show off her curves either, a thought which has always sullied even the best pornography. Far better, she was stripped casually for his gaze, totally unaware, her very innocence making the exposure of her body infinitely more thrilling.

Daniel's cock was sore, but he was still masturbating, unable to stop as he watched. Unfortunately, Katie didn't seem to have turned herself on after all, merely completing her ablutions before putting her robe back on and leaving the bathroom. Daniel switched to her room, watching as she entered and sat down on the bed to brush out her hair. He was wondering what she wore at night, and whether a skimpy silk baby-doll nightie or full nudity would be more exciting.

As it was, she pulled on a pair of pyjamas, which while nicely taut over her bottom and breasts lacked the sexual implications he had hoped for. His frustration grew sharply as he realised she wasn't going to be dirty with herself. Instead, she got into bed, reading a magazine about horse riding. Quickly he flicked between the other monitors, but, while Paige was now in the bathroom, she had kept her robe on while she brushed her teeth, showing nothing.

He sat back, feeling at once frustrated, guilty and cross with himself, yet unable to tear his eyes from the monitor screen. None of the girls was doing anything remotely sexual, which seemed grossly unfair, almost as if it were a deliberate taunt to him as a Peeping Tom. Again and again he ran through the five screens, his cock slowly deflating in his hand until it was completely limp. He sighed as he clicked on Katie's window for what he was telling himself would be the last time.

Katie

Feeling more than a touch of frustration, Katie put her magazine down. It was no good, she had to do it, however shameful. Holly, however common, was simply too like Tia, both in looks and in personality. Just to hear her laugh or see her smile was painful, inspiring feelings of regret and excitement, embarrassment and lust, but in the end there was no denying what she wanted to do, and only one way to soothe her feelings.

Deeply ashamed of herself, she pushed her bedclothes down and lifted her knees, then her hips, allowing her to push her pyjama bottoms to her ankles. As she undid her top across her breasts, there was the distinct feeling that it was all rather mechanical, masturbation not so much for pleasure as an attempt to make her feelings go away, an attempt she knew was doomed to failure.

That didn't stop her as she closed her eyes and let her hands stray to her sex and breasts, stroking the soft hair of her pubic mound and one already stiff nipple as she tried to get her head around the idea of coming over her housemate. It was immensely shameful, and even as she began to stroke her sex lips her thoughts were being led further down that same path, imagining how it would feel to go down on her knees and lick Holly to ecstasy, even to kiss the black girl's bottom.

She forced her mind away, determined to retain at least some dignity, and instead imagined how it might be if Holly were to give her the same service. Unfortunately, it was hard to imagine the tough outspoken girl doing anything remotely subservient, at least without an excuse. Reverting to an old favourite, Katie imagined how it would be if the four of them got drunk together over a game of cards. That way there would be an excuse, first to have the removal of their clothes as forfeits for any girl whose money ran out, and then the exchange of sexual pleasures.

Her back arched as her fingers found the warm moist crevice between her sex lips. The fantasy worked very well, as it always had, allowing her to express her desire without worrying too much about reality. After all, she herself had been teased out of her clothes in a card game, long before she had come to identify as lesbian. It worked, and maybe it would work with Holly? Yes, the black girl was no prude, just the opposite. She'd strip for the hell of it, too proud to back down, maybe even when it came to sex.

Katie slid her hand lower, briefly penetrating her slippery easy hole before spreading her sex lips wide to the air, two fingers holding them apart, a third stroking the soft wet flesh between. Her eyes closed and her mouth came wide; the hand on her breasts began to squeeze one full globe as she imagined how it would be.

Holly wouldn't be taking the game seriously, but playing the clown as usual, so she'd soon be out of money. Katie would suggest playing for clothes, making it a challenge, so that Holly looked weak if she backed down. That would work, without doubt, and the black girl's clothes would come off, soon leaving her nude. They'd be drunk, very drunk, drunk enough to make Holly dance naked the next time she lost, and then, then would come what Katie really wanted.

She'd suggest it, something rude but still playful, maybe a spanking. Yes, that would be perfect, and she would give it, holding the naked defiant girl across her lap and dishing out a firm punishment in front of the others. The thought of spanking Holly's beautiful bottom was enough to come over, but Katie held back, teasing herself as she sought the perfect climax.

Maybe the spanking would even turn Holly on, maybe enough to go all the way. Not in front of the others, perhaps, that was too much, but later, in one of their rooms. Holly would come in, still nude, flushed and excited. They'd talk. They'd kiss. Before long, Holly would be on her knees at Katie's feet, licking.

Katie's back arched tight, lifting her bottom from the bed as she rubbed furiously at her spread sex, right on the edge of orgasm as she imagined the feel of the black girl's body, first the plump fleshy bottom cheeks under her hand as the spanking was dished out, then warm and resilient as they cuddled, and, lastly, her tongue. Knowing full well that the object of her desire was immediately on the other side of a wall, Katie bit her lip as she started to come, only for the momentary break in concentration to change her fantasy.

Suddenly, it was her across Holly's knee, having her bare bottom smacked in front of Olivia and Paige, her coming shyly into Holly's room in the hope of something more intimate still, and her being put on to her knees to apply her tongue to the black girl's sex. She tried to stop it, but couldn't, her thighs contracting hard around her hand as she came with her teeth pressed tight to her lip and her breast caught hard in her grip, unable to push away the images of her own shaming as she rode her orgasm. But even as she came down she was wondering if it might not be possible to turn fantasy to reality after all.

Olivia

As she stepped on to the platform of Winchester Station, Olivia was doing her best to hold her poise, and failing. Her plan had seemed both simple and sensible in the privacy of her room, but now, when she was about to meet Mistress Anastasia herself, it seemed unutterably foolish and doomed to failure. The woman was older than her, and far more experienced, and surely she would see through Olivia's deception in an instant.

Mistress Anastasia's reply had been curt, telling Olivia to catch a particular train and meet at the station. None of the people on the platform looked even remotely like the Mistress, so Olivia made for the exit, glancing around for the towering formidable figure she expected, only to stop in surprise as she emerged from the broad double doors. There was a woman standing just a few yards away across the broad pedestrian area that fronted the station; slim, elegant and clad entirely in black, as Olivia had expected, but different in one important detail. Mistress Anastasia was no more than five foot four. Feeling considerably more confident, Olivia stepped forward, smiling as she approached the woman.

'Hi, you must be Mistress Anastasia?' she introduced herself. 'I'm Olivia.'

'Yes,' the woman answered, her voice haughty, cold and somewhat contrived. 'Come with me.'

Mistress Anastasia turned on her heel and started off. Olivia followed, unsure what to say in the face of the woman's brusque, even aggressive attitude. As she caught up, the woman spoke again.

'Two paces behind.'

Olivia slackened her pace a trifle, reminding herself that she was there under false pretences and so should swallow the insult. Evidently, Mistress Anastasia intended to express her dominance from the start, which at least made it easier for Olivia to play her own role. Falling back to walk as she had been ordered, she followed the woman to a parked car, not, as Olivia might have expected, some large and ancient saloon, but a perfectly ordinary runabout.

'You will drive,' Mistress Anastasia stated.

'I don't have my licence,' Olivia pointed out, 'or any insurance.'

Mistress Anastasia seemed nonplussed for a moment before replying. 'Then one of your tasks will be to learn, with suitable encouragement.'

'I can't afford the lessons,' Olivia said.

Mistress Anastasia sighed. 'We shall see what can be done. Get in.'

Olivia obeyed, climbing into the front beside Mistress Anastasia, who didn't comment. They set off in silence, through the centre of Winchester and out along a long straight road back in the direction of Silbury, turning off at an estate of houses not dissimilar to Number 47 Myrtle Road. The one Mistress Anastasia stopped outside was no different from the others, save perhaps for a particularly well-tended front garden, once more reducing Olivia's sense of awe for the dominatrix.

Nevertheless, she was careful to fall into step behind Mistress Anastasia as they approached the house, and to wait silently while the door was opened. Inside, the house again seemed perfectly normal, with an open door showing a living room furnished in cream, pale wood and glass, and a completely average kitchen at the end of the corridor.

Without speaking, Mistress Anastasia ascended the stairs, unlocked a door directly across the landing and ushered Olivia inside. The smell of leather caught

Olivia's nose even before she stepped through the door, giving her both a warning and a familiar tingle of excitement as she finally found herself in the sort of environment she'd been expecting.

The room was large and square, with an enormous mirror on one wall making it seem more substantial still. Both walls and ceiling were painted crimson, with a carpet in the same rich shade, while the furnishings were in dark wood, black leather and bright metal. But they were no ordinary furnishings. Bars covered most of one wall, a tall wooden cross with leather cuffs attached was fixed to another, while a series of shelves and hooks on a third held every sort of cane, whip and paddle she had ever seen and several she hadn't, also a great deal of rope, chain and leather strapping. The floor was occupied by a stool apparently designed to have a man bent over it for whipping, a large metal cage and two chairs, one a fantastic device of black leather and straps, the other absolutely plain.

'Great dungeon,' Olivia admitted, genuinely impressed and not a little envious. 'All this gear must have cost a bomb.'

'Enough,' Mistress Anastasia admitted. 'You are not shocked?'

'No,' Olivia answered. 'I've always dreamt of having somewhere like this to play in.'

'What we do is *not* play,' Mistress Anastasia responded. 'That is one important lesson you must learn . . . among many others.'

'I'm willing to learn. I want to learn,' Olivia responded, biting down her instinctive response to what seemed a foolish and pedantic attitude.

'So you have said,' Mistress Anastasia responded, 'but I wonder, do you truly understand what it means to seek to be a domina?'

'Yes,' Olivia answered, struggling to keep the indignation out of her voice. 'It's what I've always wanted. It's what I am.'

'It is what you might be able to become, with training,' Mistress Anastasia informed her. 'I hope you understand that in order to achieve this you must follow my rule absolutely and without question?'

'Yes, I understand that,' Olivia lied.

'Then at least learn to address me properly. While we are together, alone or in the presence of one of my slaves, you will address me as Mistress, always.'

'Yes ... Mistress,' Olivia managed, forcing the words out with difficulty.

'Good. Perhaps there is hope for you after all.'

'When do we start, Mistress?'

Olivia cast another glance around the room. It was everything she had imagined. The thought of putting a man through his paces with the equipment was exciting to say the least, and also represented the culmination of years of desire. With luck, Mistress Anastasia had had the sense to arrange something for the afternoon.

'Now,' Mistress Anastasia stated and Olivia's heart jumped.

'Cool!' Olivia answered. 'I mean, I'm pleased to hear it, Mistress.'

'First,' Mistress Anastasia went on, 'I am going to spank you, hard, and on your bare bottom.'

'Spank me!?' Olivia echoed in horror.

'Yes, I am going to spank you. Do you imagine you can learn to give without ever having received?'

'Yes! I mean, that's the whole thing about being dominant, isn't it? A true domina gives and she never receives, that's right, isn't it? Isn't it? It says so in all the magazines.'

'Magazines read by men, and yes, so far as men are concerned, a Mistress never, ever receives punishment. Nevertheless, it is essential that a girl like yourself understands how it feels, physically, and to submit herself, which is why I am going to spank you.'

Mistress Anastasia was trying to keep her voice cool and level, but there was no hiding the relish in the last few words. Convinced that the awful woman merely wanted an excuse to smack her bottom, Olivia struggled for the right thing to say, and was still trying to find the words when Mistress Anastasia spoke again.

'You may leave now, if you wish, Olivia, or at any time, but there is no middle ground. You must obey me, or leave.'

'I . . . look, is it really necessary –' Olivia began, only to stop.

Mistress Anastasia sat down on the plain chair, her knees extended to form a lap. Olivia remembered all the times she'd imagined taking a man across her knees for a spanking, and all the pictures she'd seen with the woman in that same pose, usually with some well-deserving male about to get it. Now it was she who was expected to assume that unspeakably humble position, laid across a woman's knee with her bottom the highest part of her body, for her jeans to be taken down, for her knickers to be taken down, for her bare cheeks to be smacked.

'No, I can't,' she managed. 'it's just not me. I'm dominant!'

'Then leave,' Mistress Anastasia replied calmly.

Olivia began to step away, only to hesitate, thinking both of her plan and her bank balance. Yet it was impossible to allow herself to suffer such an undignified fate as a bare-bottom spanking, from anyone, let alone the infuriating Mistress Anastasia. Still she hesitated, fidgeting as she stood there wondering what she could possibly say to get her out of it and knowing that she would feel almost as small and as ridiculous if she fled as if she took her medicine.

Mistress Anastasia spoke again, not unkindly. 'There is another reason for this, Olivia. As a domina you will quickly learn that there are those who would make a mockery of you, seek to exploit you or put a stop to what you do for moral reasons. I never accept a client without a preliminary interview, which includes a spanking, because no reporter or anybody who is not genuine will ever accept that. So what is it to be?'

'I'm genuine,' Olivia protested. 'You know that. You saw my ad.'

'Which might very well have been placed by a reporter,' Mistress Anastasia pointed out.

'Yes, but I'm a student, and I can prove it. I have my Union card.'

'I don't doubt that you are a student, but that doesn't mean you don't intend to go to the papers. Now choose.'

Olivia began to answer, and stopped. She could see the sense in what Mistress Anastasia was saying, and to know that it would be a test diluted the shame of what she was being asked to do somewhat. It was still enough to make her want to cry, and yet she knew that if she walked away she'd be in tears anyway. To be spanked was intolerable, a complete reversal of her sexuality, and yet it was from another woman, and there was a good reason for it.

'Um ... maybe on the seat of my jeans?' she offered, choking out the words. 'And standing, not across your knee.'

Mistress Anastasia shook her head. 'If you are to

111

be spanked, Olivia, you must be spanked properly, over my knee, and bare bottom.'

'Oh come on!' Olivia pleaded. 'You know that's not necessary.'

'I think you know it is, Olivia,' Mistress Anastasia answered.

'No,' Olivia protested, despite knowing full well that had the roles been reversed she would have insisted on the same complete submission now being demanded of her.

'Yes, Olivia,' Mistress Anastasia insisted, and patted her lap.

Olivia managed a single miserable sob in response, and suddenly she knew she was going to do it. Before she could stop herself, she had gone forward, the lump in her throat so big she was unable to speak as she laid herself down across Mistress Anastasia's lap, bottom up, the humiliation already burning in her head, the tears already welling in her eyes.

Mistress Anastasia didn't say a word, but began to prepare Olivia for the spanking in a calm matter-of-fact manner, as if introducing young girls to corporal punishment was nothing out of the ordinary. Maybe, Olivia realised, it wasn't. Maybe Mistress Anastasia had spanked plenty of girls. That made no difference. Now it was she, Olivia, who was laid across the woman's lap, who was having the button of her jeans fumbled open, who was having the taut denim eased down over her bottom.

A sob escaped her throat as Olivia's knickers came on show behind and the first hot tear escaped from the corner of her eye. Mistress Anastasia made no comment, and didn't stop, but adjusted Olivia's jeans to leave the full width of her panty seat exposed, then took hold of the waistband. Olivia shut her eyes, squeezing fresh tears from beneath the lids, and bit her lip in an effort to stop herself snivelling as her knickers started to come down, pulled slowly but surely off her bottom and inverted around her jeans to leave her fully bare behind.

She knew she was showing not just her bare cheeks but also the rear lips of her sex, and with that realisation she burst into tears, no longer able to hold back her emotions. Mistress Anastasia merely clicked her tongue in mild disapproval, took Olivia firmly around the waist and began to spank. It hurt, a sharp, stinging pain that had Olivia gasping and kicking her feet almost immediately, which earned a rebuke.

'Do try not to be a baby, Olivia.'

'I can't help it!' Olivia sobbed.

Still she bit her lip, struggling to retain what little dignity was left as she thought of how many times she'd imagined how she'd taunt any man who lost control while he was under punishment, tell him how pathetic he was, mock his inability to cope with the pain. Maybe she was crying for good reason, because she should never, ever be the one getting the spanking, but that was no excuse for making a fuss over how much it hurt.

Not that she could stop herself; she was fighting to control her body as the smacks got harder but was giving in almost immediately. First, her feet began to kick again, then her head to toss and her body to squirm, until with the smacks now raining down hard on her bouncing bottom cheeks she finally let go completely, wriggling in Mistress Anastasia's grip and thrashing desperately from side to side in her futile, pathetic attempts to escape the pain, only managing to make a yet more embarrassing display of herself.

Soon the tears were streaming down her cheeks as she bawled her eyes out, her legs pumping hard in her lowered clothes and her body bucking up and down so wildly that her cheeks had begun to part, showing off her bottom hole to her persecutor, and with that final humiliating exposure she realised that her spanking was absolutely necessary, and that there was no other way she could truly understand what it meant to be punished across a woman's knee.

Instantly she was babbling apologies and asking brokenly for the spanking to go on, sobbing out her words as the slaps continued to rain down on her now burning cheeks. Mistress Anastasia merely adjusted her position slightly, bringing Olivia's bottom up higher so that the big cheeks were open enough to show off her anus and the rear lips of her pussy. Olivia accepted the added humiliation meekly, now kicking only a little as the spanking continued.

The pain had gone, her bottom now glowing hot, her pussy too, and as she found herself wanting to stick her cheeks up to the smacks she realised an awful truth: the spanking had turned her on. With that, fresh tears burst from her eyes, but there was no denying it, she felt she wanted to lift her bottom not just for smacks but for penetration or, better still, for penetration *and* smacks, a good hard fucking on her knees while her blazing cheeks were smacked up hotter still.

It was too much for her, too shameful, too intimate. She began to fight, begging Mistress Anastasia to stop and struggling to climb off, not because she didn't want to be spanked, but because she did.

For a moment, Mistress Anastasia kept her grip, but Olivia was too big, too strong and too determined, lurching free only to lose her balance and sprawl on the floor, legs spread wide to the woman who'd punished her and also taught her a thoroughly humiliating truth.

'That will do, I suppose,' Mistress Anastasia stated, doing her best to retain her authority. 'I trust you now understand why that had to be done?'

'Yes – yes, Mistress,' Olivia admitted, despite a private determination never to reveal the full truth to anybody. 'Now I understand a lot more, and I hope you accept that I'm for real?'

'Yes,' Mistress Anastasia admitted. 'Now let me give you a hug.'

Olivia hesitated, knowing that to accept the comfort being offered would be another admission of her inferior status to Mistress Anastasia, but only for a moment before crawling across and allowing herself to be taken into the woman's arms. It was a hideously shameful position, kneeling with her jeans and knickers still down over her blazing bottom as she was cuddled and her back and hair stroked, but it was impossible to deny that it also felt soothing, and she even allowed Mistress Anastasia to kiss her mouth before finally getting to her feet.

She could see herself in the big mirror, her hair and clothes dishevelled, tear-streaked face and bare red bottom making it quite obvious she'd been given a spanking, her chest still heaving with emotion. It was hard to imagine a less dominant image, especially as she looked thoroughly sorry for herself. She quickly began to adjust her clothes as Mistress Anastasia spoke.

'There is an important point to be learnt there, Olivia. If I have to spank you again, I will certainly give you a hug afterwards, and should you ever find yourself in a relationship with a man who likes to be spanked then you will also find it best to hug him afterwards, but hugs are for friends. Never hug a client.'

'How do you mean, if you have to spank me

again?' Olivia asked, so horrified that the rest of what Mistress Anastasia had said barely registered.

'It may well be necessary to spank you again,' Mistress Anastasia responded coolly, 'but rest assured that it will always be in private. Now, perhaps you would like me to show you how to use some of this equipment?'

Olivia nodded but gave no answer. She couldn't, rendered speechless by the thought of a future of bare-bottom spankings across Mistress Anastasia's knee.

Paige

Her essay complete, Paige closed the commentary on Milton she had been working from, placed her pen neatly on her desk and sat back in her chair. She had got up early to finish it so that she'd be able to go riding with Katie and not have to worry about work. The absolute quiet of early morning had made it easy to concentrate, and she was finished before she'd expected to be, giving her time to get Katie's things ready as well as her own while her friend got up.

It was impossible not to feel a touch of chagrin as she polished Katie's riding boots, but there was no denying the pleasure she took in serving the object of her adoration. Not that Katie seemed to notice, but that was probably just as well. After all, a woman like Katie Shalstone was hardly going to be interested in Paige, or any other woman.

As she worked, she began to fantasise about who Katie might like. Undoubtedly, it would be a truly exceptional man, somebody both strong and sensitive, handsome and wealthy, the sort of man who would never look twice at Paige. Maybe, just maybe, Paige would be allowed to be a bridesmaid, and just the thought of basking in Katie's reflected glory made her tummy flutter, for all that it also brought a flush of shame.

She imagined how it might be if Katie used her as a surrogate. No doubt the gorgeous boyfriend would sometimes be aroused when Katie was indisposed or simply not in the mood, in which case Paige would have to suck his cock or even allow him to put it inside her. It would be done whenever and wherever he pleased, regardless of Paige's feelings, her sole reward the satisfaction of pleasing Katie. Also, if there was anything he liked but Katie didn't, then Paige would have to act as substitute, accepting any dirty sexual act, and with Katie watching. The idea made her shiver, and she had just begun to enlarge on what actually might be required of her when Katie herself appeared, now in full riding gear but for her boots.

'Are we ready?' Katie demanded.

'Yes,' Paige answered, and watched as Katie pulled on her now highly polished black riding boots one by one, a sight that always made her feel weak.

'I thought we might ride up to Bramwell Heath today,' Katie remarked as they left the house.

'That would be nice,' Paige responded automatically, despite knowing that it would mean missing her nine o'clock lecture.

They set off for Greymartens, where Katie signed in and put the costs of the day on her father's account while Paige busied herself getting the horses ready. As had become their habit, they started off along a bridleway which climbed the long chalky slope to the downs. For most of the way, they were obliged to go in single file, but once up on the more open ground of Bramwell Heath they were able to ride side by side. After a gallop, with Katie inevitably leaving Paige behind, they reined in together and continued at a sedate walk.

Katie had been unusually silent, which Paige had respected, but now she spoke, her voice unusually diffident. 'Your school was all girls, wasn't it?'

'Yes, St Mary's Lytham,' Paige replied.

She'd mentioned it before, several times, but Katie never seemed to remember that sort of thing about other people.

'So was Roegate,' Katie went on. 'It seems funny now, doesn't it, the silly games we used to play and all that sort of thing.'

'How do you mean?' Paige asked.

'Oh you know,' Katie answered. 'Truth or dare, and spin the bottle. Don't tell me you didn't do that?'

'No,' Paige admitted, 'or, anyway, some girls did, but the sisters were very strict about that sort of thing.'

'That's a shame, it was fun,' Katie went on. 'I suppose we're all a bit old for that sort of thing now, or don't you think so?'

'I – I don't know,' Paige responded, already wondering what Katie was getting at. 'Do you mean you'd like to?'

'It would liven up the evenings a bit, don't you think?' Katie went on.

'Just you and I?' Paige asked, trying desperately to keep her voice level, despite a rapidly growing sense of embarrassment mixed with a wild hope.

'It's no fun with two, silly!' Katie laughed. 'I mean all of us.'

'What about Daniel?' Paige asked, swallowing her disappointment.

'Daniel?' Katie responded. 'Oh no, I don't think so. So how about it? If I try to get a game going, would you back me up?'

'Yes, I suppose so,' Paige admitted, 'but what would we do exactly?'

'Whatever takes our fancy,' Katie told her. 'You know how it goes.'

Paige didn't, but she was fairly surely Katie just intended an exchange of secrets. Maybe it was even Katie's way of making a careful pass, although she'd have expected her friend to be more open, bold even. Still, it was intriguing and, while the idea also seemed somewhat silly, she knew that if it happened she would be drawn in.

Daniel

For three full days, Daniel had held back from spying on the girls, not for any moral reason, but because watching Katie masturbate had left his cock so sore that any further stimulation risked injury. He had always suspected that posh girls were the dirtiest of all underneath, but to see her bring herself to orgasm apparently over something in her riding magazine had allowed his always fertile imagination to reach new limits. By the time she had come he'd been long finished, but had still been rubbing his cock, and only when she'd finally adjusted her pyjamas and covered up had he realised just how much damage he'd done to himself.

A brief inspection showed that he really ought to wait another day, but his need for orgasm was getting close to desperation, a situation not helped by the continuing hot weather and the abundance of nubile flesh on display in the town it caused. That afternoon had been particularly difficult. First, as he walked back from the supermarket with the day's shopping along his usual route through the park, he'd seen that some of the locals had fixed a rope swing above the river and were using it to swing out over the water. The group had included girls, and he had been unable to resist taking the longer path along the riverbank in the hope that there might be something worthwhile on show.

He had not been disappointed. Of the three girls there, two were already soaking wet, their tops plastered to pleasingly ample breasts, and as he had approached they'd been trying to catch the third as she ran screaming and laughing in her efforts to avoid her fate, which was obviously to be thrown in the river. Daniel had put his shopping bags down, pretending to tie a shoelace, and so managed to delay himself just long enough. The girl had been caught, rolled on her back and picked up by her ankles and wrists, wriggling all the while and with her tiny skirt rucked up so high that he'd had a clear view of a pair of cheeky pink bottom cheeks barely covered by tiny blue panties. Despite her struggles and playful protests, she'd been thrown in the river, and for one joyous moment as she sailed through the air her thighs had come apart, rewarding Daniel with a brief but exquisite flash of her pussy with the panties pulled up so tight that her bare lips showed at either side of the taut blue cotton.

Sure that he would attract attention if he lingered, Daniel had been forced to move on, his cock a solid bar in his pants and the image of the girl's helpless display of cunt fixed firmly in his head. Even before he'd reached the house he'd been trying to work out how best to masturbate without renewed chafing, but then had come the second shock. Holly had been outside the house with her Greek boyfriend, wearing nothing but a skinny top and a pair of cut-down jeans, and seated on the bonnet of Katie's car in such a way that an extraordinary volume of her full black bottom was spilling out behind.

Despite his nervousness in the presence of the large and aggressive boyfriend, he had been unable not to stare, drinking in the way her flesh bulged as she moved and quivered to her laughter as the boyfriend made some humorous remark. Worse still, as he'd drawn near, she'd bent to pick a piece of gravel from her sandal, so that for one glorious, agonising moment the full spread of her bottom had been stuck out towards him, her abundant flesh straining out of her shorts to what looked like breaking point in a perfect ball of juicy female bottom.

They'd barely noticed him as he passed, let alone acknowledged him, leaving him with a strong sense of pique in addition to his sexual frustration. Now, alone in his room once more while they continued their conversation outside, he was hoping they'd come in and go to Holly's room for sex so that he could watch her put through her paces on his undoubtedly huge cock.

Only the prospect of something better later prevented him from taking out his cock and finishing himself off, but while there might be a chance of Holly and her boyfriend coming upstairs he felt unable to leave the room, so that he spent the next hour seething with frustration, only for the boyfriend to leave.

Cursing his own uncontrollable lust, he went downstairs and made himself a solitary dinner before retiring once more to his room.

Paige

Paige closed her book as she reached the end of the chapter she had promised herself she would complete before allowing her mind to turn to other things, and specifically her conversation with Katie that morning. She had thought it through again and again, and the only reasonable conclusion was that Katie wanted some form of probably mild sexual contact with herself and maybe Olivia and Holly too. Nothing else fitted the facts, and yet she was surprised her friend hadn't been more open. Surely Katie realised that Paige worshipped her? Or maybe not.

She was frowning as she put the book back on the shelf, and struggling to think rationally without allowing her overpowering crush to get in the way. Maybe it wasn't so obvious? Maybe Katie wasn't as worldly wise as she seemed? Maybe her feelings even reflected Paige's own?

Just the thought was enough to set her heart hammering, and also to fill her with guilt. She knew, in principle, that lesbianism was perfectly acceptable. There was even a university society for lesbians. Admitting that she was that way inclined herself was a very different matter, despite her long history of crushes on other girls. It was just silly, and also sinful, something she would undoubtedly grow out of and until she did should hide as best she could.

At least, that was what her upbringing told her, but she had already rejected most of the teachings the nuns at St Mary's had tried to impose on her, including the very existence of God. Why, therefore, should their opinions on sex hold any more authority? Why was it wrong anyway? If both she and Katie wanted it, how could it be anything more than harmless pleasure?

She was still wracked with guilt as she tried to decide whether she should suggest to Katie the sort of game they had spoken about, and also scared of rejection. Katie had made it clear she wanted all four girls to play, but maybe that had just been an excuse, made so as not to risk too much intimacy in the event of Paige rejecting her? Still standing, she began to chew thoughtfully on her lip, her mind moving between the guilty joy of undressing in front of her friend according to the turn of the cards and the pain of possible rejection. Finally, she reached a decision.

Daniel

After hesitating twice, once through guilt and once for the state of his cock, Daniel switched on the monitor. Within seconds, the programme had sorted itself out and he was able to look in on the girls' rooms. Only Paige was visible, and she was doing nothing in particular, and yet the sense of relief as the pictures came up was vast, as if all his cares were draining away. He recognised his reaction as a symptom of addiction, and told himself that he would stop before his need to spy got out of control, despite knowing full well that it already had.

His door was locked, his clothes off, his dressing gown undone to allow easy access to his cock once things got fruity, as he was sure they would. After all, even without Holly and her boyfriend to watch the girls had to undress for bed, and that was enough, more than enough, especially when he knew that both Olivia and Katie liked to masturbate over what seemed to be the most outrageous fantasies before going to sleep.

As Paige was the only one there, he left her window up, watching as she moved idly about her room and considering her virtues as a subject for his voyeuristic lusts. Her being shy was good, as it added to the exciting feel of intruding on her privacy, while despite being relatively short she probably had the biggest breasts of all, in proportion. She also had a fine bottom, round and firm, which wiggled as she walked, doubtless quite unconsciously.

He licked his lips at the thought of watching her strip down, but she didn't seem to be ready for bed, or to want to do anything else. Rather, she seemed agitated, as if she didn't quite know what to do with herself. Daniel watched with interest, wondering if she was trying to get over her guilt before indulging herself in some especially dirty piece of masturbation, even though it seemed unlikely. Finally she acted, burrowing into the travelling trunk she kept under her bed to pull out a square green box.

Daniel recognised the box as a role-playing game, increasing his curiosity. Rather than unpack it, Paige just extracted two dice, one yellow, one black. At her desk, she began to roll them, and his heart rate picked up as he wondered if she was going to play some dirty little game with herself, perhaps relying on the fall of the dice to make herself do things she'd otherwise have felt too guilty about, a practice he'd indulged in many, many times.

To his disappointment, she merely continued to roll the dice, only to suddenly catch them up and stand once more, as if she had reached some sort of decision, perhaps based on the numbers she had scored. More puzzled than ever, Daniel watched as she went to her door and left, disappearing from his view. He could now hear her in the corridor, and for one thrilling, almost panic-stricken moment he wondered if she might be coming to him to suggest a game of dice.

She didn't, but walked down the corridor and rapped gently on another door. Daniel quickly switched windows, first to Holly's room, which was dark and presumably empty, then to Katie's just in time to see the blonde girl answer the door to Paige.

Paige

'Come in,' Katie said, opening the door.

'Thank you,' Paige answered, hoping that all the embarrassment, doubt and self-recrimination within her didn't show. 'Are you doing anything this evening?'

'Nothing in particular,' Katie admitted. 'I was going to finish my essay.'

'Oh,' Paige answered. 'I'd better go then.'

'That's all right, it can wait,' Katie went on. 'Would you like a G and T?'

'Please, yes,' Paige answered, eager for the alcohol although she hated the taste.

Katie went to her miniature fridge, leaving Paige to sit down. What she wanted, what she hoped for, seemed insane, an impossible and ridiculous fantasy, and yet she could remember Katie's words. Telling herself she had to speak up or risk losing her courage completely, she forced the words she needed to say from her mouth.

'I was wondering. Would you like a game ... of dice? I mean, it's just that you mentioned playing a game this morning, and I thought ... well, maybe, if you don't mind just me ...' She trailed off, her face

125

burning, sure Katie would realise and be horrified or, worse, laugh at her.

Her friend didn't even turn around, but continued making the drinks, using a tiny sharp knife to slice pieces of lime. Paige waited for the answer, trying to ignore the voices screaming at her from within her head, one telling her she was an idiot, another a shameless slut.

At last Katie turned around. 'If you like.'

Paige felt her stomach tighten. It was going to happen. Or maybe not. Katie had spoken casually, with no sign of tension, much less desire.

'I suppose we should take bets?' Paige asked hopefully.

'Of course, silly,' Katie responded as she passed Paige a drink. 'We need something for chips. Shells will do. I used to use these at school, sometimes.'

As she spoke, she reached back for a lamp, the base of which was a squat rounded bottle weighted down with sea shells, some of which she tipped out into her hand.

Paige took a swallow of her drink as Katie began to count out shells, her enthusiasm and excitement rising once more at her friend's mention of playing similar games at school.

'The cowries can be a pound,' Katie explained, pushing several of the tiny round shells aside. 'These little limpets can be five, and the dog whelks ten.'

'OK,' Paige agreed, wondering if she was going to end up in debt instead of naked.

Daniel

As the girls began to play dice, Daniel watched with his usual mixture of strong emotions and with one

126

hand caressing his cock. Common sense told him that Katie and Paige were merely having a game to pass the time, and neither had said anything to suggest that it was remotely sexual. Yet both his eternal sense of hope and everything from his fantasies suggested otherwise.

'Be a pair of little lezzies,' he muttered under his breath. 'Please turn out to be a pair of little lezzies.'

He could hear the girls talking quite clearly, and it was easy to imagine that their laughter held more than simple companionship, perhaps even the nervous anticipation of those who knew they'd soon be stripping down together for the first time. Then again, he considered, perhaps it wouldn't be the first time? Katie and Paige went riding together almost every morning, after all, and it was all too easy to imagine what they might get up to out among the lonely hedgerows and copses of Salisbury Plain. There was definitely something subservient about Paige's behaviour as well, so that it took no great stretch of the imagination to picture her stripped bare in the woods, perhaps with her glorious bottom decorated with welts from Katie's riding crop, down on her knees and eagerly licking cunt.

At present there was no suggestion of anything of the sort. The dice were going Paige's way, although she was so cautious in her betting that she had made only a small dent in the pile of shells Katie was using for chips. Katie, on the other hand, was bold, putting out large bets on low chances, so that she had lost more through her own reckless play than Paige had won through careful attention to the odds.

Both were laughing, and Katie had put the bottle of gin and some miniature tonics on the table between them. Both were drinking quite fast, increasing Daniel's hope that even if their game was innocent they might end up in a drunken tangle, and whatever happened it was clearly going to be a slow process. Yet, with both Olivia and Holly elsewhere, there was nothing to do but watch and fiddle with his cock.

Katie

'I'll get you in the end.' Katie laughed as she pushed over another handful of shells to Paige. 'Your turn.'

'I'll bet two, no, three, that I can get less than eight,' Paige said, using one finger to place three cowries in a precise line in the exact centre of the table.

'Taken,' Katie agreed, and quickly put out her own shells.

Paige took up the dice and rolled, scoring a two and a three. Smiling, she scooped her shells in. Katie took the dice. Her remaining shells were worth fifteen pounds, and while she knew it was only fair not to take too much from Paige, she didn't like to lose.

'Five of mine against twenty of yours that one of my dice is a six,' she suggested.

'OK,' Paige agreed after an instant of calculation.

Katie threw, scoring a double one. She sighed as she pushed one of her two remaining limpets forwards, as she did so remembering first how Tia and the others had laughed the night she'd ended up naked and had to stick her bottom out to be smacked with a ruler, then thinking of how it would feel to be in the same shameful situation in front of Holly. Paige was nice, but too wet to provide the same thrill, and maybe too innocent even for a bit of harmless fun. Or maybe not? After all, Paige had suggested the game.

'I'm going to be daring,' Paige said. 'I bet five that the yellow one comes out at least two higher than the black.'

'OK, five,' Katie agreed, adding a little pile of cowries to the neat line Paige had set out.

Paige rolled the black die, scoring a five.

'I win, for once,' Katie said, raking in the cowries.

She swallowed the last of her gin and tonic, refilled her glass and topped up Paige's drink. Already she felt a little drunk, more than a little nostalgic, and also beginning to feel bored and frustrated, making her wonder if it would be fun to play naughty with Paige, if only to try and recapture some tiny spark of what she'd lost.

'I'll bet,' she said, pushing the entire pile of shells into the middle of the table, 'my fifteen against everything you've got that I can throw a double six.'

Paige's face flickered with some unknown emotion, but she pushed her pile of shells forwards to join Katie's, who lifted the dice. Now it was going to matter, because whatever happened one of them would end up with nothing. Then she could make her suggestion for how they should continue, just something silly, something to test Paige, but which she could easily back down from if she had to.

She rolled, scoring a six, and a four.

'Bother!' she exclaimed.

Paige scooped her shells in, although she didn't look too happy with her victory.

'Are you going to let me get my own back?' Katie asked.

'You don't have to pay me anything,' Paige said quickly. 'I don't mind playing just for fun.'

'A bet's a bet,' Katie insisted. 'At school we used to smack each other if anyone ran out of chips.'

'Smack each other?' Paige asked, her face going pink.

'With a ruler,' Katie said, feeling the heat start in her own face, 'on the bottom.'

She'd laughed as she said it, as if it meant nothing, but she knew she was blushing. So was Paige.

'Your turn,' Katie said before their mutual embarrassment could get the better of them.

Paige nodded silently as she pushed out five cowries, then a limpet, and finally a dog whelk into the centre of the table.

'I'll give you a chance to get back into the game,' she said.

'That's twenty smacks if I lose,' Katie said, the familiar blend of excitement and humiliation already welling up inside her.

'Let's say I have to roll a double to win,' Paige offered.

Disappointment and relief joined Katie's tangled emotions. It was hard to imagine anything more humiliating than being smacked by Paige, who was such a little brown-nose, but that made her feelings all the stronger.

'Here goes,' Paige said, and rolled.

Katie watched, speechless, as first the yellow and then the black came to a stop, both showing three spots.

Daniel

His mouth slack, his eyes wide, his hand clutching convulsively at his erection, Daniel watched as Katie stood up. Her face was full of chagrin, but that didn't stop her as she went to her desk and took an old-fashioned wooden ruler from the drawer.

130

'You can use this,' he heard her say, and saw Paige nod dumbly as she accepted the ruler.

'Oh fuck,' he mouthed as Katie turned her back to Paige, and to the camera, 'she's going to spank her, oh fuck, oh fuck, oh fuck!'

'Twenty?' Paige queried.

'Twenty,' Katie confirmed, and Daniel's cock jerked in his hand as she stuck her bottom out to be smacked.

She was in jeans, one of the best designer labels, perfectly fitted to her inexpressibly gorgeous bottom, the tight dark-blue denim and rich-yellow stitching following every exquisite contour, every bulge and tuck.

'Oh fuck,' he repeated, now hammering at his cock, his eyes locked on Katie's bottom.

'Go on,' she said, 'don't make me wait, that's not fair.'

'I – I wasn't,' Paige stammered, and smacked the ruler down across the seat of Katie's jeans.

Daniel came, a fountain of spunk erupting from his cock to splash over his belly and the keyboard, but he didn't stop, wanking furiously as he watched Paige apply the ruler to Katie's well-thrust-out bottom. It wasn't hard. In fact, it was rather pathetic, but that didn't matter. He was watching one beautiful buxom girl spank another, actually spank her; the sort of kinky, dirty girl-on-girl sex play he had imagined so often, come over so many, many times, but never seen, not for real.

Magazines weren't the same. The internet wasn't the same. That was all posed, girls playing sexy with girls because they'd been paid, or at best to show off to male watchers. This was infinitely better, something he'd never even been completely sure happened, two perfectly ordinary young girls playing dirty together, not for money, not for anyone else, but for each other.

By the time twenty smacks of the ruler had been applied to Katie's bottom, Daniel was slumped back in his chair, dizzy with ecstasy and triumph, the spunk dribbling slowly down his hand and over his belly.

On screen, Katie made a face, put one hand briefly to her smacked cheeks, and sat down.

Paige

Her hands wouldn't stop shaking as Paige arranged the pile of shells on the table. Her heart was hammering, her throat dry, her head full of excitement and guilt and uncertainty; she was also dizzy with drink. She'd smacked Katie's bottom, something at once so desirable and so inappropriate that it was impossible to get her head around it. Yet she had done it, and if she won again she'd be doing it again, because there was no question of stopping now. The only problem was that she was winning, while there was nothing she wanted in the world more than to have the tables turned on her, for all the agonising embarrassment she would feel if they were. Katie was giggling.

'I'm going to get you, Paige! If it's the last thing I do. Right, another twenty says I can throw a ten or better. And there's another rule: If I get it again, it has to be on my knickers, then bare.'

Paige nodded, her stomach tight as Katie took up the dice and threw them out on to the table. One showed a five, the other a six, and Katie clapped her hands together in delight. 'Yes! At last, some luck. That's twenty you owe me, Paige.'

As she pushed her shells across, Paige was making a rapid calculation. She badly wanted to lose, the mere thought of being spanked by Katie enough to make her feel weak with desire and soak her panties, but it would also mean she owed her friend fifty pounds, which she couldn't really afford. Unless she bargained.

'Can – can we just play for smacks?' she suggested, her cheeks blazing to a new heat as the words came out.

'That's usually the way it ends up,' Katie answered, smiling. 'Your turn then.'

Paige took a nervous swallow of her gin and tonic. The gin bottle was now close to half empty, having been nearly full when they started, but she felt she needed more. She topped up Katie's glass, then her own, before a thought occurred to her.

'I think, maybe we should lock the door,' she suggested.

Katie hesitated, but got up and did as Paige had suggested. Just to hear the click of the lock sent a powerful shiver down Paige's spine. Now she was locked in with Katie, locked in so that they could be naughty together, so that she could have her bottom smacked maybe, maybe more, even some of the unmentionable things she had imagined in her fantasies.

'Play then,' Katie urged.

'OK,' Paige said. 'I bet fifty that I throw a seven.'

'Something tells me somebody wants to lose.' Katie laughed, and Paige felt the blood rush hot to her cheeks one more time.

She took up the dice and rolled, already imagining the exquisite shame of pushing her bottom out to be smacked with the ruler, even as the yellow came down on a two and the black a five.

'Shit!' Katie swore, her eyes wide as she stared down at the seven little spots. 'You bitch!'

'Sorry,' Paige said immediately. 'If you don't want to –'

'You have to pay your losses, or it's no fun. I wouldn't let *you* off.'

'No, but –' Paige began, and stopped.

Katie had already stood up, her hands on the button of her jeans. 'It has to be on the knickers the second time, that's the rules,' she explained once more, as if she felt she needed to excuse her behaviour.

'OK,' Paige agreed, despite feeling that she was committing the most appalling outrage by having Katie take her trousers down.

Even with the button undone, Katie's jeans were so tight she had to wiggle her bottom out of them, leaving her blushing pink as her lacy dove-grey silk panties came on show, already half down over her cheeks. Paige's face was more flushed still, and she paused with the ruler in her hand as Katie adjusted herself behind and pushed out her bottom to make a target of herself.

'Thirty smacks,' Katie said, 'and – and you can do them a little bit harder, or – or there's no point.'

'OK,' Paige answered, and smacked the ruler down across the seat of Katie's knickers.

'Ouch!' Katie said, and made a face.

'Sorry,' Paige said quickly.

'Don't be, it just stings a little with no jeans,' Katie answered. 'Anyway, it's supposed to hurt. I'm paying a forfeit, aren't I?'

'I suppose so,' Paige agreed, and applied a second smack to Katie's bottom, hard enough to send a tremor through the big cheeks.

This time Katie merely made a soft noise in her throat, not so much pain as desire. Telling herself that it was all right if she was giving her friend pleasure, and thrilling to the thought, Paige began to spank to an even rhythm, bringing the ruler firmly down across Katie's bottom. Katie took it giggling and gasping, all the while with her bottom pushed well out to keep her panty seat taut over her cheeks, a sight that filled Paige with desires she could barely cope with even as she applied the spanks.

At last, the fiftieth stroke was done, but Katie stayed as she was for a moment, perhaps hoping for more before she managed to collect herself. Paige put the ruler down, her hands shaking harder than ever as Katie craned back to look at her smacked bottom.

'Am I red?' she asked.

'A bit, round the edges of your panties,' Paige replied.

'It feels warm,' Katie said, and sat down as she continued. 'Now I'm going to get you. I bet every shell you've got and ten more that the black comes out higher than the yellow, but, if you win, I – I have to go bare, and you can do me properly. I mean . . . in the nude, and bent over your knee.'

Katie had swallowed twice as she spoke. Now there was no doubting that what they were doing was erotic, but Paige merely nodded, still unsure of herself, how far she could go and how far Katie would want her to go. She pushed her shells into the middle as Katie caught up the dice, watching as the yellow rolled out to score a five.

'Oh, shit,' Katie said softly, and rolled the black. 'Bother.'

The black had landed on a two. Paige bit her lip, saying nothing as Katie climbed slowly to her feet. She knew her friend wanted what she was about to get, and the thought of giving it thrilled her even though she'd far rather have been the one about to go nude to be spanked across the knee. Katie's humiliation was very real too, her face red and her hands shaking as she began to unbutton her blouse.

'I have to take it all off, everything,' Katie said softly, as if to confirm her own fate, 'and you're to spank me properly, Paige.'

'If you're sure?' Paige asked.

'It's supposed to hurt, or there's no point,' Katie said for the second time. 'You have to *really* spank me, as if you were punishing me for real.'

Katie's blouse was open, showing off a bra in the same dove-grey silk as her panties, with a lace trim covering the upper surfaces of her breasts. She took it off, shaking so badly she kept fumbling with the catch but at last letting it fall to bare the heavy globes of her breasts. Paige found herself wondering if her own were any bigger, and how it would feel to hold Katie's in her hands, maybe to suck her nipples, or to be bare herself, undressing to have her bottom smacked.

'You can use the ruler, or your hand,' Katie said as she once more unbuttoned her jeans.

'Which would you prefer?' Paige asked.

'Your hand, please,' Katie answered, and she had pushed her jeans and panties down as one, exposing her bare bottom behind and the neatly trimmed V of her pubic hair at the front.

A moment more to kick off her shoes and socks along with her jeans and panties, and Katie was in the nude. Paige pushed her chair back from the table, struggling to cope with what she was being asked to do even as Katie stepped forwards to lay herself into spanking position.

'Now do me, spank me, as long as you like,' Katie breathed, and Paige brought her hand down across her friend's bare bottom.

Katie's flesh felt hot and resilient, infinitely desirable, although as Paige began to spank and draw out little squeaks and gasps from her victim she was wishing she could kiss the beautiful flushed cheeks better, maybe even bury her face between them to atone for the grossly inappropriate sin she was committing.

'Harder,' Katie urged suddenly. 'Come on, Paige, punish me.'

Paige began to smack harder, making Katie's cheeks wobble and bounce. The response was a soft groan and, as Katie began to push her bottom up, the last scrap of pretence that what was happening between them was anything but sexual vanished. Katie's cheeks were open, the lips of her sex on full show, soft and puffy and moist between, as was her anus, the tight pink hole in slow, rhythmic contraction.

Shocked by her friend's openly sexual reaction, still Paige spanked, now vigorously, with a touch of the disapproval for sexual display the nuns had spent so much effort drumming into her now showing in the force of her smacks. Katie just moaned all the louder, sighing too, and now up on her toes to lift her bottom into full prominence, her thighs wide and the scent of her excited fanny rich in the air.

'Really hard,' Katie gasped suddenly, 'and do it over my pussy.'

As she spoke, her hand went back to find her sex, rubbing and patting at her swollen lips as her moans grew louder and more urgent. Paige was now spanking as hard as she could, unsure if she was punishing Katie or simply helping her friend masturbate, but with no intention of stopping. Katie's whole bottom was pink, her cheeks squeezing as they were smacked, her anus winking lewdly between, fluid dribbling from her excited sex. She cried out, begging Paige to spank harder still, and again, in a gasping, grunting orgasm, the last of her inhibitions snapping as she began to rub herself on Paige's leg in her ecstasy.

Daniel

Wincing with every step, Daniel struggled to walk normally as he approached the park gates. It was not easy, his cock so sore that every tiny motion against the inside of his pants hurt, and yet he didn't regret a single moment of the session of near-demented masturbation which had left him that way. His first orgasm as Paige had applied a smack to Katie's bottom had been largely involuntary, yet as it became clear that the girls had no intention of stopping he had quickly begun to regret his impulse.

By the time Katie had taken her jeans down to accept the second set of smacks across the seat of her panties, he'd been erect again, and after that their conversation alone had been enough to keep him rock hard and wanking. When she began to undress he came for the second time, just as she lifted her bra to flop out her divinely large and firm breasts.

He'd been unable to stop, still tugging at his slippery half-stiff cock as she stripped nude, and he was almost weeping with desire as she crawled into spanking position across Paige's knee. The camera angle had been near perfect, not quite rear view, but close enough so that he could not only catch glimpses of cunt and even anus as she wriggled her way through her smacking, but also the pained ecstasy on her face. She'd wanted it hard and he'd thrilled to her pain, imagining how it must feel as he drove himself

138

closer to orgasm. When she had begun to rub her cunt on Paige's leg, it had been too much, his cock emitting a pathetic trickle of spunk as he jerked himself to a third orgasm within the space of half an hour.

Guilt and self-recrimination had followed, as always, and he had tried to soothe his feelings by turning the monitor off as the girls tidied up, only to find himself unable to do it. Watching them was just too compulsive, and he'd remained glued to the screen throughout the rather embarrassed conversation they'd held afterwards, and until Paige finally left and Katie went to wash. By then, he'd been hoping that Katie might return the favour by making Paige come, or that the two of them would sleep together. It hadn't happened, which – he reflected as the chafed skin of his cock gave another twinge of pain – was probably just as well.

It was so bad he'd begun to limp, and passers-by were giving him funny looks, as if they knew exactly what was wrong, and why. He sat down to rest, only for a pair of perfect little cuties to go by on roller blades, their tiny skirts barely covering their panties, long bare legs flashing in the sun to their movements. Again he winced as his cock stirred in reaction, and he got up, eager to reach the less dangerous environment of the supermarket.

Unfortunately, the girls of Silbury seemed to have conspired to torment him. First he found himself walking behind two young housewives with low-cut jeans tight over ripe wiggling bottoms, and he was forced to pause, only to discover there was a group on the rope swing, including a girl in a yellow bikini who seemed to be indifferent to the fact that her pants had pulled so far up between her cheeks that she might almost have been bare.

He hurried on into the supermarket, but it seemed impossible to escape the erotic display. Every well-formed breast beneath a top, every hint of nipple showing beneath a bra, every curve of cloth-covered bottom cheek seemed a deliberate provocation. Even the gigantic backside and wrinkled stockings of a matron from the local hospital caused his cock to twitch, as if, in revenge for his peeping, the last of his self-control had been taken away. Yet if anything his guilt was worse than before.

As he shopped he pondered his situation. Basically, his peeping scheme had been *too* successful. With four girls to watch, all of whom could at the very least be guaranteed to undress and wash every single night, he simply had too much to wank over, although the abundance of female flesh had done little or nothing to reduce his urge to capture each and every private moment. Katie and Paige indulging in lesbian spanking games made restraint harder still, while Holly and her boyfriend and Olivia's peculiar habits didn't exactly help.

For a while, he considered the possibility of recording each evening's peep show and restricting himself to one really good evening of masturbation a week, or possibly two. Unfortunately, there were problems. He could only record from one camera at a time, but if he monitored them to see who was giving the best show he knew full well he'd be unable to resist pulling himself off anyway, while if he chose at random he might get little or nothing. The thought of recording two hours of Katie's empty room while she and Paige got dirty together in the other was unbearable.

Then there was the problem of evidence. He wasn't at all sure if once a recording had been made he would have the willpower to erase it, and yet if he built up a collection there would be an ever-increasing risk of being caught out, especially by Olivia, and both Holly and Paige had also begun to borrow his computer. The thought of being caught made him sick to the stomach.

He even wondered if there might be something he could take to reduce his sex drive as needed, but the thought of explaining the situation to the doctor, or rather trying to find a convincing lie, made him cringe with embarrassment. Yet some sort of restraint was clearly necessary.

Holly

Andros lay on the bed, his expression more smug than excited as he watched Holly work on him with her mouth. He was fully dressed, but with his fly open and his cock and balls bulging from the opening. She was holding his cock and tugging gently at the shaft as she licked and kissed at his balls, already excited, and not only for having him to indulge herself with, but for the striptease she had performed first. It had felt wonderful to go nude in front of him, utterly different to how it had felt in the clubs and bars where she'd worked, even though she'd gone through much the same moves. Now it was Andros she was pleasing, and her excitement reflected his own.

Opening her mouth as wide as it would go, she took the full wrinkly bulk of his scrotum in and began to suck on it, with her hand still moving on his thick rubbery shaft. He was taking his time to get hard, presumably because it was only a couple of hours since he'd had her up against the wall of an alley behind the university, first in her mouth and then with her bottom pushed out for rear entry. The risk of being caught had added a delicious thrill to the fucking, and even as she mouthed on his balls she was thinking of how it would feel to be watched.

'Get your mouth around my dick,' Andros said suddenly.

Holly obeyed, letting his scrotum slip from her mouth and giving the bulging sac a last kiss before running her tongue up the full length of his shaft and popping it in. He was now close to full erection, his cock fat enough to fill her mouth to capacity as she took him deep. It felt as good as ever, and she wondered if it would be best to rub herself off while she sucked, or if she should wait to see if he was going to fuck her.

He was beginning to react, groaning with pleasure as her mouth worked on his cock, now fully erect. Holly ringed the base of his shaft with her fingers, masturbating him into her mouth as she sucked on the thick band of his foreskin, now enjoying his cock so much that it was impossible to hold back from her own pleasure. Her spare hand slipped low, between her thighs, to where her pussy felt swollen and sensitive and wet, ready for her fingers.

As he realised that she was masturbating, he spoke again. 'Ah, you dirty little bitch, Holly. OK, I'll give you something to get off on.'

Holly looked up, still sucking, as he reached down to take a firm grip in her hair. Thinking he was going to make her gag, she braced herself and began to rub harder between her pussy lips, but he merely took control of the blow job, easing her head up and down on his shaft while he masturbated into her mouth. She managed a muffled thank you as her other hand came free. Now she could touch herself properly, teasing her breasts and stroking the sensitive skin of her bottom and thighs as she sucked, and all the while with one finger busy with her cunt.

She was getting close, her muscles already in contraction, her mind fixed on how she must have looked in the alley with her jeans and knickers pushed down, her top and bra up to let her tits swing free as he pumped into her from behind. He'd come all over her bottom, forcing her to walk home in sticky knickers, which had been disgusting at the time but now made a deliciously dirty memory. She pictured the white spunk on her dark skin, and as Andros spoke again she realised that his thoughts weren't so very different.

'I'm going to do it in your face, Holly . . . right in your face . . . spunk in your face.'

He finished with a grunt and whipped his cock free, wanking furiously as she tilted her head back, mouth wide to catch his come, thrilling to the thought of having her face spunked on as her own orgasm kicked in.

'Do it,' she gasped. 'Do it in my face, and in my mouth too.'

'Dirty bitch!' he grunted, and a jet of white erupted from his cock.

Holly was coming as the spunk splashed down across her face, the sticky streamer catching her in one eye and across her cheek to end dangling from her lip. The second spurt went into her mouth and down her chin, the third higher, soiling her hair and closing her other eye. A last blob was wiped on her nose before he'd stuck his cock back in her mouth, slippery and tasting of salt as she began to suck once more, riding her orgasm in delirious ecstasy as his spunk trickled slowly down over her face.

Daniel

Three times Daniel walked past the sex shop before finding the courage to go inside. It was the only one in Silbury, located in a back street where the main shopping centre began to give way to business premises and insalubrious flats. The inside was more or less as he had anticipated; a dirty floor of red linoleum, a counter with a bored-looking man behind it, shelves and racks displaying videos, magazines and tawdry underwear, along with a few sex aids. There were no other customers, and he managed a weak smile as the man behind the counter looked up with a single incurious glance before returning to the biking magazine he'd been reading.

Relieved that he wasn't going to have to explain himself, Daniel crossed to the display of sex aids. There were dildos, vibrators, two varieties of blow-up doll so hideous he could barely bring himself to look at them, and very little else. The only thing even vaguely in the same category as the highly specialised cock restraint he wanted was a black leather collar with the word 'BITCH' inscribed on it. Telling himself that he'd be better off risking a credit-card purchase through the internet after all, he stepped back, only to freeze as the man behind the counter spoke.

'You all right, mate? What're you after?'

'Um, I er – I don't think you've got it,' Daniel stammered, the blood rushing to his face.

'Something a bit kinky, eh?' the man chuckled. 'Nice pair of handcuffs to keep the missus in order?'

'Er – do you have that sort of thing?' Daniel asked tentatively.

'No, but I can get it in for you,' the man answered.

'No, I, um, I really need it right now,' Daniel blustered, desperate to avoid having to explain what he wanted, or to wait weeks for the privilege of being overcharged.

'Desperate, are we?' The man laughed again. 'Back home gagging to be tied up, is she? Look, I got these.'

He came around from behind the counter, rummaging behind a display of nylon baby-doll nighties to extract a pair of plastic handcuffs lined with some fluffy material in shocking pink.

'Um ... er ... yes, those will do,' Daniel blurted out, now desperate to get out of the shop.

'How about one of these to go with them?' the man asked, indicating the nighties.

Before Daniel could find it in himself to refuse, the man had taken the garment down and was walking to the counter. Far too embarrassed to stop the transaction, Daniel waited numbly as the handcuffs and baby doll were put into a bag and the total rung up. He paid in cash and retreated as fast as he could, the presence of an elderly couple walking past the door as he emerged adding the final touch to his overwhelming embarrassment.

Olivia

As she sat down at the computer, Olivia was running the events of the day through her head over and over again. Despite having been something she'd anticipated for some time, her first involvement with the domination of a man had been a strange experience, almost surreal.

Rather to her surprise, Mistress Anastasia had been as good as her word, inviting Olivia to witness a two-hour punishment session for a rotund middle-aged businessman. He had been far from attractive physically, but his grovelling subservience to both Mistress Anastasia and herself had been everything she'd anticipated and more. Even having her watch had brought him to a new level of ecstasy, or so he'd claimed, at which Mistress Anastasia had provided a useful lesson in trapping a man into a punishment.

When he said how wonderful Olivia was and how much her presence enhanced his pleasure, Mistress Anastasia demanded to know if that meant his previous visits had been unsatisfying. The man had immediately denied it, babbling apologies, only for Mistress Anastasia to then ask if he was now saying that Olivia didn't count for anything. He was thrown into utter confusion, unable to answer without earning himself further punishment.

Mistress Anastasia made him kneel and placed an elegant booted foot on his back, asking question after question, each of which could not be answered without insulting either herself or Olivia. Inevitably, he failed to satisfy her and, with each answer, another six smacks of her riding crop were applied to his porcine backside, until he was left squirming on the floor in a lather of submissive ecstasy. Finally, he was permitted to masturbate into his own hand and eat the yield while the women looked down on him with what in Olivia's case was real disgust.

Afterwards, with the man still deeply deferential to both of them, despite no longer being in role, he was full of praise and booked another session for the following fortnight. Of the four hundred pounds he paid over for the privilege of being beaten and humiliated, Olivia was given fifty, with her travel expenses on top. Telling herself that it was only the start, and that she had learnt a great deal, she had swallowed her feelings on being made so very much the junior partner. She was also pleased that she had escaped without having her own bottom smacked, although there was a touch of traitorous disappointment as well.

Now, as she tried to catch up with the work she was supposed to have done while in Winchester, she was finding it increasingly hard to concentrate. Images of the businessman crawling on the floor in nothing but a collar and lead kept crowding her head, along with speculation on what might be to come, and as to whether, as Mistress Anastasia claimed, all men were at heart submissive.

Only when she had convinced herself that she didn't need to read any more on the political consequences of the Black Prince's death did she allow herself to look for anything other than history. A quick surf through some of her favourite female domination sites only whetted her appetite for more, and made her wonder about men in general. The man she had helped to dominate had been wealthy and confident, arriving at Mistress Anastasia's house in a large, new Mercedes and dressed in an expensive suit, the very image of masculine achievement, even arrogance. Yet there he had been, naked, collared, beaten, masturbating at her feet as he called himself a worm, a piece of filth, and worse.

According to Mistress Anastasia, he was simply expressing what was natural to all men if only they could admit to their true feelings, but Olivia had her doubts. Certainly, most of those she had met had shown no sign of any such behaviour; just the opposite if anything. Idly, she began to wonder about Daniel. On the surface he seemed more dull than anything, and yet Mistress Anastasia assured her that it was always the quietest men who hid the darkest fantasies. Possibly his login might provide some clue?

It was password protected, but a click on the question mark brought up a hint: 'What Paige is', which was more than a little intriguing. Feeling both guilty and mischievous, she tried to think of something that distinguished Paige. She tried 'Brainbox', 'Mouse' and 'Butterball' before deciding that she was going the wrong way about it. It wouldn't be how *she* saw Paige, after all, but how *Daniel* saw Paige.

Sitting back, she considered Paige's most obvious sexual characteristics – her breasts, which looked huge on her small frame and were undoubtedly even more awkward than Olivia's own. She tried 'Breasts', 'Tits', 'Boobs' and 'Knockers', even though they didn't seem to fit the question, with no success. What she needed was either a noun or an adjective to describe a girl with large breasts, maybe both.

Despite her own physique and a long history of compliments or supposed compliments from men, it wasn't that easy. She tried 'Milkmaid', 'Boobie Baby' and 'Melon Farmer', all without result, then gave up, telling herself that there were many thousands of possibilities and she was probably on the wrong track altogether.

The front door banged, and she quickly returned to her own login, just in time as Daniel himself appeared in the doorway.

Holly

'But I don't know how to cook stuffed vine leaves,' Holly protested.

'You just stick them on the barbecue for a few minutes,' Andros told her. 'Come on, love, how hard can it be?'

'OK, I'll try,' Holly promised, 'but I thought blokes liked to do barbecues.'

'Not this bloke,' Andros answered, and sat down in the single garden chair, where he pulled a tab from a can of beer and made himself comfortable.

Holly turned back to the barbecue with a mild frown. For all the appeal of his abundant masculinity, his attitude could be annoying at times, both when it came to not getting her pussy licked and being expected to wait on him pretty much hand and foot. Not that she minded cooking, but the barbecue was an ancient battered contraption left by the previous owners of the house. Andros had insisted on resurrecting it, which mainly involved having Holly wash it down with the garden hose, then buying charcoal and what he considered suitable food; lamb chops marinated in red wine and herbs, pitta bread and the stuffed vine leaves. Holly had already done the preparation, and was obviously expected to cook it too.

There was at least plenty to drink, and once she'd managed to get the charcoal burning she helped herself to a large glass of the strong red wine he'd suggested to go with the meal. It was good, rich and smooth, sliding down her throat so easily that she had swallowed her first glass in a couple of mouthfuls and quickly poured another. By the time she'd put the meat on, that was gone too, and the level in the bottle continued to fall as she cooked.

Andros watched and drank beer, providing only the occasional instruction and occasionally making a remark on the shape of her bottom in her jeans or the way her breasts filled out the top she was wearing. As always with him, she found herself unable to resent remarks that would have earned any other man a sharp come-back or even a slap, and instead found herself growing gradually aroused, just as she was growing gradually drunk.

Daniel

It was exactly what he wanted, a cage made of stiff rubber bars that fastened with a tiny padlock to enclose a man's genitals, leaving him unable to get at his cock without it first being unlocked. Worn over his pants, it even looked as if it would be comfortable, while having to pee sitting down was a price he was prepared to pay.

The price of the cage was another matter, over a hundred pounds plus post and packing. Yet it was more or less exactly what he needed, the sole problem being how to prevent himself from getting at the key when the urge to masturbate grew strong at the wrong time. It was hardly practical to give it to anybody else, both for reasons of embarrassment and because it would very likely lead to the discovery of his secret life. Nor was it sensible to lock himself up in the cage and then put the key in the post, as he very definitely did not fancy a trip to the local Accident and Emergency when the Post Office failed to deliver.

Discouraged by the price and the difficulty of the key, he added the website to his list of favourites and moved on, deliberately avoiding pornographic sites. The camera system was off, but none of the girls was in their rooms anyway, reducing temptation for the time being. Later, he knew it might be difficult. Paige had not yet come back from the university, and Katie had been out all day, but Holly and her boyfriend were in the garden, cooking and drinking wine and beer. Olivia joined them after she came off his computer. It seemed inevitable that the meal would eventually be followed by drunken dirty sex between Holly and Andros, which from his perspective meant the opportunity for a full-on live sex show. It was hard to resist.

Deliberately avoiding the camera monitor, he settled down with one of his favourite science-fiction adventures.

Holly

Swallowing the last of her wine, Holly let her body go slowly limp, tilting back her head to look at the sky. It was now dark, with the dull orange glow from Silbury reflected on a few high scattered clouds and the stars beyond, the whole scene merging and separating as she struggled to focus properly. She knew she was drunk, and she was happy to be drunk, allowing her to completely relax into the arousal which had been growing all evening. Immediately after the barbecue, she'd been too full, but now she was ready for sex.

'Let's go to bed,' she sighed.

'All three of us?' Andros joked, throwing a glance to where Olivia lay propped up on one elbow with a glass of wine in her hand.

'Don't be a pig!' Holly chided. 'Sorry, Olivia, he can be such a bastard.'

'I don't mind,' Olivia answered casually. 'I'll whip his arse while the two of you fuck, if you like?'

Holly burst out laughing at the immediate expression of horrified indignation on Andros's face, and spoke again as she took his arm. 'That'll teach you, big pig.'

Andros didn't reply, but suddenly twisted around and down to catch Holly around her thighs and haul her squealing across his shoulder, her bottom the highest part of her body as she was carried into the house and upstairs. Despite her repeated demands, he didn't put her down until they were in her room, and then only to dump her unceremoniously on the bed.

Katie had seen them, leaving Holly in a state of giggling drunken embarrassment as she wriggled around to face Andros, only to find him in the act of unzipping himself.

'Get your mouth around me,' he demanded, flopping out his cock and balls as he stepped close to the bed.

Holly's intended rebuke died in her throat as she caught the scent of him. Bouncing quickly into a sitting position, she nuzzled her face against his cock and balls, extending her tongue to lick at the rubbery flesh, kissing his scrotum and the fleshy hood where his heavy foreskin hid his helmet, then rolling it back with her lips to suck. Andros groaned as she began to mouth on the sensitive helmet of his cock, and again as Holly began to tickle him under his balls.

'You really know how to suck cock,' he sighed. 'Do it tits out, yeah? I want to see those tits.'

Nodding around her mouthful, Holly paused in her tickling to pull up her top and bra, freeing her breasts into her hands as he had asked. They felt good, heavy and sensitive, her nipples already stiff with excitement, and all the better for being asked to show them off. She began to play with herself as she sucked, holding one plump breast in each hand and stroking her nipples as his cock grew in her mouth, his helmet now poking out of his foreskin of its own accord.

Andros gave a grunt of appreciation as he saw

what she was doing, his eyes fixed on her breasts and the junction between his cock and her mouth as she sucked. He began to thrust with his hips, fucking her mouth as his shaft stiffened, until soon he had a full-size erection rearing up from his belly for her to suck and lick and kiss. She took him in hand, masturbating him into her mouth, but quickly stopped, determined not to waste such a glorious erection in her face.

'Fuck me, doggy style,' she demanded, bouncing around on the bed.

She stuck out her hips even as she wrestled her jeans open and down, showing off her bare black bottom with just her tiny bright-blue thong to cover her, so small that the full spread of her cheeks and even a little of her anal star would be showing to him. Andros needed no further encouragement. One big hand found her bottom, spreading her cheeks to make a target of her cunt, his cock head poked against her flesh, guided in past her panties, first to rub in the slippery crease between her sex lips, then to slide in up her ready hole.

Holly's mouth came wide in bliss as she was penetrated. He took her by the hips, driving his cock deep in up her hole, until his balls were pressed to the tiny triangle of panty material now taut over her cunt and his belly pressed tight to her naked bottom cheeks. Her fingers were clasping at the bedclothes as her fucking began, the motion of cock in cunt growing faster and harder until she was gasping and shivering in ecstasy, her tits swinging beneath her chest and the bed creaking to his thrusts.

Daniel

Daniel shifted uneasily on his bed, his mind flickering between the complexities of robot morality and the rhythmic thumping noises coming from down the corridor. Once more he tried to get into his book, only for a cry of female passion to break his concentration, this time completely. With a curse as much for his own weakness as for Holly and Andros, he put his book down and rose from the bed.

Again he hesitated, but another squeal of girlish delight broke the last of his resolve and his hand moved to the monitor switch. He sighed as he sat down, telling himself he'd simply watch, or maybe record what was going on, but not masturbate to it. The screen came to life and he quickly clicked on Holly's camera, to discover a scene that instantly doubled the envy and lust which had been building up inside him since the couple had come upstairs.

Holly was kneeling on her bed, her jeans pushed down behind and her top pulled up, leaving her glorious bottom and the heavy brown balls of her breasts bare. She still had her panties on, a bright-blue thong, but it covered next to nothing, and hadn't stopped Andros from fucking her, with his hands gripped tight to her hips as he slid what looked like a truly monstrous erection slowly in and out of her body.

'Oh fuck,' he sighed, his hand moving to his crotch, only to pull back. 'Oh no, not again . . .'

He trailed off, his mouth falling slowly open. Andros had withdrawn from Holly, holding on to his cock as he quickly pulled down her panties before guiding it into her body once more. She gave an ecstatic grunt as she was penetrated and Andros repeated the action, pulling his cock free then insert-

154

ing it back in her cunt, and again. Daniel could only stare, his envy rising to a maddening level, and not just for what Andros was doing, but for the size of his cock. It was easily half as long again as Daniel's, also considerably thicker, with a swollen bulbous head and an upward curve to the shaft that gave the impression of a near-godlike virility.

'Oh I wish . . .' he groaned, and this time, when his hand moved to his crotch, it stayed there, easing down his zip to extract his own member, which now seemed utterly pathetic.

Ignoring the sharp twinge of pain as he rolled back his foreskin, he began to masturbate, and as his cock grew quickly in his hand he was telling himself that his excitement was all to do with Holly's naked beauty and what was being done to her – and nothing whatever to do with Andros's extraordinary manliness.

Holly

'That's nice,' Holly sighed as Andros entered her one more time.

She wiggled her bottom, encouraging him to carry on the delicious cycle of withdrawal and penetration, which was driving her higher and higher still each time he filled her cunt. Andros responded by pushing himself into her as deep as he would go, before pulling slowly out once more to leave her sex a gaping hole for an instant until once more filled with thick hard cock. She moaned as she was filled, and gave another wriggle on his cock, at which he began to fuck normally once more, slapping at her bottom as he drove himself in and out.

Almost out of her senses with pleasure, Holly clung on hard to the bedclothes, gasping and panting as his cock moved inside her. Already she wanted to reach back and rub herself off while he was in her, but she was simply too far out of control to do it, her body jerking helplessly on his cock and her flesh quivering beneath the slaps to her bottom as she was fucked and spanked.

He grunted, and suddenly he was on top of her, his hands groping for her breasts, catching them up and squeezing hard at the two fat globes even as he got on to her back, still with his cock working in her cunt hole, but now mounted up like a dog with his bitch. Holly could do nothing had she wanted to, pinned beneath his weight as they fucked, out of her mind with pleasure. She began to scream and to beg to be fucked harder, swearing at him and calling him a pig and a bastard even as she demanded more. He gave it, driving into her at a furious pace, until she could barely breathe, his grunts growing louder as his thrusts grew harder, and still more, rising in a furious crescendo, only to suddenly stop.

Holly realised he had come inside her, but she was too far gone to really care. For a moment he held himself deep up her, before pulling his cock free and wiping it across her bottom. With his weight now off her back, Holly snatched back to find her sex, already near to orgasm as she began to rub between her lips. She could feel his spunk oozing from her hole, wet and slippery under her fingers as she masturbated in a frenzy of lewd drunken arousal.

He sat back, watching, and called her a slut, which only drove her feelings higher still. She was kneeling near nude in front of him, her mouth full of the taste of his cock, her tits swinging bare beneath her chest, her bottom spread to show off her bumhole, her well-fucked cunt oozing spunk, and it was perfect, exactly how she should be in front of him. Her orgasm kicked in, wringing a scream of unrestrained ecstasy from her lips, and a second before she collapsed whimpering on to her bed, her hand still between her thighs.

Daniel

As he watched slack jawed, Daniel was wondering if he'd ever seen such an open display of female ecstasy, and he was sure the answer was no. When Holly gave herself, she gave herself completely, showing no inhibitions whatsoever, and incidentally making one hell of a show of herself. That made the guilt of his intrusion all the stronger as his cock went slowly limp in his hand, but for once that was a secondary emotion. He'd rubbed himself sore again, worse than before, and as he climbed painfully to his feet he decided to order the cock cage and worry about what to do with the key once he actually had it. It was that or end up explaining to some doctor why his cock appeared to have had a nasty accident with a cheese grater.

Katie

'Did you hear Holly and her boyfriend last night?' Paige asked as she slowed her horse to a walk beside Katie.

'She's a common . . .' Katie answered, and stopped, thinking of what she and Paige had done together and how much noise she'd made during her spanking.

157

She been too drunk and too aroused to care, but the morning after she'd realised that her housemates had almost certainly heard, which had filled her with mixed feelings. Presumably they'd guessed what was going on, but nobody had said anything to her, let alone criticised, which made her wonder if her desire to get Holly involved in a similar game was a real hope. Obviously, the black girl was highly sexed, and if she had a clear preference for men, then so had most of the girls Katie had played with at Roegate.

The only fly in the ointment was Andros himself. Katie found him impossibly coarse, while the thought of him with Holly made her burn with jealousy. He always seemed to be around as well, sometimes even while he was supposed to be at work, which made the task of arranging an all-girls evening harder still. Yet she was determined to do it, her spanking from Paige having reawakened many of her old feelings, including a desire for the sort of playful revenge she and Tia had indulged in so often. That Paige would be willing she had no doubt whatsoever, and now that they were well up out on Bramwell Heath she had the perfect opportunity.

'This is a pretty place,' she stated as she reined Achilles in beside a copse of elder. 'Let's stop for a while.'

Paige agreed without hesitation. They dismounted and led the horses to a patch of shade before Katie pushed in deeper among the elders. She could feel her heart rate picking up, but all her uncertainty was gone. Paige had a crush on her, and had even admitted as much, while she could hardly deny the fairness of having her own bottom smacked after what she'd done to Katie.

There was a little hollow at the heart of the copse, with a patch of chalky ground dappled with sunlight, quite invisible from outside. Katie turned on Paige, who looked nervous and had evidently guessed at least something of what was going to happen. Feeling bold and full of mischief, Katie cocked her head a trifle to one side as she regarded her friend.

'I think you should be spanked, don't you?'

Paige said nothing, her eyes wide and her lower lip trembling.

'Come on, it's only fair,' Katie insisted. 'You did me.'

This time Paige nodded, a barely perceptible movement of her head but enough to tell Katie that she'd been right. She could do precisely as she wanted.

'Take your jodhpurs down then,' she demanded.

Paige fumbled her jodhpurs down over her hips, inspiring both arousal and cruelty in Katie as soft white flesh came on show, plump thighs and belly, a chubby pussy mound encased in white cotton tight enough to hint at the slit. She was shaking badly, her eyes huge and moist, but she pushed her jodhpurs right down to the top of her boots.

'Your knickers too,' Katie instructed. 'You don't think I'd let you get away without going bare bottom, do you?'

Paige shook her head and pushed her thumbs into the waistband of knickers, only to stop as Katie lifted a finger.

'Uh, uh, we do it the rude way. Stick that big fat bum out and take them slowly down so I can see, but only when I say.'

Paige swallowed hard, but turned around, pushing her bottom out to make a fat white ball, her knickers taut over her big cheeks, a little dampness showing between her thighs where she'd grown wet while riding. Katie was enjoying herself immensely, far too much to let her friend off a single detail of her

159

torment, and counted silently to twenty as Paige waited in her lewd pose before speaking again.

'Now take them down. Slowly.'

A faint sob escaped Paige's lips as she began to push her knickers down, slowly exposing the globe of her bottom, first the swell of her cheeks and the top of the deep slit between, then the full mass of overweight girl flesh, the tight pink dimple of her anus, the tubby meaty tuck and a sweetly turned and distinctly wet cunt.

'Right down,' Katie ordered, and Paige's knickers joined her jodhpurs at boot level. 'That's better. That's how you should be, Paige, with your big bottom bare, your breasts too. Come on, get your jacket off and open your blouse.'

Paige reacted with a soft whimper, but hurried out of her riding jacket and hastily unfastened her blouse, fumbling with the buttons in her eagerness to obey. She turned around, and met Katie's eyes as she lifted her bra to flop out her fat heavy breasts, both nipples already stiff with excitement.

'You like to be bare in front of me, don't you?' Katie demanded.

'Yes,' Paige admitted, her voice a whisper.

'That's just as well, because you are going to be – a lot. I hope you like being spanked too, because I intend to do you quite often.'

'I – I don't know. I've never been spanked before, but – but I'd like to be, by you.'

'That's just as well then, isn't it? How would you like to go? Over my knee? Standing? Maybe touching your toes?'

'However you like.'

'We'll start with you touching your toes then. Bend over.'

Paige tried, but couldn't quite manage it, grasping

her legs instead. The position left her bottom pushed well out, with the lips of her cunt peeping out from between her thighs and her cheeks open enough to make a full show of her anus. Katie smiled, enjoying the view and how easily Paige could be made to do rude things. Already she wanted to do more than just spank, but there was no rush, and no question in her mind that a hot bottom would do Paige the world of good before she was asked to do anything yet more intimate.

Stepping close, she put her hand on one of Paige's cheeks, feeling the smooth resilient flesh, soft and yet meaty, so like Tia's that she had to restrain a sob as she lifted her hand to apply the first smack. Paige gave a little gasp as Katie's hand hit her bottom, a second with the next smack, and the spanking had begun, each impact followed by a soft cry as Paige's flesh began to bounce and shiver. Soon the big white cheeks were picking up colour, uneven pink marks quickly blending to a rich flush that covered both porky cheeks from hip to hip and from slit to thighs.

Paige was juicing heavily, the thick white fluid oozing from the mouth of her now open cunt and running sticky and glistening down the insides of her thighs. Katie could smell her friend's excitement, and knew her own sex was responding too, moist and sensitive in her knickers. She was spanking hard too, each smack firm enough to make the big cheeks squash and wobble and send shivers through the flesh of Paige's belly and breasts, and getting just the sort of blended reaction of pain and arousal she enjoyed, only perhaps with a touch more pain.

'Tough little thing, aren't you?' Katie said, delivering another hard smack across the seat of Paige's now red bottom cheeks. 'Let's see if you're so tough when I use my crop, shall we?'

The response was a soft whimper, but Paige made no move to stop her as Katie retrieved her riding crop from where she'd hung it on a broken branch. Paige was looking back, her big eyes wide with fright, her flesh trembling, but still she stayed in position, even as Katie lifted the crop. It felt good, delightfully cruel, to have her friend so obedient and so eager to accept pain.

'This is going to hurt,' Katie warned, but Paige merely nodded.

Katie brought the crop down, slashing it hard across the full fat width of Paige's bottom, to wring a scream from her friend's lips and leave a long white line across the reddened flesh that quickly coloured up to a rich purple. Paige was whimpering badly and shaking her head, obviously in pain, which filled Katie with sadistic glee.

'Another?' she asked. 'Come on, ask for it.'

Paige let out a single, bitter sob before speaking. 'Whip me, Katie . . . if you want to . . . whip me.'

'Do you want it?' Katie demanded.

'Yes,' Paige sobbed, and Katie brought the crop down a second time, harder than before.

The cut caught Paige low across her bottom, sending her staggering forwards so that she nearly lost her balance and producing a second crimson welt. Katie's heart was pounding, her mind and her body thrilling to the pleasure of whipping her friend. Again she brought the whip down, not bothering to ask, this time drawing a long squeal from Paige.

'You sound like a pig!' Katie laughed. 'Just like a pig! I think that's what I'll call you, Miss Piggy – no, Piglet. You can be Piglet, Paige!'

She laid in another stroke, laughing openly, and another, thrashing Paige's wobbling, squirming bottom cheeks as her cruelty rose to fever pitch, only to stop as her victim finally tripped over her jodhpurs and knickers to sprawl in the leaf mould, where she lay, gasping and sobbing, her well-whipped bottom thrust high, her sopping cunt on plain show between her open thighs.

'Go on, rub yourself off,' Katie laughed. 'I know you want to.'

'Whip me while I do it,' Paige sobbed, and her hand had gone back to her sex.

'You dirty little tart!' Katie called out in delight, and began to belabour Paige's bottom with the crop.

It took just moments, Paige's sobs and squeals turning to moans almost immediately, her thighs and bottom cheeks squeezing, her anus starting to wink between her well-splayed cheeks, her fingers busy in the wet mushy flesh of her open and quite obviously virgin cunt. She cried out, begging Katie to whip her harder, and again, declaring her love and her undying worship even as she was thrashed.

'I never thought you'd be so dirty!' Katie gasped as Paige finally subsided.

Paige didn't answer, merely turning to Katie with a sheepish expression on her pretty face. She was a mess, her skin wet with sweat, her hair bedraggled, her riding hat gone, her breasts smeared with leaf mould, her bottom rosy all over and criss-crossed with a dozen or more thick purple welts. Her face was red too, with embarrassment for her own behaviour.

'I'm sorry, Katie, I –'

'Don't be,' Katie interrupted. 'We all get carried away sometimes. Look at me. Just do as I ask, will you? You've turned me on.'

'Yes, anything.'

Katie didn't need any further encouragement, her inhibitions quite gone, and she pushed down her jodhpurs and knickers with one smooth motion.

Paige looked on, wide eyed and open mouthed, as Katie arranged her riding jacket on a convenient low branch and sat down, legs splayed to the cool sunlight, her pussy wide and wet.

'Do you know what to do?' she demanded.

'I – I suppose so,' Paige answered, and she began to crawl across the ground.

A smile lit up Katie's face as she watched her friend come to her, huge naked breasts swinging beneath her chest at the front and big red bottom wiggling behind. Reaching out, she took Paige by the hair, then pulled her in to make sure there was no last minute change of heart, and sighing as her friend's face nuzzled in her slit.

'That's my Piglet,' she sighed. 'Like that, only with your tongue too.'

Paige responded, cautiously at first, then with rising enthusiasm, her tongue flicking over Katie's sex lips and between. Katie sighed, pulling Paige further in as her eyes closed in bliss. It had been so long, *too* long, and, if the girl licking her wasn't Tia or even Holly, then neither of them could ever have been so obedient, nor allowed themselves to be spanked and whipped and so thoroughly humiliated.

She turned her thoughts to Tia anyway, only to get a twinge of guilt. It wasn't fair, not when it was Paige whose face was buried between her thighs, Paige who had yielded so well to a beating, more willing by far than Tia. Her mouth opened to call out her friend's name as her thighs began to tighten, telling Paige she was beautiful, and sweet, and not really a pig at all as the orgasm swept through her.

Daniel

The cock cage was a snug fit, and not only prevented him from masturbating but also provided relief in a quite unexpected way. When wearing it, he felt an almost religious sense of fulfilment, both repentance and absolution, as although it was essentially a punishment, it also prevented him from committing the act which provoked his guilt. It had also provoked a new fantasy, to have a woman be the key holder for him, a need so strong that only his absolute conviction that all women would react to the suggestion with disgust prevented him from asking.

Now, as he sat waiting for Olivia to finish with his computer, the sensation of the cage around his cock and balls was pushing him to an erotic high quite different to anything he had known before. He wanted to tell her, and to beg her to be his key holder, but even to think of uttering the words made him feel sick to the stomach, while cold logic told him that he would be rejected. After all, what would a beautiful young girl like her want with him, even if she clearly did have a penchant for sadism.

'There, I'm done,' she said, pushing the chair back.

Olivia

As Daniel stood up to go to his computer, Olivia stole a covert glance towards his crotch. There was something wrong with him or, at least, with the way he walked, while his genitals seemed to bulge in a way she was sure they never had before. As he sat down, she was wondering if he'd done himself an injury and was having to wear some sort of truss, although his condition was oddly similar to that of a man she knew only as Dog, and who she and Mistress Anastasia had put through his paces two days before.

Dog liked bondage, and particularly to have his cock and balls in restraint, so that when he arrived she had been told to put him in a peculiar device. It was a male chastity belt of sorts, which encased his genitals and allowed his hands to be fastened behind his back, while also keeping him in an upright stance by means of a rigid bar leading from the back of the belt to a steel collar.

Obviously, whatever Daniel was wearing was far less complicated, and yet there were definite similarities in the way he held himself and the way Dog had, at least before Dog had been whipped. She shook her head, telling herself it was just her imagination and perhaps also inspired by Mistress Anastasia's insistence on all men being inherently submissive. She still kept an eye on him, but with her back turned as she pretended to adjust an eyelash in his Jack Daniels mirror, but now for different reasons.

He had sat down at the computer and was typing in his password. Olivia watched carefully, trying to note which keys he pressed, but with only partial success. He typed slowly, using a single finger, but his arm obscured the left-hand side of the keyboard. Whatever he'd typed began with an M and an O, contained a space and ended in an O and an M, but that was all she could be sure of. There might also be a B or V, and either a U or and I.

She left the room feeling more intrigued than ever, and determined to have another attempt on his login as soon as possible, in the hope of discovering that he was indeed a masochist. After four visits to Mistress Anastasia, she not only felt ready to take on somebody herself, but was growing increasingly resentful of her share of the pay, especially with respect to the amount of work she did. Also, while she had still not been spanked again, the threat was always there, while she got all the dirty jobs, including wanking off those clients who had paid to be masturbated after their sessions. Dog had been particularly bad, coming with such power that he had not only spunked all over her hand but also splashed her shorts and top, and the bare skin of her midriff. Mistress Anastasia, meanwhile, never touched the men at all, which Olivia felt was a more properly dominant attitude.

Paige

Lying face down on the bed with her skirt turned up and her panties pushed down to leave her bottom bare, Paige was in a state of bliss she could never have imagined was possible to achieve by being beaten. Yet she had been beaten by Katie, which had kept her in a state of near-constant arousal for days, punctuated by exquisite highlights; each time she masturbated over what had been done to her, as she admired her bruises in her mirror or lay with her bottom bare to reinforce her memory, but, best of all, when Katie made her take her panties down for an inspection.

They had been far more intimate since that day, almost lovers, although in a way she did not fully understand. Katie seemed to regard what they did as play, a guilty secret not to be taken entirely seriously. Paige didn't mind, too swept up in the excitement of being in a relationship at once so daring and so desirable. So often she had watched and listened with quiet envy as friends went through the rituals of pairing up and having sex. She herself, shy and with little confidence in her own appeal, had always assumed that the game was for other bolder spirits, but now she was doing things most of them would never have considered in their wildest moments.

Just to be lying on her bed with her bottom bare kept her in a state of constant mild arousal, but as she caught the familiar sound of Katie's Mini pulling up a thrill of far greater power ran through her. She was alone in the house, and Katie was sure to come up to her, to catch her bare. The thought of the possible consequences was enough to have her biting her lip with need, and she listened to the sequence of noises as Katie came indoors with rising anticipation, culminating in a sharp exquisite shock at the click of her own door handle.

'Hello, Piglet,' Katie began, and paused. 'What are you up to, you bad girl?'

'Just nursing my bottom,' Paige answered, blushing. 'It feels better with my knickers down.'

'You do like to make a fuss, don't you?' Katie laughed, and sat down on the bed beside Paige. 'I suppose I did whip you quite hard, but the bruises are nearly gone. It can't hurt that much, surely?'

As she spoke, she placed a hand on Paige's bottom, very gently tracing the still tender skin where she had applied her riding crop. Paige closed her eyes in bliss, thrilling to the touch and the casual way Katie was inspecting her bottom.

'It – it doesn't really hurt any more,' she admitted, 'not much. I just like to be bare, and remember what happened.'

'Slut,' Katie joked, and planted a gentle slap across the crest of Paige's bottom cheeks.

Paige sighed and stuck her hips up, earning a

second slap before Katie went back to her inspection, tracing each now faded welt with a single finger.

'That does feel nice,' she said. 'You can spank me if you want.'

'Maybe I will,' Katie responded. 'You like to be spanked, don't you?'

'By you, yes,' Paige admitted.

'How about by somebody else?' Katie asked, as she began to do it, smacking lightly at Paige's cheeks, one after the other.

'I want to be yours,' Paige said, but she was already familiar with the games Katie liked to play, 'but, maybe, if you let somebody do it to me.'

'You'd love that, wouldn't you?' Katie asked, going back to caressing Paige's bottom. 'How about Holly, and Olivia? Maybe if I was to spank you in front of them and then let them take turns with you over their knees? Would you like that?'

A sharp pulse of mingled pleasure and shame hit Paige at Katie's words, but there was no doubt about the answer.

'Yes,' she sighed, and gasped as a firm smack was applied to the crest of each bare cheek.

'Bad girl,' Katie chided. 'Yes, I bet you would, with your big fat bottom all bare and wriggling in front of them. Think how they'd laugh, and how hard they'd smack when their turn came.'

Paige responded with a sob and pushed her hips higher still, offering her bottom to Katie. She got another pair of hard smacks for her trouble before Katie went back to teasing her, now using one finger to tickle in the deep sensitive slit between Paige's cheeks.

'Maybe they'd like to play dice?' Katie suggested. 'That would give you a good excuse to get your clothes off in front of them, and you can count on me to see you get your bottom smacked.'

'Yes, please,' Paige sighed, now lost in the fantasy as she imagined the shame of having her panties pulled down for spanking in front of her housemates.

Katie didn't reply, but continued her slow and increasingly intimate exploration of Paige's bottom, alternately spanking and caressing, her long fingers tickling between the cheeks, and lower, touching between the thighs, and brushing the sex lips. Paige groaned with pleasure and stuck her bottom higher still, knowing she would now be showing the rear of her sex and her anus. Katie rewarded her with a dozen sharp slaps before easing a finger deep into Paige's slit to tickle the tight pink rosebud at the very heart.

'We're alone in the house,' Katie said softly.

'I know,' Paige answered.

'Roll over then,' Katie ordered.

Paige obeyed without hesitation, rolling on to her back and quickly struggling her panties off down her legs. Katie was in a light summer dress, which she shrugged off with a single easy motion before hurrying out of her bra and panties. Seeing her lover nude, Paige tugged up her own top and bra, then opened her arms as Katie came back to the bed. A moment of hesitation and their mouths met for the first time, their lips touching once, twice, and then opening together in a full-blown kiss.

With her arms tight around Katie's back, Paige wanted nothing more than to melt into her lover's kisses, at least for the time being. Katie was more practical, one hand behind Paige's neck to tickle the sensitive spot just below the hairline, the other already going lower. Paige pushed her chest up as Katie's fingers found her breasts, caressing the heavy curves and teasing the nipples to erection before moving on, over the soft swell of the stomach to her goal.

Completely surrendered, Paige let her thighs come wide as Katie's hand found her sex. Their kisses became more urgent still, and Paige allowed her own hands to wander, one to the nape of Katie's neck to return the exquisite sensation, the other taking a handful of firm bottom flesh. Katie clung closer, her hand now busy between Paige's thighs, only to suddenly pull back.

Paige gave a squeak of surprise and delight as Katie mounted her, scrambling quickly around to bury her face where her fingers had just been with her thighs cocked wide, bum to face. Dizzy with pleasure and overwhelmed by the sheer rudeness of what they were doing as her sex was licked for the first time in her life, Paige lay back, gasping in ecstasy. Katie's bottom was right in her face, and she knew she was expected to return the favour, so she took hold, licking eagerly as she squeezed at her friend's cheeks.

Katie stopped, rocked back, and Paige's face had been smothered in full firm bottom, her mouth still to her lover's sex, her nose pressed into the moist cavity of the anus. For a moment she struggled to change her position, only to give in, licking as before. She heard Katie sigh and her breasts were taken in hand once more, moulded and gently slapped, squashed together and the nipples pinched as she wriggled under her faceful of bottom.

'Lick me,' Katie demanded, her voice hoarse with excitement, 'lick me all the way, but first, you have to kiss my bottom hole, Paige . . . you have to.'

A sharp intensely shameful thrill ran through Paige at Katie's words, but her friend had already risen a little, her hands back to spread her bottom cheeks. Paige stared at the tiny wrinkled knot of flesh she had been told to kiss, another girl's anus, an act so unspeakably dirty she could hardly take it in, and yet she already knew she was going to do it, because she'd been told to, and because she wanted to. Still she hesitated, her lips puckered up for what she knew would be her final act of surrender to Katie's will. Then her head came forward, her face was once more smothered between her lover's bottom cheeks and she was doing it, kissing Katie's anus, a second time and a third, and as her desire got the better of her completely she had begun to lick at the tight fleshy knot.

'Oh, you bad, bad girl!' Katie sighed. 'You lovely, bad, bad girl. Don't stop.'

Paige obeyed, licking Katie's bottom hole with an eager busy tongue, lost in pleasure for what she was doing and what it made her do. Only as Katie's bottom settled back into her face did she stop, returning her attention to her lover's sex with the now sloppy bumhole once again pressed to her nose. Katie was in ecstasy, wriggling her bottom in Paige's face and laughing in delight at her pleasure and her conquest. Paige licked all the harder, on her back with Katie's bottom in her face while her own was pink and tingling from spanking, knowing that she was exactly where she deserved to be and should be as often as possible.

Katie came, squirming her bare sex against Paige's mouth and crying out in abandoned ecstasy, again and again as she was licked, until at last she collapsed sideways on to the bed. Paige was left gasping, her face sticky with Katie's cream and her own spittle, her tongue sore and her own sex so badly in need of a touch that her hands had gone between her thighs on the instant. Katie propped herself up on one elbow, her face set in a knowing smile as she watched Paige masturbate, before moving close to share a somewhat sticky kiss as the orgasm hit home.

Daniel

Placing the key into the lock of his cock cage, Daniel gave a single gentle twist. It sprang open, filling him with an instant sense of relief. He had held off for the best part of a week, until he was absolutely sure his cock was in sound wanking condition once more and his erotic needs had come to fill not only his every waking moment, but also his dreams. It had been torture, but an exquisite torture, with every hint of female display becoming increasingly pronounced until the mere glimpse of a pair of well-filled jeans or a straining top would leave him shivering with desire.

Yet he had managed to hold off, by the simple expedient of hiding the key under the carpet in Paige's room. She was the tidiest of the four, and also the most regular in her habits, so that he could always guarantee quick and safe removal without having to move anything that might arouse her suspicions if he didn't replace it properly. He also found her the least frightening, while she was undoubtedly the most buxom – both factors in his final decision.

Now, with the house empty except for himself, he had retrieved the key and was looking forward to an evening of happy masturbation once the girls were home. It promised to be a good one too. Holly and Andros had become increasingly bold, using her room for sex, both of them apparently unable to get their fill. Better still, Katie and Paige were now in a full-blown lesbian relationship, indulging not only in spanking games and mutual masturbation, but in a range of girl-on-girl action almost as great as what he knew was possible from his extensive surfing of both real and posed lesbian websites. Only Olivia seemed unlikely to provide him with anything worthwhile, as she was absent from the house for ever-increasing periods and always seemed to be tired when she came in. It had occurred to him that she might have found a lover, but, if so, she was being remarkably discreet about him.

Just to have his cock free was making him want to masturbate, so he decided to go and fetch a take-away, thus avoiding temptation until he had something to watch. He heard the front door go as he was pulling his trousers back up, and quickly hid the cage in a drawer of his computer desk, with the key still in the lock. It was Olivia, who came straight upstairs, so that she nearly caught him doing up his belt.

'Hi, can I go online?' she asked.

'Sure,' he told her. 'I was just going out anyway.'

Olivia

Olivia sat down, waiting only for the bang of the front door before clicking on Daniel's login. The box for his password came up, and she once again called up the clue, just in case he might have changed it. As before, it was 'What Paige is', and after typing an M and an O into the password box she sat back, again wondering as to the clue.

It seemed likely that the first word would be 'More', and refer to something at which Paige excelled. There were two obvious choices, her intelligence and her more than voluptuous curves. Daniel was a man, so it likely to be the second choice. She also knew that the second word was only five or six letters long.

After a long pause, she typed in 'More Bouncy', only to be rejected. 'More Busty' was met with the same response and she sat back to think again, trying to find a word meaning the same but with an O and an M. Unable to think of an answer, she returned to her own login, called up the word processor, typed out 'Busty' and clicked on the thesaurus. The word at the top of the list was 'Buxom', and she was smiling as she returned to the login page, only for her expression to move back to a frown of annoyance as 'More Buxom' was rejected.

Immediately, it occurred to her that Paige would only be *more* buxom than one other girl, while between four of them she would the *most* buxom. Smiling again, she typed the two words in, clicked in the green square and punched the air in triumph as the blue screen vanished, to be replaced by a picture of a pretty dark-haired girl in the act of pulling a bright-red bikini top up from a pair of truly enormous breasts. She was in.

She glanced down at her own chest, feeling slightly invaded at the idea of Daniel admiring her in the same way, only to dismiss the thought, telling herself not to be naive. It was hardly a surprise that a man like Daniel enjoyed looking at girls with ample chests, or porn for that matter. What she wanted to know was what he would have liked to *do* to the girl, or perhaps, what he would have liked *her* to do to him.

Feeling a little guilty and very mischievous, she called up Internet Explorer and clicked on the icon for Daniel's favourite sites. A long list came up, and as she read down Olivia's mouth came open in surprise and even shock. Nearly every link he had saved was pornographic, and they could be divided into three categories: those dealing with busty girls; those dealing with girls with big bottoms; and those dealing with voyeurism. Only one stood out as even close to what Mistress Anastasia's theories might have led her to expect, a site called 'One Stop Sissy

Shop'. She immediately clicked on it, to find herself faced with a selection of garments and apparatus not dissimilar to some of the gear at Mistress Anastasia's.

The site specialised in clothing, including huge heavily flounced dresses in an assortment of pastel shades, frilly knickers ranging in size from medium to colossal, and every other type of female garment but in a grotesquely exaggerated style. She was grinning to herself as she imagined Daniel dressed up like one of the men shown modelling the clothes, and yet the site seemed curiously at odds with his other choices.

Wondering what he had actually bought, if anything, she clicked on the History icon and worked back until she found his last visit to the site. Two more clicks and she had the answer, the confirmation page for his shopping basket, recording the purchase of a lockable cock cage. As she admired the item, she was nodding thoughtfully, already working on the best way to confront Daniel without giving herself away. It would take tact, but she could already imagine him grovelling naked on his knees with his cock and balls encased in the thing while she gave him a peep show, which would seem to cover his fantasies, and would hopefully more than cover her rent.

Holly

'That was good,' Holly said appreciatively, pushing her plate away. 'You're a great cook, Paige.'

'Thanks,' Paige answered.

'Would you like some more wine?' Katie asked.

'Yeah, why not,' Holly answered, extending her glass so that Katie could fill it with the rich red Italian wine she'd provided to go with the vegetarian pasta Paige had cooked for them.

'It was good, thanks,' Olivia put in.

Holly sat back, sipping her wine, with one hand resting gently on her tummy. For all Katie's annoying airs and graces, there was no denying her generosity. She had bought four bottles of wine, and didn't seem to expect a contribution from anybody. It was only a pity that Andros had chosen the same evening to go out drinking with his mates, because she already knew she was going to get drunk, and that would inevitably leave her wanting him.

'Shall we go through to the living room?' Katie suggested, rising to pick up her glass and the bottle.

If the bottle was going to the living room, then so was Holly who followed immediately, making herself comfortable in one of the armchairs, as did Olivia, while Katie and Paige took the sofa. Katie poured out more wine, and for a while the four of them talked casually, discussing their courses and the university in general, the quality of the shops in Silbury, Daniel's virtues and vices as a landlord and a number of other topics.

The bottle was finished, then another, the third out of four, leaving Holly feeling pleasantly tipsy and their conversation a great deal more intimate than it had been, with Paige now pink faced with embarrassment as Olivia described the shortcomings of an ex-boyfriend. As Olivia finished, Katie shifted her position on the sofa and threw out a pair of dice, one black, one yellow.

'Who likes to gamble?' she asked.

'I don't mind,' Paige answered immediately, somewhat to Holly's surprise.

'I'm up for it,' she put in herself.

'I'd love to, but I'm broke,' Olivia added.

'That needn't be a problem,' Katie responded. 'We can play for truth or dare if you prefer?'

Daniel

Knowing that every moment until the girls began to go to bed would be agony, Daniel had chosen to eat out instead of collecting a takeaway. The strategy had worked, at least in that his sense of propriety was strong enough to prevent him taking his cock out in a Chinese restaurant, but his erotic fervour had not abated in the slightest. As he ate he had found himself speculating on the possibilities the evening might hold and wondering if it was more exciting to watch Holly put to Andros's monstrous cock, or Katie and Paige playing their dirty games.

Nor was that the only distraction from his food. The staff of the restaurant included two waitresses, both tiny compact Chinese girls, whose dresses of brilliant green and gold silk clung to the contours of their bodies like a second skin, so that he was constantly taunted by the elegant, enticing movements of round little bottoms and pert breasts. By the time he'd finished his meal, his erection was so rigid it refused to go down, causing him immense embarrassment as he attempted to leave without anybody noticing.

It was no better out in the street. As he started towards Myrtle Road, he found himself behind a group of girls going out for the night. Two were in jeans so tight they might as well have been painted on to their bottoms, and so low that their hips and the waistbands of their brightly coloured thongs were visible. The third was in a miniskirt, so short that the full glorious length of her legs was on show, while her every step threatened to provide a glimpse of panties or, if she shared her friends' taste in underwear, bare bottom cheeks.

He was terrified one of them would turn around and notice the raging erection in his trousers, but they took not the slightest notice of him and presently turned off, leaving him with the images of their rear views as he made his way up Myrtle Road. To his disappointment, Andros's car wasn't in its usual place halfway across the drive, but the moment he walked in he caught the sound of girlish laughter, then Holly's voice raised in delight.

'Read 'em and weep, Katie! OK, so what I want to know, is this . . .'

Holly stopped as the front door banged behind Daniel, then said something in a voice too quiet for him to make out her words. Clearly, they were having a girls night in, and he knew that his presence would be unwelcome, so he contented himself with poking his head around the door and saying hello before going upstairs. The brief glimpse had shown the four of them seated around the living-room table, and apparently playing dice, also drinking wine.

Upstairs in his room, he immediately sat down at his computer, his fingers shaking as he manipulated the mouse. He had caught the look of distaste on Katie's face as he came in, making the prospect of peeping at her all the more exciting, while, if she and Paige were drinking wine at the rate suggested by the empty bottles on the table, he could hope for a very fine show indeed later that evening.

It was all he could do not to get his cock out immediately, and as he typed his password in he was already in a lather of frustration and expectation. Knowing that to visit even the mildest of his pornographic sites would be more than he could bear, he began to read the news in a desperate attempt to calm himself down.

Katie

Katie swallowed the lump in her throat, close to tears of frustration. Three times she had attempted to engineer a game between the four of them, and three times Holly had been going out with Andros. Now, with all four of them in a good mood and Andros firmly out of the way, she had felt a real hope of success, only for Daniel to come back and immediately ruin the mood.

Holly had already admitted to putting on rude shows with other girls at the strip clubs where she'd worked, and enjoying the experience, which was enough to set Katie's pussy tight between her thighs. Olivia had admitted she owned a vibrator, and even Paige had bashfully recounted how she'd once been caught as she peed at a rock festival. Then had come the perfect moment, when she had scored a double one to Holly's eleven, meaning that she had to answer whatever question the black girl posed, or pay a forfeit. It had been the perfect opportunity ... and then Daniel had walked in.

Ten minutes more, maybe a show of her breasts or a few playful smacks on the seat of her jeans, and sex would have become part of the game. They could have moved up to her room, locked the door and Daniel would no longer have mattered. As it was, even Holly was a little subdued and had asked a question so tame Katie had felt unable to opt for a forfeit. She collected the dice, determined that at the very least the game would go on.

'Four and two, six,' she said as the dice came to a stop.

Paige picked up the dice and gave Katie a worried look before she threw. Katie returned a weak smile, knowing exactly what her friend was thinking. Paige knew what Katie wanted, and found the idea exciting, but had specifically said she was not prepared to risk embarrassment in front of Daniel or Andros.

'Three, just my luck!' Paige said as the dice rolled to a stop.

Olivia picked up the dice and rolled, scoring seven, then Holly, who only managed a two. It was Olivia's turn to ask Holly a question, and Katie relaxed a little, sure that Holly could cope.

'OK,' Olivia said slowly. 'Holly, have you ever whipped a man?'

Paige had gone bright red, but neither of the others noticed, as Holly gave her answer in deliberately casual fashion.

'Sure I have. We used to have SM nights at the Pussycat Club and I'd dance with a whip. Usually I'd just put it around the guys' necks so I could pull them in close, but once or twice when some arsehole was giving it all that I'd flick him with the tip.'

Olivia smiled and took up the dice again, rolling a five and a one. Holly followed and scored seven, Katie just three and Paige a double six. Katie felt her tummy go tight. It was the perfect opportunity, but, as their eyes met, Paige looked doubtful.

'Oh dear, me again,' Katie sighed, praying Paige had the courage to do as she had agreed.

'Ask her something about her posh school,' Holly suggested.

'Do they still have the cane in girls' public schools?' Olivia put in.

'It's not your question,' Katie pointed out, 'and, anyway, the answer is no.'

'Shame!' Olivia laughed. 'Come on, Paige, make it a good one.'

'Um,' Paige began, and stopped. 'OK, Katie, describe the last time you had sex . . . in detail.'

Olivia laughed, and Holly's mouth twitched up into a smile. Katie felt herself go pink at the memory of sitting on Paige's face, even though the question had been prearranged.

'I – I really can't answer that, not truthfully,' she managed after a long pause.

'Oh yeah?' Holly queried.

'You get a forfeit then,' Olivia pointed out. 'What's it going to be, Paige?'

Paige was blushing more fiercely than Katie and, when she managed to speak, her words came out as a mumble. 'A spanking.'

'Sorry?' Olivia queried. 'I didn't catch that.'

'A spanking,' Paige said, fractionally louder as her face flared to crimson.

'A spanking?' Olivia echoed. 'OK then.'

'A spanking!' Holly crowed in delight. 'Oh yeah, *that* I want to see, little Miss Rich Bitch gets a spanking!'

Katie's face seemed to be on fire, as did her pussy, every single one of Holly's cruel words sending a powerful shock through her. It was what she'd imagined so often, in a hundred variations, and now she was going to get it, in the way she wanted best of all. Knowing full well it would make her fate all the worse, and all the better, she turned to Paige.

'Oh, come on, Paige! That's a bit strong, isn't it?'

Paige merely shrugged.

'It's a fair choice,' Olivia put in. 'If you don't want it, all you have to do is describe your last sexual experience.'

'Yes, but, a spanking –' Katie began.

'Get that booty up, Katie girl!' Holly demanded. 'And if you don't want to give her it, Paige, I am well up for it.'

Katie felt her tummy tighten, now so full of emotion she was close to tears. She glanced at Paige, not wanting to hurt her friend's feelings, but guessing that the answer would be what she wanted.

'I – I think I'd rather you did it, please, Holly,' Paige said quietly.

'Oh, yeah, this is good,' Holly replied, 'this is *really* good. Come on, Miss Katie, you get that bum stuck out, right at me – actually no, I'm going to put you right down across my knee and spank you like you were some squalling little brat.'

Katie got up, shaking badly as Holly adjusted her position to make a lap. She could feel the tears of raw emotion starting in her eyes as she laid herself into position. Holly took her firmly around the waist, and she quickly hung her head so that her hair would make a curtain to hide her crying, which began as a hand was placed squarely across the seat of her dress. She was about to be spanked by Holly, and in front of both Paige and Olivia, a prospect at once frightening and thrilling, and which took her right back, pushing aside the last of her regret for her lost time.

Holly's hand lifted, and a smack landed across Katie's bottom, delivered hard enough to make her squeak, a second, a third, and as the rhythm picked up she began to wriggle in a glorious blend of pain and shame and excitement, with the tears running freely down her face. It felt so good, to be spanked across Holly's knee with an audience to enjoy the view, so good, but as Olivia's voice cut through the sound of hand applied to bottom it stopped.

'Hey, come on, Holly, take her knickers down for her. That's half the fun.'

'You've got a point there, girl,' Holly answered, and she began to lift Katie's dress.

'No!' Katie protested. 'Nobody said anything about going bare! No, Holly!'

She began to struggle, but not hard, as, if there was one thing she wanted more than anything else, it was to have her knickers pulled down while her tormentors thought it was against her will. It was going to happen too, with Holly pinning her firmly in place. Katie reached back, grasping for her dress and catching a handful, only for the other side to get jerked up, exposing part of her knickers.

'Give me a hand here, Olivia,' Holly demanded, and a moment later Katie's arms had been pulled up into the small of her back.

Still she struggled, kicking and wriggling across Holly's knees, but either they knew she wasn't serious or they simply didn't care. In an instant her dress had been pulled high and pinned beneath her trapped arms, leaving the broad black seat of her lacy knickers on show. She began to struggle harder, certain she would be stripped anyway, and, sure enough, Holly's thumb had been hooked into the back of her waistband.

'Not my knickers, please!' Katie begged, but was ignored.

'I am really going to enjoy this,' Holly said, jerking Katie's knickers down.

Her shame-filled sob as her bottom came bare was not entirely false, nor was her squeak of pain as a heavy swat landed across her cheeks. She was being spanked, bare bottom, by Holly, a common little tart from some housing estate and a stripper as well, and, if it was ecstasy, it was also impossibly humiliating. It

184

was happening too, whether she liked it or not, Olivia keeping a firm grip as the smacks landed, now hard and fast, to set Katie gasping, kicking and squealing at an ever rising volume.

After maybe thirty spanks, a soft voice broke in through Katie's swirling emotions.

'Um . . . what if Daniel hears?' Paige asked doubtfully.

'Who cares?' Holly laughed. 'I'd like him to watch. How about that, Katie?'

'No, not that!' Katie snapped back in genuine panic. 'Spank me, but not in front of Daniel. I couldn't bear that, not Daniel . . .'

'Oh do shut up!' Holly broke in, and went back to spanking Katie's bottom.

'Hang on,' Olivia said after another half-dozen hard slaps had been delivered to Katie's wiggling cheeks. 'Take her knickers right off, and I'll show you a trick.'

The spanking stopped. Holly took a firm hold on Katie's knickers and they were drawn down the full length of her legs.

'What are you going to do?' Katie demanded.

'I'll show you,' Olivia answered, taking Katie's knickers from where they'd been left dangling from one ankle. 'Open wide, Katie.'

'Look, Olivia, no –' Katie began as she realised what was going to be done to her, but, before she could finish her protest, her discarded panties had been pushed into her half-open mouth.

She tried to struggle, wriggling across Holly's lap and looking up at Olivia in furious consternation, but her nose was held and her knickers forced well in, filling her mouth with dry cotton that tasted more than a little of her own sex. Only a tiny scrap was left hanging out, and she found it all too easy to imagine how absurd she would look as the spanking began once more, lying bare bottom across the black girl's knee with a scrap of her own knickers hanging out of her mouth as her cheeks were slapped.

Holly

Holly was enjoying herself immensely as she worked on Katie's bottom, making sure every square inch of the full pale cheeks got an even share of slaps and was turned a rich glowing pink. Not only was it satisfying to see the smug superior Katie in such a humiliating position, but it was also turning her on, and she was pretty sure it was turning her victim on too. She knew enough about faking pleasure to recognise the real thing, and there was no mistaking the tone of Katie's muffled sobs, nor the state of the neatly turned cunt she could glimpse when the harder smacks made the hapless girl kick her legs apart or lift her bottom. Knowing that Katie got excited by spanking was almost as good as dishing it out. Nor was she in any hurry to stop, but at last Olivia spoke up.

'I think that's enough, don't you?'

'Yeah, I reckon that's dealt with her,' Holly answered, and planted a last heavy slap to each of Katie's cheeks. 'Only you keep those knickers off, girl, and sit on it bare.'

Katie gave a single weak nod as she rose from Holly's knee. Her hair was a mess, her face streaked with tears, her eyes unfocused, but far from complaining she simply extracted her now soggy panties from her mouth and sat down as Holly had ordered, with her skirt lifted and her bottom bare on the sofa.

Paige immediately moved close, to give Katie a long loving hug, which was returned, and as the two girls clung shivering in each other's arms, Holly and Olivia exchanged a knowing look.

'Do you think so?' Olivia whispered.

'I *know* so,' Holly answered. 'That's public-school girls for you. Go on, Miss Katie, you can kiss her, we don't care.'

Katie hesitated, but a moment later her mouth had opened against Paige's in an open kiss. Holly watched, wondering just how far it was going to go and happy to watch the show, but neither girl seemed interested in doing more than kiss and cuddle.

'So, are we playing or what?' she finally asked, taking up the dice.

'I'm playing,' Katie answered as she broke away from Paige. 'I want to get my own back.'

'No way, girl!' Holly laughed. 'I'm sticking to truth.'

'Coward,' Katie answered, and Holly felt her cheeks flare hot in annoyance.

'You want your big arse smacked again?' she demanded.

'Maybe,' Katie answered coolly, and Olivia laughed.

Knowing she would only make herself look a bitch if she kept on, Holly threw out the dice.

'Five and six, eleven,' she said as they came to a stop. 'Maybe you're going to get it sooner than you think, Miss Katie.'

Olivia took the dice and threw a seven, followed by Katie, who for all her bold comments looked distinctly apprehensive. A double four kept her safe, but Paige could only manage a three, leaving her wide eyed and shamefaced as she looked up at Holly, who laughed.

'First I get to spank Miss Katie, then I get to spank her girlfriend! This is turning out to be one great evening.'

'You have to ask me a question first,' Paige pointed out, 'and anyway, I – I don't mind playing around, but not with Daniel in the house.'

'I'll deal with Daniel,' Olivia answered confidently. 'Don't do anything until I get back.'

She walked from the room, leaving Holly to formulate a question that Paige would be sure to refuse and wondering if Katie should be made to look at her girlfriend's face or bottom as the punishment was dished out.

Daniel

Never in his life had Daniel known such frustration. Something was going on downstairs, involving all four girls, and unless he was very much mistaken one of them had just been given a spanking by another. He had no idea who had done what, but it didn't matter, any one of them could have dished it out and any one of them could have taken it, but just knowing that it had been done, and in front of the others, was almost more than he could bear. It was physically painful, making his stomach feel weak and his throat tight, while his cock was an iron bar in his trousers. Yet he was determined not to touch, not until the girls came upstairs and he had something to watch, because he knew that if he did he would end up as sore as he had before.

'The bitches!' he muttered, despite knowing that the circumstances were entirely of his own making.

Cursing himself for not installing a camera in the living room, he turned back to his book in what he knew would be a futile effort to clear his mind of the images of the girls with their bare bottoms stuck out to each other. It was impossible to concentrate on the text, let alone lose himself in the story, and after no more than a dozen lines he threw it down in annoyance, only to stop as he heard a footstep on the stairs. For one moment of wild hope, he wondered if they might not be going to invite him to join in, only to realise that it would just be somebody coming up to use the loo. Then came a knock on his door and his hope surged once more, and higher still as Olivia's head poked into his room.

'Hi,' she said.

Daniel smiled.

'Look,' she went on, 'we're playing a game down-stairs, which is strictly girls only. Not meaning to be nasty or anything, but we really don't want you around. You won't come in, will you?'

'No, of course not,' Daniel managed as his dream collapsed around him. 'I'm just reading.'

'Well, make sure you stay reading,' Olivia told him, and shut the door.

For a long moment, Daniel stayed as he was, staring at the point in space where her head had been, his mouth open. He felt as if he was going to cry, and yet deep down he knew it was a perfectly reasonable request. After all, if they were going to play dirty games together, he was the last person they'd want, but that knowledge only went so far to quell his rising resentment, and within a minute or less he had decided not only to record whatever the girls had to show in their bedrooms, but also to put some of the images up on the internet.

Paige

As Olivia returned to the room Paige cast a nervous glance in her direction. Olivia merely smiled and returned to her seat before she spoke.

'That's sorted. I told him we were having a girls-only evening and he promised to stay in his room.'

'Do you think he really will?' Paige queried.

'Yes,' Olivia confirmed.

'Look, sod Daniel,' Holly added, and got up to quickly push a table against the door so that the handle was jammed up.

Paige managed a weak smile as Holly came back to her seat. Her tummy was fluttering, with some serious misgivings warring with the excitement in her head, but she knew that whatever she was asked to do, whatever she was *told* to do, she would be unable to refuse.

'Here's your question,' Holly was saying. 'Have you ever given Miss Katie head.'

'I –' Paige began, her face flaring crimson.

'She means, have you licked her out?' Olivia supplied helpfully.

'I know what she means,' Paige answered, and hesitated, facing the hideous embarrassment of having to admit to her lesbian antics or go for her forfeit, which seemed more than likely to be a spanking across Holly's knee.

It was just too much, too shameful, too frightening, for all she had done with Katie. This was different, a spanking not from her lover and in front of other people, while, even if Daniel couldn't see, she was sure he would hear, and somehow know it was her being punished. Yet the thought of admitting to licking Katie's pussy was almost too much to bear, so that in the end she only managed a feeble nod.

'So what's that mean?' Holly demanded. 'That you lick cunt, or you're going for a forfeit.'

'I – I don't think I can handle a forfeit,' Paige admitted.

'So you lick cunt?' Holly demanded, her face alight with sadistic pleasure.

Again Paige nodded.

'Say it,' Holly ordered.

'Play fair,' Katie put in, also blushing pink. 'She's admitted it.'

'I want to hear her say it,' Holly answered. 'Come on, girl, tell us how Miss Katie likes it. Do you go sixty-nine, or down on your knees to her? Does she sit on your face, or what?'

At Holly's final words, Paige's blushes grew darker and hotter still. Both Holly and Olivia burst out laughing, the black girl slapping the arm of her chair in delight as she cried out.

'Oh, yeah, we know it. She likes to sit on your face, doesn't she? Come on, girl, admit it, you get Miss Katie's bum in your face, yeah? What – does she make you kiss her arsehole too? I bet she does!'

Paige shrugged, unable to speak for her embarrassment, despite a powerful thrill in the admission, which made her feel both sexual and wanted, and not the shy little mouse she had always been.

'Say it,' Holly demanded once more. 'Say what you do.'

'She . . .' Paige managed, 'she – she likes to sit on my face.'

Holly burst out laughing once more, clapping too, also Olivia, both of them showing open delight in the revelation. Katie was blushing and smiling at the same time, and exchanged a shy glance with Paige before she picked up the dice.

Olivia

As she watched Katie roll, Olivia was praying she would win the next round. Watching Holly dish out a spanking had done more for her than she would easily have admitted, not only for the pleasure of watching Katie get it, but in response to her own humiliating treatment at the hands of Mistress Anastasia. To do it herself would be a greater thrill by far, not perhaps the ideal, which would be a young attractive man, but infinitely better than playing second fiddle to Mistress Anastasia with her invariably middle-aged clients.

'Six,' Katie said, and darted a worried glance to Holly that made Olivia's heart skip.

Paige took the dice and threw, to roll a ten. Olivia cursed quietly as she in turn picked up the dice, and she gave them a good shake in her closed hands before throwing them out. Both landed with two spots uppermost and her heart sank. Holly threw in turn, scoring a three and a four, which left Olivia telling herself it would be easy to answer whatever question Paige came up.

'I win,' Paige said. 'Olivia, what do you do when you go to Winchester?'

'How do you know I go to Winchester?' Olivia retorted in shock and surprise.

'There was a train ticket in your jeans when I did the wash for you the other day,' Paige answered. 'That is where you go, isn't it?'

'Yes,' Olivia admitted, suddenly flustered.

'What do you do, then?' Paige insisted.

'Yeah, what do you do?' Holly added.

Olivia hesitated, knowing she couldn't possibly admit the truth, especially in front of Katie, and wondering whether she should lie and, if so, what she

192

could say that would be convincing. There was also a nagging little voice at the back of her head telling her that she had the perfect opportunity to get another spanking without admitting she liked it.

'I'm sorry, but I can't say.'

'Forfeit then,' Holly said immediately. 'What's it to be, Paige? Make it something strong.'

'Thanks a bunch, Holly!' Olivia answered, her stomach fluttering at her friend's words.

'I – I'm not sure,' Paige said.

'Spank her,' Katie advised.

'I – I thought, maybe, she should have to – to wet her knickers, in front of us,' Paige said, her cheeks burning scarlet at her own words.

For a moment, there was absolute silence, all three girls staring at Paige, before Holly burst into raucous laughter.

'Yes!' she exclaimed. 'You go, girl. Come on, Olivia, tell us the truth or you have to piss your knicks.'

'Hang on,' Olivia began, but went quiet as Katie broke in.

'Those are the rules, Olivia, and it's not as bad as being spanked.'

'Yes it is!' Olivia gasped.

Holly laughed to see her friend's embarrassment. Katie gave a satisfied nod, and Paige was smiling. Olivia made a face, once more considered lying, or backing out, only to realise that if she did it was likely to spoil the game, which would rob her of a chance to punish one of the others.

'Oh, all right!' she snapped. 'But you're a dirty bitch, Paige.'

Paige gave an embarrassed shrug, but said nothing.

'I'll get a bucket from the kitchen,' Holly offered, grinning.

Olivia stood up, shaking with emotion, to stand in the empty space beyond the end of the table, where everybody would be able to see. Not wanting to risk ruining her boots if the pee ran down her leg, she kicked them off, and after a moment's thought her socks too. It was obviously best to take her jeans off too, and she'd just put her hands to the button when Holly came back.

'Hey, wait for me!' the black girl demanded.

'I haven't done anything,' Olivia pointed out, pushing her jeans down around her hips.

'No, but you're going to,' Holly answered her, passing across the bucket. 'You're going to pee in your panties, girlie.'

Olivia made a face, then reached down to pull her jeans free. Her bladder already felt taut from all the wine she'd drunk, and there was a horrible weak feeling in her stomach, making her wonder if she could do it without having a full-blown accident in her panties. With her jeans gone, she stood up once more, now bare legged, with the front of her black satin knickers on show to the room.

'Couldn't I just pee in front of you?' she asked.

'Uh, uh,' Holly responded instantly.

'In your knickers, Paige said,' Katie agreed, and Paige nodded.

Olivia swallowed, casting a last imploring look at the three watching girls but found only curiosity and lust in their eyes. Squatting down over the bucket, she lifted her top to get it out of the way and show her panties off properly, only to discover that for all the tension in her bladder the pee wouldn't come, not into her panties and while she was watched.

'Come on,' Holly urged. 'You must want it. You've drunk nearly a whole bottle of wine.'

'I do,' Olivia sobbed. 'It's just not easy when you're watching me!'

Even as she spoke she pushed, and suddenly she was doing it: a gush of hot yellow piddle erupting into her panty crotch, and through it, splashing in the bucket below her, even as it soaked into the tight satin encasing her pussy and the turn of her bottom cheeks. Paige giggled, Holly laughed out loud and Katie put on a smug grin.

Olivia shut her eyes, shaking badly as the pee squirted out through her knickers and the wet patch spread slowly up over her pubic mound and around her bottom cheeks. Some pee had run back into her slit too, wetting her anus and making her want to let go completely. She held off, sobbing with emotion, the pee now gushing through her panties at full force, and running out of the side as well, to trickle down her thighs.

'It's going on the carpet!' she squealed, but too late, the piddle already dripping from her leg to soil the floor.

'You're going to have to clean that up, you know.' Holly laughed.

Olivia's answer was a weak sob. She'd given up, her eyes closed in bliss as she let the last of her pee trickle out into the bucket and down her leg. Her panties were soaked, her bottom too, and her pussy, wet and sticky in the clinging satin, but, if what she'd done had excited her, she wasn't the only one.

'Show us the back,' Holly demanded as Olivia finally rose, her top still lifted to display the wet triangle of soggy black satin plastered tight across her sex.

Turning, Olivia stuck out her bottom, deliberately showing off her sodden panty seat with her top held up to make sure they all got a good view.

'I think you'd better clean up your mess,' Katie suggested. 'And you can stay bare, like me.'

Olivia made a face, but nodded and began to peel off her soiled panties.

Holly

'Come on!' Holly urged as she watched Olivia crawling on her hands and knees as she sponged the pee stain from the carpet.

As agreed, Olivia was naked from the waist down, her bottom still wet and glistening from the hasty wash she'd taken after wetting herself for them. It felt good to have both Katie and Olivia bare bottomed, and Holly was determined to add Paige to the line-up just as soon as she could. Her luck seemed to be in with the dice, so it was only a matter of time.

'OK, I'm done,' Olivia answered, and stood up to drop the sponge into the bucket, which now had soapy water in it in place of her pee. 'Just let me dry my bum.'

She'd brought a towel down from the bathroom, and briefly applied it to her bottom before resuming her place.

'Right,' Holly said, 'from here on in, the loser has to take a piece of clothing off, even if she goes for truth. OK?'

Nobody protested, and Holly threw out the dice, smiling as they came to rest on five and four. Olivia leant forwards as Holly sat back, taking her throw to score an eight. Holly chuckled, sure she'd soon have either Paige or Katie at her mercy once more. Katie threw, scored nine, and Holly was grinning openly at Paige.

'You're going down, girl,' she said happily, 'and this time you get your bum spanked.'

'Maybe,' Paige said bravely, and threw the dice, both of which landed with six spots uppermost.

'You can't ask the same question twice!' Olivia said quickly.

'That's fair,' Paige agreed. 'OK then . . .'

'Get that top off first, Olivia,' Holly interrupted.

Olivia made a face but quickly hauled her top up and off, leaving her in just her bra.

'I'll ask a question for your bra then,' Paige said. 'Did you get turned on by what you just did?'

Olivia hesitated, then quickly put her hands behind her back, speaking as she unclipped her bra. 'I'm not answering that!'

'Yeah, 'cause we all know you did, slut!' Holly laughed.

Olivia stuck her tongue out as her bra came lose. A quick tug, and she'd lifted it over her breasts to leave them lying round and heavy and naked on her chest, the nipples erect. She was blushing a little, but quickly gathered up the dice and threw them once more, scoring a seven.

'Shit!' she swore. 'It's just not my night.'

'No, it's mine,' Holly answered. 'Make it snakes eyes, Katie, and you can lick . . . my . . . cunt.'

She said the words slowly and carefully, looking full into Katie's face to leave the posh girl blushing and confused as she took up the dice. Holly laughed, well pleased with herself, and watched closely as Katie threw, scoring six. Katie made a face and pushed the dice towards Paige.

'You'll do,' Holly remarked. 'How d'you fancy my big black bum in your face for a change?'

Paige blushed but said nothing, then rolled the dice.

197

'Eight,' Holly said as the dice came to a stop. 'Oh, well, looks like it's Miss Katie after all.'

She threw, completely confident, only to find herself staring in horror at a three and a one.

'Shit! That can't happen, I'm supposed to win,' she gasped. 'Fuck it! You better go easy on me, Paige, or you're in big trouble.'

'Don't let her off, Paige,' Olivia insisted. 'Make her strip.'

'What's the point of that?' Katie responded. 'She does that anyway. I suggest a spanking, from each of us in turn.'

'You've had it, Miss Katie,' Holly warned. 'Just you wait.'

Katie merely stuck her tongue out and sat back, then abruptly leant close to whisper something into Paige's ear.

Paige smiled, then spoke. 'You must take your top off, first.'

Holly gave an indifferent shrug and peeled off her top.

'This is your choice,' Paige went on, 'either you have to play with yourself in front of us, or you tell us which of us you'd most like to go to bed with.'

'Who says I want to go to bed with any of you?' Holly retorted.

'You enjoyed spanking me,' Katie pointed out.

'What's not to enjoy, beating some rich bitch on her bare arse?' Holly queried. 'But yeah, I'll take you to bed, with my Andros, and I'll hold your head while he fucks you up the arse. How's that?'

Katie went scarlet and Holly laughed.

'Next one please,' she said as she picked up the dice. 'Right, I want to see sixes.'

She threw, and scored a double, but fives, which still left her grinning as she settled back in her seat.

Olivia threw a seven, Katie the same and Paige a five.

'So what was it you wanted me to do, Paige?' Holly asked. 'Frig off in front of you? Right, so I want to see you do the same, only with your posh bitch girlfriend licking your pussy.'

'I didn't lose,' Katie pointed out, 'and, anyway, you have to give her a choice.'

'Sod that,' Holly answered. 'Let's just go for the forfeits.'

Katie hesitated, but Paige spoke up. 'I have to have the choice.'

'Let's vote on it,' Holly suggested. 'Who wants to play for forfeits – oh, and get your top off, Paige.'

'Forfeits only,' Olivia agreed as Paige reluctantly peeled off her top.

Katie nodded.

'Looks like you're on your own,' Holly told Paige. 'Jesus you've got big tits. You'd make a packet stripping, if you lost a bit of weight.'

'I could never do that,' Paige said.

'Better than me, are you?' Holly answered. 'OK, if Katie won't lick, that's your forfeit, a striptease, all the way.'

'I – I'm not really very good at dancing,' Paige answered.

'You can do it,' Katie urged, reaching out to squeeze Paige's hand.

Olivia stretched back to reach the sound system, and after a moment fiddling with the controls managed to get the start of a pop song. Paige stood up, looking if possible more embarrassed than before, and began a clumsy hesitant dance. Holly watched, enjoying Paige's rising shame as the clothes began to come off.

By the end of the song, Paige was still in her bra and panties, her face burning with blushes, but as the next started she seemed to gather a little in confidence, deliberately teasing with her bra before allowing it to fall from her massive breasts, then turning her back to ease her panties down and show off her bottom. At last, with her panties kicked off, she turned to stand full-frontal nude, her arms lifted to show every detail of her body.

'Not bad, for an amateur,' Holly admitted, clapping. 'So what now? I think we need Miss Katie's tits out.'

She scooped the dice up and tossed them casually out on to the table, scoring a six and a two. Eight was fair, and she nodded complacently as she sat back. Olivia took her turn, heavy breasts swinging forward as she reached for the dice, which came out as a two and a one. Holly gave a cluck of amusement. Katie threw a four and Paige a six, leaving Holly victorious one more time.

'Time you were spanked, my girl,' Holly stated, and snapped her fingers to indicate her lap as she moved forward in her chair.

Olivia returned a resentful look, but came anyway. Already nude, she had no clothing to disarrange, her bottom naked and vulnerable as she put herself into spanking position across Holly's knees. Holly set to work, her mouth set in an amused smile as she applied several dozen firm smacks to Olivia's quivering bottom, leaving her friend red behind and holding her cheeks as she rose.

Katie

Katie had been aroused since before she'd had to go across Holly's knee, and was getting towards the point where the game was no longer an excuse to express her desires but a distraction. As Olivia sat down on her hot bottom, Katie was hoping to be given the same treatment herself for a second time on the very next go, and to be made to strip into the bargain. A little pressure and she'd have given into Holly's demands that she lick Paige, and she knew that once she was nude there would be no more resistance.

She took another gulp of wine and rolled the dice out on to the table, scoring a ten, which provoked more disappointment than satisfaction. Paige could only manage four, and Holly five, which after Olivia's nine left Katie in charge.

'Come on, Piglet,' she joked, reaching out to guide Paige down over her knee.

Paige went without resistance, lifting her plump bottom high to make a thoroughly rude rear view for Holly, and gasping and giggling her way through the spanking. Katie did it hard, knowing Paige could take a lot more and keen to indulge herself with her girlfriend's bottom in front of the others. When it was over, they hugged and kissed once more, and might have abandoned the game in favour of having sex together in front of the others if Olivia hadn't taken up the dice.

Katie lost the round and part of her wish was granted; her clothes were lost and she was fully nude, blushing and smiling as she sat down once more, with her nipples rock hard in excitement.

Again, the dice were rolled out and again she lost, to be put across Paige's knee in turn to have her bottom warmed for a second time, which left her more excited still.

Paige

Drunk, naked and horny, Paige had finally got over her inhibitions, making a display of Katie's bottom as she spanked it, and even kissing both hot cheeks better once it was done. It had been fun, but she no longer wanted to win. Only Katie had spanked her, and she wanted it badly from both the others, which no longer even felt like a betrayal. After all, Katie obviously didn't mind.

Glancing at Holly, she threw the dice, hoping for a low score that would get her over the black girl's knee for a hard spanking as the other two watched. She scored eleven, and sat back in frustration as Holly in turn took up the dice, which came out as a double one.

'Shit!' Holly swore and threw Paige a warning look. 'If you win, girl . . .'

Holly left the sentence unfinished, and Paige felt a delicious little shiver at the prospect of having to submit to some awful revenge.

Olivia took up the dice and rolled a seven, as did Katie.

Paige looked at Holly. 'Um . . . you can do a strip, if you like?'

'Good idea, about time she got her clothes off,' Olivia put in.

'It's always a treat to watch a professional at work,' Katie put in.

'You better watch it, all of you,' Holly answered, but she was smiling. 'OK, so you want to see me strip. I'll show you how it's done.'

The music was still on, but she turned it up before stepping to the open space. Her strip was very different to Paige's, slow and sensual, teasing from the start as she gradually exposed herself. Paige and the others watched entranced, and by the time Holly had kicked off her knickers Katie had one hand between her thighs. Paige wanted to do the same, but couldn't quite find the courage, even when Holly finished by stepping close and lifting her bare breasts.

'Put them in her face, Holly,' Olivia suggested, and Paige was immediately smothered in warm brown flesh, leaving her shivering with desire.

All four girls were silent as Holly sat down, the air tense with sexual excitement. Katie took up the dice and rolled, but only scored four. Paige followed, and her heart leapt as a two and one came up, but Holly only managed a five herself. Olivia threw and Paige watched the dice bounce and roll, to come up on a double four. As she looked up, Olivia had extended a single crooked finger, beckoning.

'Over my knee, now,' Olivia ordered.

Olivia

To Olivia, the feel of Paige's bottom under her hand was pure heaven, the skin smooth and hairless, the flesh soft and resilient, sexier by far than any of the men she had punished. Paige was obviously turned on too, her breathing deep and even, her bottom lifted to Olivia's caresses. There was no hurry to start spanking, no need to pretend it was just a game, and Olivia took her time, enjoying the full contours of Paige's heavy bottom, squeezing the ripe flesh and tickling in the deep slit until her fingers were just inches from the girl's pussy and anus. Soon Paige had begun to sob with passion, and at last Olivia began to spank, just gently, alternating the smacks with caresses as both Katie and Holly looked on in fascination.

Katie's hand was between her thighs, gently massaging herself as she watched her girlfriend punished. Olivia gave her an arch look and began to spank a little harder, making Paige's bottom quiver and grow slowly pink. Katie responded by letting her thighs come wide, now openly masturbating as she watched Paige spanked. Olivia began to slap harder still, and shifted position a little, allowing Katie to see full between Paige's thighs. Katie gave a weak sob and began to rub harder, and to pat at her pussy.

'Do it,' she sighed. 'Punish her, Olivia ... spank her ... spank her hard ...'

Olivia obliged, applying hard smacks to Paige's bottom to make the flesh bounce and the big cheeks part, showing off her bottom hole to Katie. Paige began to react, whimpering and gasping, wriggling her bottom and kicking her feet. Olivia spanked harder still, putting the full force of her arm into every blow, to set Paige squirming and pumping her legs, thighs spread wide to show the plump juice-smeared lips of her cunt between.

Katie cried out, her legs spread wide and her own cunt on open show as she brought herself to a gasping, shaking orgasm in front of them, with her back arched tight and her breasts thrust high. Olivia watched in delight, still spanking, but the moment Katie was finished she stopped, pushing Paige to the floor.

'Get down there,' she ordered. 'Lick me out.'

Paige cast a single glance to Katie, but gave no resistance as she was put to the floor and her head pulled in between Olivia's thighs. Olivia sighed as Paige's tongue found her sex, and she lay back to be licked, her head buzzing with what she'd done, and what she was doing.

'I'll have some of that,' Holly said, and beckoned to Katie. 'Get here, you.'

Katie came more than willingly, scrambling quickly around the table on her hands and knees to bury her face between the black girl's thighs, licking obediently.

Holly made herself comfortable and took a gentle grip in Katie's hair, making sure she stayed in place. Her other arm went to her breasts, caressing the stiff black nipples and stroking the plump chocolate-coloured skin. Olivia looked across, grinning at the sight of the two girls on their knees, busily licking cunt.

'This is the life, eh?' Holly remarked.

Holly

Sitting back, Holly let the pleasure of having Katie's tongue work on her sex wash over her. It wasn't the first time another girl had licked her, but Katie was doing it as if she couldn't get enough, and plainly saw it as more than straightforward sex. That was good, to have a posh girl on her knees, in the nude and licking cunt as a gesture of submission, making Holly wonder just how far Katie would go. She slid a little further down the chair and lifted her legs, exposing the turn of her bottom and her anus as she spoke.

'Lick my arse, you stuck-up bitch.'

Katie responded with a sob, but hesitated only an instant before her head went lower. Holly laughed as a gentle kiss was planted on her bottom hole, and she sighed as Katie began to lick the tight little ring. It felt different, but almost equally nice, while just to know that Katie was licking her anus gave a thrill all its own.

'She's only fucking doing it,' Holly gasped. 'She's licking my bumhole, Olivia! Fuck but that feels nice . . . go on, bitch, get your tongue up me.'

Olivia's answer was a gasp of surprise, then she spoke. 'She's doing it too . . . and my one didn't even have to be told.'

They shared a grin and reached out to slap their hands together, both now having their bottoms licked, both with a girl on her knees at their feet. Katie had begun to work her tongue in up Holly's bumhole, as ordered, a sensation too exquisite to be ignored. Holly sat back, her eyes closed in bliss as she rolled her legs higher still to let Katie get deeper in, but the feeling and the knowledge that she had Katie licking her bottom was too much for her. Her hand went down, snatching at her sex. Her mouth came wide in a long ecstatic sigh. Her knees came higher and wider still, spreading her bottom in Katie's face.

'Do it while I come,' she ordered, gasping out her words, as she began to masturbate. 'Lick my bumhole, you little bitch, taste it, taste my arse.'

Katie licked all the harder, wriggling her tongue deep in up Holly's now open anus. She was using her hands too, to knead Holly's cheeks and pull her face yet more firmly in. Beside her, Olivia groaned in ecstasy, even as Holly's mouth opened wider still and her muscles began to contract. Holly's finger was pressed hard to her clit, as Katie's tongue was as deep up her bottom as it would go, and she started to come, gasping and shuddering her way through a long glorious orgasm that surpassed even those she'd enjoyed with Andros.

At last the spasms of pleasure died down, and as her body went slowly limp one thought stayed firmly in her head. She'd made Katie Shalstone lick her bottom hole.

Daniel

Daniel awoke to a bitter sense of disappointment, but only as his head cleared did he remember why, with the events of the night before coming slowly back to him. In a lifetime of sexual frustration and guilty relief, never had he known either emotion so keen. For some two hours he'd been in a state of need so bad it had hurt, yet always hoping, only to ultimately be denied, at least more than the briefest taste of what might have been.

He'd listened as the girls played, to their laughter and to their voices, to the slaps of hands on bottom flesh and the cries of the victims. Sometimes he'd even been able to make out what was said, enough to know that at least one of the girls had ended up licking cunt for another. There had been spankings, cunt licking and at least one striptease, that much he knew, and his imagination was more than capable of supplying the rest, filling him with yearning, lust, regret and, above all, self-pity, yet all the while he'd held off from touching his aching cock, convinced that the girls must eventually come upstairs.

They had, but not to play. From their giggling, drunken conversation as they came upstairs, it was clear that they had already indulged themselves to the full in the living room, and were too exhausted to do more. He had managed a few peeps as they took turns in the bathroom, and Katie and Paige had gone to bed together, but their naked flesh was no longer enough, not when he knew they'd been playing dirty lesbian games immediately before.

He'd come anyway, realising that it was his last chance to get any visual stimulation at all, watching Paige in the shower while Katie talked to her, stark naked and careless of what she was showing. It had been a weak orgasm, far inferior to what he had expected, although a long one, which left several days' worth of come dribbling down his fist as his cock deflated.

Now, in the cool of morning with brittle autumn sunlight filtering through his curtains, he felt both exhausted and depressed. Rising slowly from his bed, he tried to tell himself that what had happened once would happen again, but he was by no means sure of it. The girls had got drunk, and would probably be ashamed of themselves when they woke up. Even if they weren't, for him there would still be the pain of rejection, and the way Olivia had spoken to him, making it absolutely clear that he was unwanted.

The house was silent, all four of the girls still asleep, but he washed and made coffee as fast as he could, not wanting to have to face them. He was sure they'd be embarrassed, both for what they'd done and because he knew, which would no doubt mean they didn't want him around. Perhaps they would even tell him to get out, of his own house, and he knew he'd do it.

Feeling thoroughly fed up, and with his thoughts swinging between guilt and a desire for revenge, he went out, hoping to catch a glimpse of nipple or panties in the park.

Olivia

'What do you suggest?' Olivia asked as she accepted the mug of coffee from Mistress Anastasia.

'He is a typical man,' Mistress Anastasia answered, 'submissive at heart, but having difficulty coping with his real needs in the face of social pressure. You should find this cock cage of his and spell out your terms to him, openly and without evasion. Men respond better to the direct approach.'

Olivia nodded. For all her doubt when it came to Mistress Anastasia's theories, the advice seemed practical. The Mistress certainly had plenty of experience at any rate. Olivia had decided to ask her, knowing that with Daniel in Silbury she would still retain full control of the situation, while Mistress Anastasia seemed to presume her loyalty.

'I'll do that,' she said, and paused, wanting to talk about what had happened two days before when she played dice with the other girls, but both slightly embarrassed and feeling it might be taken as boasting. She tried a question instead.

'How do you feel about women submitting to other women?'

'It is not a question of how I feel,' Mistress Anastasia answered, 'but of how it should be. Spankings between women are not inappropriate, in the right circumstances, and perhaps rather more, but it must never be done for the gratification of men.'

Olivia nodded her agreement before going on.

'Do you mean spankings and stuff for pleasure, or only for discipline?'

'There is pleasure in discipline, surely you know that?' Mistress Anastasia answered.

'Yes, of course,' Olivia said hastily.

Mistress Anastasia took a sip from her teacup, and as she lowered it her mouth was curved into that wry smile which invariably meant trouble for somebody, although usually a client.

'I have a little exercise for you, Olivia,' she said. 'You are to confront this man with the evidence of his submission, to make him accept it, and to whip him. I shall require a photograph of the end result as proof. Fail, and you'll be going across my knee.'

'I'll do my best,' Olivia promised.

Daniel

Sitting at his computer, Daniel stared from the window of Number 47 Myrtle Road. Outside, it was a perfect autumn day, warm enough for the girls to be in skimpy clothing, while the approach of winter would soon mean they were wearing coats, which always spoiled the opportunities for voyeurism. Yet he had no desire to go out.

Well-shaped jean-clad bottoms were no longer enough, or even the occasional teasing flash of panties. He wanted more, far more; to watch Paige as her gloriously cheeky bottom was smacked up to a rosy glow, to see Holly perform an intimate striptease in front of the other girls, to watch Katie lick cunt on her knees, to see Olivia apply a whip to a nicely fleshed bottom.

So desperate had he become that he was even reluctant to leave the house for fear of missing something, despite the fact that the four girls had done nothing remotely similar since. Yet he knew it would come. Katie and Paige were now sleeping together openly, while the four were generally much more intimate. Even Holly and Katie seemed to be getting along, albeit with a lot of good-natured teasing. Sometime it would happen again, of that he was sure, and, when it did, he intended to be watching.

A bug in the living room was evidently a necessity. He had already purchased it, and adjusted both wiring and software to allow him to switch from the bathroom camera to the living room with a simple change of one USB connection. All that remained was to install the bug itself and wire it into the system, but for that he knew he would need at least two hours of uninterrupted work time.

That meant waiting until all four girls were out, and he was fairly sure he was about to get his moment. Paige and Katie had gone riding in the morning as usual, but had also gone into the university together, in Katie's car, and he knew they intended to lunch together. Holly was also at the university, but was seeing Andros in the afternoon, which left only Olivia, who had just left the house with a heavy bag. The bag contained library books, as he knew from watching her pack them on his monitor, and he had listened into their conversations that morning.

He waited until she had disappeared from view, then quickly extracted the bug from its hiding place. Taking the stepladder and his tools from the cupboard under the stairs, he went into the living room. The girls had played their game seated around the central table, so the ideal view seemed likely to be from one of the end walls, where he'd have the best chance of a decent display of cunt when one got spanked. Unfortunately, neither wall provided much in the way of hiding places, while if he concealed the bug in the shadows provided by the top of the curtains and the French windows he would be unable to get a decent view of any action that took place in the two armchairs. There was also the problem of how best to conceal the wires running from the camera.

Finally, he decided that the best course of action was to set the bug high in one corner, which would give him a good view of the sofa and at least one of the chairs. It also meant drilling through brick to reach the outside, from where he could run a wire up to the level of the attic behind a drainpipe. He set to work, put down newspaper to catch the dust, positioned the stepladder and fited the correct bit into his electric drill.

Olivia

It was the ideal moment, or so Olivia hoped. With Katie, Holly and Paige all busy, Daniel was in the house alone and likely to be for the rest of the day. She already knew where the cock cage was, in the drawer of his desk, which left only the crucial confrontation. With luck she could also catch him masturbating, which she was sure he did at every opportunity.

Ten minutes had passed since she had left the house, surely enough time for him to get busy, but not enough for him to have finished. She turned the corner, walking up the next road and along a footpath to rejoin Myrtle Road beyond the house. Now in sight of his window, she hurried down the road, not stopping until she was in the concealment of the front door. Listening, she caught the sound of an electric drill, but was uncertain which house it came from. After a moment it stopped, then began again, helping conceal the noise as she carefully slid her key into the lock and eased herself in at the front door.

Knowing how the door banged, she shut it carefully, in absolute silence. The drill had stopped again, but she could hear Daniel in the living room. Obviously he wasn't masturbating, but she had little choice but to go on, for if she was unable to provide a photo of his whipped buttocks by that evening she could expect a trip over Mistress Anastasia's knee.

He was obviously busy with some DIY, and she decided to slip upstairs, fetch the cock cage and confront him with it in the living room. Everything went smoothly, and she was soon in his room with the cock cage in her hand, when it occurred to her that she'd be in a stronger position if she could find more evidence of his submissive nature. After a moment to listen, she went to his chest of drawers, easing each one wide in turn. The first two contained nothing more unusual than a pair of purple Y-fronts, but with the third she struck gold.

At the bottom, carefully hidden beneath some trousers, was a bright-pink frilly baby-doll nightie of the cheapest and nastiest sort. It was still in the wrapper, but Olivia had no doubt at all why he had bought it, for his own humiliation. Several of Mistress Anastasia's clients liked to cross dress, and there was a distinction between those who enjoyed female clothing for its own sake and those who found it shameful to be dressed as a girl. The first group generally did their best to look like real women, but the second preferred to look as ridiculous as possible. Looking at the baby-doll, Daniel was obviously in the second group, although possibly he'd yet to pluck up the courage to dress up.

Below the baby-doll was a pair of furry handcuffs, suggesting that he not only liked to cross dress, but to be put in restraint as well. That implied a need to be punished as well as humiliated, precisely as Mistress Anastasia had predicted.

Now sure that she had everything she needed, Olivia made her way downstairs. She was confident, well used to handling submissive men, and sure Daniel would be no different. He was using the drill again, giving her the perfect opportunity to enter the living room without being noticed. Sure enough, he had his back to her, standing on a stepladder as he used the drill to make a hole in the top corner where the walls and ceiling met.

Olivia made to speak, only to stop, wondering what he was doing. Various bits of equipment had been laid out on a newspaper that covered the central table; tools, a coil of wire, a small pot of paint and an electronic device still on its card, which bore the clear legend 'Microcam VS10'. There was no doubt whatsoever about what Daniel was doing, but it still took a moment for the sheer outrage of his behaviour to sink in for Olivia, at which point he stopped drilling. As the room fell silent, he turned, looking directly into Olivia's face.

'You slimy little bastard!' she gasped. 'You're planting a camera on us, aren't you? You heard us the other night, didn't you, and you were going to peep on us if it happened again, weren't you? You little shit!'

Daniel said nothing, his face frozen in the horror of discovery, until he took in what Olivia was holding, at which his mouth began to work in an agony of shame and contrition, although he was still unable to speak.

'Yes,' Olivia said. 'I've got your dirty little things, you pervert, but I'm not worried about that. I want to know what the fucking hell you think you're doing? Where do you get off, you filthy little creep, spying on us? I'm calling the police, right now.'

'No, please, Olivia, please!' Daniel gabbled, finally finding his voice. 'Don't do that, please. I didn't mean any harm, I really didn't. I just had to see . . . I just had to. You don't know how it feels, you really don't. I just wanted to see!'

His face was screwed up, obviously close to tears as he begged and Olivia felt her anger soften a little. She drew her breath in, telling herself that she'd be much better off taking advantage of the situation than making sure he got what he truly deserved. Besides, she'd caught him in time, before any real damage was done.

'OK,' she said, keeping her voice level and a little stern, 'I won't report you, either to the police or to the others, but I'm not letting you get away with this.'

'What – what are you going to do?' Daniel asked.

'You'll see,' Olivia answered him. 'First, clear this up, then go up to your room and put these on. I'll have this.'

She threw the cock cage and baby-doll down on the sofa and picked up the miniature camera in exchange, keeping the handcuffs. He stood dumbstruck, his face working with emotion, and he didn't react until she spoke again.

'Come on, get on with it, do as you're told.'

Daniel nodded weakly, and Olivia left the room. Her heart was beating fast, but she was confident that he'd do as he was told. She had given him his excuse, something many men, and women, needed to live their fantasies, as Mistress Anastasia had explained. He'd soon come to accept his place as her personal slave, but it needed to be done in style.

In her room, she quickly stripped out of her ordinary clothes, right down to her knickers. Her leather gear went on instead, the top and shorts, her collar and boots. A touch of makeup and her whip left her in full gear, along with the silly handcuffs and her mobile phone. As she climbed the stairs, her sense of dominance was undercut by only the slightest uncertainty, which vanished as she entered Daniel's room. He was ready, as she had instructed, looking as submissive and as ludicrous as any one of Mistress Anastasia's clients in his cock cage and baby-doll, while his eyes were full of fear and longing as he in turn took in the way she looked.

'On your knees,' she ordered, pointing to the floor at her feet with her whip.

'What are you going to do with me?' Daniel quavered as he got down.

'Shut up,' Olivia answered. 'Stay like that.'

She held up her mobile phone, but Daniel quickly turned his face away. 'Not a picture!' he whined. 'That's not fair, Olivia!'

'It's just for me,' Olivia lied, 'to make sure you behave yourself in future. Now stay still, and from now on every complaint you make will earn you an extra ten strokes, the same if you fail to obey me promptly.'

'Are you going to beat me?' Daniel asked, throwing a worried glance at Olivia's whip.

'Yes,' she answered.

His eyes grew wider and more terrified still, but within the tight rubber cage his cock had started to swell.

'I thought so,' she said, nodding to herself. 'Now watch the birdie.'

She took her picture, grinning as she admired the result. Daniel stayed as he was, shaking visibly, while

Olivia quickly sent the picture and an accompanying text to Mistress Anastasia, assuring her mentor that it was only the start of the session.

Daniel

As he looked up into Olivia's face, Daniel was torn between guilt and arousal, hope and shame. He'd been caught out, something he'd dreaded for years, not just since he'd been spying on the girls, but since his peeping habits had first gone beyond mere covert glances at what pretty girls had to show. His feelings in response were every bit as bad as he had imagined, and yet Olivia was not reacting in the hysterical accusatory manner he had anticipated.

Nor was she reacting with the complicity he had occasionally imagined in his wilder fantasies, although never daring to hope for in reality. Instead, she seemed determined to use his helplessness for her own ends, which seemed to be perverse to say the least. Not that what she intended seemed unfair, far from it. That he should be punished seemed entirely appropriate, but it in no way reduced his fear of the whip in her hand, nor his shame that it should be necessary at all. She had also sent his picture to some unknown person, making it all that much worse.

'Who did you send that to, please?' he asked.

'Shut up,' Olivia answered, 'and when you speak to me you address me as Mistress.'

'Yes, but –' he began, only to break off with a squeak of pain as she flicked her whip against his leg.

'I suggest you give yourself over to me,' she went on, 'because what I have to offer is what you really want, isn't it? And it's a great deal better than peeping at girls.'

Daniel wasn't so sure, at least not about the whip and having to kneel in the ludicrous baby-doll nightie. Olivia herself was a different matter, as desirable as any woman he'd ever peeped at, but present in the flesh and being openly sexual with him, just so long he obeyed her rules. He nodded.

'Say it,' she demanded. 'Tell me what you want.'

'I – I want to do whatever you say . . . Mistress,' he managed, hoping that whatever she did want involved contact with her body and his, particularly her magnificent tits and his straining cock, but not too much pain.

'Do you deserve to be punished?' she demanded.

'Yes, Mistress,' he answered truthfully, but his voice was nearly breaking as he spoke.

'I'm glad you appreciate that,' she said, 'because it is exactly what I intend to do, you dirty Peeping Tom. Let me see, ten lashes? No, six – six for each of us, for what you intended to do. Get on all fours.'

Daniel hastened to obey, shaking badly as he got down on the carpet. Olivia moved close, trapping his head between her legs, so that he could smell the leather of her boots and his vision was restricted to a small area of carpet and her heels. She bent down, taking his arms and pulling them together in the small of his back. He felt the handcuffs press to one wrist and click closed, then on the other and he was completely helpless.

'Not too hard, please,' he begged. 'I'm really not very good with pain.'

'This is a punishment,' Olivia pointed out, 'while I suspect you understand the link between pain and pleasure, even if you've yet to experience it.'

Daniel made a face, remembering how he'd got off over the thought of Katie's pain as she was spanked over Paige's knee. Now he was in the same awkward, shameful situation, worse maybe, but at least she'd wanted it. She'd even come as she was spanked, but then again for all his fear there was no denying that his cock was now straining against the bars of the cage. Maybe it was just that Katie understood the reactions of her body better then he did his own, or he certainly hoped so, because there was nothing whatsoever he could do to avoid his punishment.

'Twenty-four strokes,' she said calmly, 'bare.'

She had coiled her whip, and used the end to push down the ridiculous see-through nylon panties of the baby-doll, adjusting them to leave his buttocks completely bare and his cock and balls dangling down within the cage. A whimper escaped his throat at the feeling of exposure, and another as Olivia lifted her whip from his skin. There was a brief, agonising pause, and she brought the whip down across the buttocks.

Daniel gasped as the plaited leather thong struck home. It stung like fire, making him wonder how anybody could ever be mad enough to submit to anything of the sort, and before he could so much as protest the second cut landed. Again he gasped, and was about to yelp out a protest when he remembered what Olivia had said. He'd only make it worse for himself. Besides, he deserved it, or so he was desperately trying to tell himself as the whip smacked down across his naked flesh for a third time.

Many times he had fantasised about being taken in hand by a strong woman and beaten for his sins, but now it was happening he was regretting every one. Every stroke hurt more than the last, until he'd begun to lose control and wriggle and kick under the lash.

Olivia merely gave a snort of contempt for his weakness and struck home once more. 'Pathetic!' she snapped in response to Daniel's pained yelp. 'Truly pathetic!'

Her words sent a pulse of shame through Daniel's head. It was true. He was the most pathetic specimen of all, a voyeur and a wanker, a man who'd let a woman make him dress in a nylon baby-doll and would crawl to her for a whipping, pathetic indeed. Doubly pathetic, in fact, because his cock was straining so hard against the cage that it hurt.

'Get it up, worm!' Olivia ordered, and Daniel obeyed instantly, lifting his buttocks for the whip.

He heard the crack as it hit him and his body jerked in pain once more. One leg had begun to shake, but he didn't even try to control it, too far gone to care how much of a show he made in front of her. He was nothing, and he wanted her to realise that, so began to babble apologies and thanks as she beat him. Olivia merely laughed and brought the whip down harder still, crack after crack, until Daniel's words grew broken and then gave way to cries and a wretched snivelling, only for it to stop abruptly.

'Twenty-four,' Olivia said. 'You're done.'

'Thank you ... thank you, Mistress,' Daniel managed.

'Stay as you are,' Olivia told him.

Daniel obeyed, grovelling down on the floor as she stepped away. His buttocks felt as if they were on fire, hot all over with several spots more painful still where the lash had caught his skin especially hard. Yet his cock felt as if it was about to burst the cage and, from where Olivia had gone to sit on his computer chair, he knew she could see. His face went red with embarrassment, imagining her disgust, although deep down there was a wild hope that she might take pity on him and let him toss off in front of her.

'So,' she said, her voice slow and even, 'whatever is to be done with you? A few questions first, and you'd better be honest, because I'll be able to tell if you're lying. First, do you make a habit of peeping at girls, or was it just that the game we were playing was too much for your dirty little mind?'

Daniel hesitated, torn between the need to cover up his behaviour and the need to confess. So far Olivia had only used her power over him to amuse herself, but he suspected that if he told her the full truth she might turn him in. There was plenty to confess anyway.

'I – I peep at girls,' he said.

The whip flicked out, catching his thigh to add one more to his collection of smarts and bruises.

'I'm sorry! I'm sorry!' he spluttered. 'I know it's wrong, but I can't help it, I really can't. Just to see a girl, in jeans, or anything, it's too much for me, it's just too much . . .'

'Stop blathering,' Olivia interrupted him. 'That was for failing to address me properly. Your punishment for peeping is going to be far worse, and far longer, believe me.'

'Yes, Mistress,' Daniel answered.

'So you peep at girls?' she went on. 'That's going to have to stop. You need to learn some respect for women, Daniel, and you also need to learn your place. A man like you shouldn't even dare to think about girls in that way, but only how he can serve, never in terms of his own pleasure. Is that understood?'

'Yes, Mistress.'

'I doubt you meant that.'

Daniel winced at being caught out.

Olivia chuckled, then spoke again. 'You see, Daniel, I understand you. I understand you better than you understand yourself. You feel bad about what you do, don't you?'

'Yes, Mistress.'

'But underneath all that dirty behaviour you recognise women as your superiors, don't you?'

'Yes, Mistress,' Daniel answered, no longer sure, but eager to please and to avoid her whip.

'In fact, you worship women, don't you?' she went on. 'You feel we're untouchable, don't you? Let me dig into your foul little mind for you. When you wank, you imagine being a slave to a woman, don't you? You imagine one of those ethereal creatures you stare at taking you in hand and using you for her amusement, don't you?'

'Yes, Mistress,' he quavered.

'Yet you do not respect women,' she went on. 'You see us as objects. Objects of adoration, but still objects. Well, I'm going to teach you respect, Daniel, proper respect, so that by the time I've finished with you you'll know better than to let your dirty little eyes feast on our bodies.'

'Yes, Mistress,' Daniel replied, fighting to keep the doubt from his voice.

'You don't think I can do it, do you?' she said immediately. 'Tell the truth.'

'Um . . .' Daniel began with a worried backward glance for her whip. 'I don't know . . . I just think it's natural to look at girls, isn't it?'

'Are you an ape?' Olivia demanded.

'Er . . . no.'

'Then learn not to behave like one!' she snapped, and the whip flicked out at the same instant, catching his thigh and drawing out a fresh yelp of pain.

'You need to be civilised,' she went on. 'You need to be taught your proper place. I will do so, and, naturally, as your teacher I expect my efforts to be recompensed.'

'I'll do anything you say, Mistress,' Daniel answered as a sudden wild vision of being made to lick her cunt rose up in his brain. 'Anything.'

'Yes, you will,' she assured him. 'For a start, I feel a reduction in my rent would be appropriate. Shall we say, one hundred per cent?'

'But . . .' Daniel began immediately as his erotic vision collapsed, only to break off with a yelp as her whip caught his skin.

'You are getting a remarkable bargain,' she told him. 'The sort of service I'm offering can cost as much as five hundred pounds an hour.'

'Yes, Mistress, but . . .'

Again the whip snapped out, making him gasp and filling him with frustration.

'Naturally you wouldn't want me to have to tell the others about your disgusting habits?' Olivia queried.

'No, Mistress,' Daniel said miserably.

'Then I suggest you accept my terms,' she said. 'Come, come, isn't it what you want, deep down, to submit yourself to a woman, completely and utterly?'

'Yes, Mistress,' Daniel lied.

'And in doing so, you naturally want to help her in every way possible?' Olivia queried.

'Yes, Mistress,' Daniel answered, and paused, afraid of the whip and telling himself he'd discuss the rent at a better time, also feeling impossibly horny, 'but, Mistress, what about my relief.'

'Disgusting!' Olivia sneered, but she kept the whip back.

'But, Mistress –' Daniel whined.

'Quiet!' She cut him off. 'After each session, if you behave yourself, I may allow you to relieve yourself in your hand. Afterwards, you go back in the cock cage, and I will be keeping the key.'

'But Mistress, wouldn't you . . .' he began once more.

'No,' she interrupted, 'I have no desire to touch your disgusting cock. I only let you show it for the good of your own humiliation, and, just for thinking that, you get another six, you filthy little shit!'

The whip snapped out as she spoke, and again, Daniel jerking and gasping as six fresh cuts were laid across his buttocks and legs. For all the pain his cock was left straining against the inside of the cage once more. Even being permitted to masturbate in front of her, or at the very least in her presence now seemed wonderful. Maybe it was even going to happen, because Olivia had stood up once more, her feet braced apart and her hands on her hips as she looked down on him with utter contempt.

'Still, I suppose . . .' she began, only to stop as the front door banged, followed by a burst of loud laughter, then Andros's voice.

Olivia stayed as she was. Daniel looked up.

'Um, may I shut the door please, Mistress?'

'No,' Olivia answered. 'I think it might do you good for Holly to see you like this?'

'No, please!' Daniel blurted out. 'You said you wouldn't tell anyone! You promised!'

'I said I wouldn't tell anyone about your peeping,' Olivia answered him, 'and I won't, just so long as you do exactly what you're told.'

'But Olivia . . .'

The whip snapped out, catching his hip, and as he rubbed at the new welt she raised a warning finger. 'One more word out of you, worm.'

Daniel went quiet, close to panic as he struggled to think of a way out. Holly and Andros were already on the stairs, laughing together, plainly drunk and also amorous.

'Holly!' Olivia called out. 'Come and see what I've got.'

Daniel shut his eyes, his entire body trembling violently as he cringed down on to the floor in unbearable embarrassment, which grew even worse as he heard Holly's voice.

'What is it? Fucking Hell! What are you doing, Olivia!'

'Just dishing out a bit of discipline,' Olivia answered coolly as she placed one booted foot on Daniel's back.

He bit his lip in an agony of emotion, close to tears, and closer still as another voice sounded, male.

'Shit! That's your landlord, ain't it?'

'Yes,' Olivia answered.

'I always thought he was a bit ...' Andros answered, and trailed off.

Holly was giggling, full of drunken amusement at Daniel's plight and her boyfriend's open disgust.

'What's he got that nightie thing on for?' Andros demanded. 'Is he some sort of poof or something?'

'He's a pervert, that's what he is,' Holly put in. 'I always thought he was like that.'

'Yeah but, wearing girl's knickers?' Andros queried. 'And letting himself get a whipping?'

'Pervert, poof, whatever,' Holly answered. 'Let's watch.'

'Watch?' Andros queried, his revulsion greater than ever.

'Yeah,' Holly insisted. 'Come on, Olivia, give him some good ones. Then I want a go.'

'But ...' Daniel began.

'Shut up!' Olivia interrupted him, 'Or else. Now you heard the lady, she wants to watch me whip you, only I think I'll make it a spanking. Over my knee, now!'

Daniel stayed as he was, unable to react for his appalling shame. Olivia responded with a derisive tut and reached down to pull him to his feet. Unable to resist, he allowed himself to be dragged upright, now facing Holly and Andros where they'd sat down on his bed.

'What the fuck is that!?' Andros demanded as Holly burst into fresh giggles. 'And look, he's getting a fucking stiffy! He likes it, he fucking likes it!'

'Of course he likes it.' Olivia laughed. 'Now come on, worm, over Mistress Olivia's knee with you.'

Daniel was whimpering pitifully as he was dragged into place, across Olivia's knee with his bottom towards the bed, the ridiculous baby-doll panties still down behind to show the cock cage and his bulging genitals within. Holly laughed, Andros gave a grunt of disgust, then another as Olivia began to spank.

'You ain't no kind of man!' he sneered.

'Not like you,' Holly said happily. 'Go on, Olivia, spank him! You don't mind if I have a go, do you Andros?'

'What's to mind?' Andros queried. 'It's not like I have to watch my back with him, is it? What a poof!'

Dizzy with pain and shame, Daniel could only lie across Olivia's knees and take it as he was spanked. Andros's words and Holly's laughter burnt into his head, yet he dared not speak up for himself, and was desperately trying to tell himself he wasn't enjoying what was being done to him. His cock gave his efforts the lie, bulging in its cage and jerking every time Olivia's hand landed on his bottom, showing exactly how he felt deep down and so bringing his misery higher still. He couldn't stop himself gasping and kicking to the pain either, and still Olivia spanked, peppering his bottom with hard slaps until it felt hot all over, when finally Holly spoke again.

'Come on, Olivia,' she urged, 'it's my go!'

The spanking stopped.

'Very well,' Olivia said. 'Get over Holly's knee, worm.'

Daniel got up, hardly able to stand, his vision blurred and his hands shaking. As he turned he found Holly looking up at him, her face full of amusement and disdain, also Andros, who showed only disgust. Daniel quickly lowered his eyes, and as Holly moved forward on the bed to make a lap he got down into spanking position. She was laughing as she took hold of him around the waist, and began to spank immediately, harder and less accurately than Olivia, to draw yelps of pain from his lips and set his legs kicking on the instant.

'What a laugh!' Holly crowed, spanking harder still. 'Yeah, look at the colour of his arse! Do you reckon we can make him do stuff, Olivia, like wash the dishes in his baby-doll and that?'

'He'll do anything he's told,' Olivia answered. 'You heard that, didn't you, worm? You're to obey Mistress Holly as well.'

Daniel didn't even attempt to answer, too lost in his private world of shame and desperate erotic need. For all the degradation of his situation it was far more intimate than anything he'd ever experienced before, filling him with a truly pathetic gratitude as well as arousal so powerful he was sure that if Holly just kept on spanking he'd spunk up in his cock cage, even though he couldn't get erect. At last she slowed down, but kept him firmly in place across her knee, applying only the occasional firm swat to his buttocks as she spoke again.

'What else can we do with him?'

'Many things,' Olivia responded. 'What would amuse you?'

227

'I don't know,' Holly said, 'the sort of things blokes like to do to girls ... I know, let's make him suck Andros's cock, yeah?'

'What!?' Andros demanded.

'You always say it's the one doing the sucking who's the poof,' Holly responded. 'Go on, I want to see him with your prick in his mouth. I've always wanted to make a john suck cock.'

'No,' Daniel managed, 'I beg you, Mistress, not that ... I'll do anything, but not –'

'Shut up, worm.' Olivia cut him off. 'You'll do as you're told, and if Mistress Holly wants to see you suck cock, then you'll suck cock.'

'But I'm not gay!' Daniel pleaded.

'All the better,' Olivia went on, 'because that way it will be even more humiliating for you.'

'Come on, Andros, get it out,' Holly urged.

Andros hesitated, but he was grinning. Daniel began to struggle, mumbling incoherent pleas and wriggling on Holly's lap, but there was no real fight in him. For all the horror of what they were suggesting he knew he couldn't stop himself. Every last jot of his self-respect was gone, the strain in his cock and the heat in his bottom blending with the sheer power of Olivia and Holly to leave him helpless.

Out came Andros's cock, thick and dark and meaty.

'You're big,' Olivia said admiringly.

'He's lovely,' Holly agreed. 'You ought to be privileged to suck a cock like this, Daniel, a real man's cock. Tell you want, I'll spank you while you suck him. I bet you'll like that?'

As she spoke she'd taken hold, hefting Andros's shaft in her hand to show off the size and thickness. Daniel could only stare in horror, barely able to take in the fact that he was going to be made to put the awful thing in his mouth and suck, suck another man's cock while his bottom was smacked. It was too much, but he was going to do it, and as Andros slid forwards on the bed a horrible realisation hit him. He wanted to do it.

Still he kept his mouth shut, desperately shaking his head as Holly tightened her grip on his waist and began to spank once more. Olivia reached out, taking him by the hair and forcing his face against the rubbery mass of Andros's genitals, to set him whimpering with emotion.

'Suck it!' Olivia ordered.

'No, I beg you, Olivia, I'll do anything!' he babbled, trying frantically to keep his face away from the cock and balls beneath him.

'You will,' she told him. 'You'll suck cock, and you'll suck it now!'

Again his face was forced down, his nose and mouth rubbing in Andros's pubic hair and on the thick cock shaft. Holly was spanking hard and fast, making it impossible to concentrate, and ever more difficult to deny the awful urge rising up inside him.

'Suck him, worm!' Olivia shouted. 'Or else!'

Daniel thought of the hold she had over him, and he had his excuse. With a final despairing sob he had opened his mouth, to allow Andros to feed in his cock, filling Daniel's mouth with the taste of man, and he had began to suck. Both girls and Andros burst out laughing to see Daniel with his mouth full of cock, and something deep inside him seemed to snap. He began to mouth urgently on the thick shaft already swelling up between his lips, drawing more laughter from the girls and a grunt of derision from Andros.

'Yay! We have one brand-new cock sucker!' Holly called in delight. 'That's right, suck him well, you dirty little boy!'

'I told you he was a poof,' Andros sighed.

Daniel shut his eyes, utterly overcome. Holly started to spank again as he began to move his head up and down on Andros's rapidly stiffening shaft. Holly was right. He was a cock sucker. It was all he was fit for, to suck another man's cock as he was spanked by a woman. To be handcuffed, to be in the baby-doll with the knickers pulled down, all of it was completely appropriate.

Soon Andros was stiff, his erection a tower of cock meat extending from his open fly into Daniel's mouth. The girls had gone quiet, both watching in fascination as he sucked, the only sounds the smack of Holly's hand on his bottom, his slurping noises and, after a while, Andros's sighs of pleasure. Both girls were excited, that much was obvious, if not as excited as Daniel, or Andros, who was about to spunk.

'Do it in his face,' Holly breathed. 'I want to see you do it in his face, Andros.'

Daniel swallowed on the fat cock head now half blocking his throat, the tears squeezing from his eyes at the thought of the final humiliation about to be inflicted on him. Still he sucked, more urgently than before, taking Andros's cock as deep as he could in imitation of girls he'd seen in pornography. He was going to get it in his face, and swallow some too, deliberately degrading himself in front of them, and as Andros grunted and whipped his cock free, Daniel had opened his mouth.

Holly gave a delighted gasp as she saw her boyfriend's cock erupt, full in Daniel's face, to splash his cheek and one eye, then fill his mouth and soil his chin before he'd pushed his head back on to Andros's erection, sucking and swallowing over and over in dirty, abandoned arousal.

Andros let it happen, but only briefly, pushing Daniel away in disgust the instant he'd got control of himself. Holly was laughing and began to spank harder than ever, calling Daniel a male tart and a pig as her hand slapped over and over on his blazing bottom. It no longer hurt, both her words and her smacks bringing him only pleasure. All that remained was his own orgasm, so he could show them how utterly low he was.

'Please, Mistresses,' he gasped, 'let me wank . . . let me wank my cock.'

Holly only tightened her grip, but Olivia nodded.

'Let the little cock sucker go, Holly.'

Holly released her grip and Daniel tumbled to the floor. Olivia undid his handcuffs and casually tossed the key to the cock cage down at his feet. After a moment of frantic fumbling he'd got it open. His cock sprang out, swelling even before he'd taken it in hand and he was wanking with fevered urgency. Both girls were staring, Olivia cool but plainly excited, Holly laughing at him as his cock bobbed in his hand. He imagined how he must look to her, naked but for his pink nylon baby-doll, his bottom spanked pink, his face clotted with her boyfriend's spunk.

He wasn't even fully hard but already he was beginning to come, with the ordeal he'd been put through raging in his head, now he'd been made Olivia's slave, stripped and whipped, dressed as a girl and spanked, but, best of all, made to suck a real man's cock all the way to orgasm. His mouth came wide as the orgasm hit him, showing off the spunk on his tongue to evoke squeals of delight and disgust from Holly. Come erupted from his own cock, spurting high to soil his belly and run down his hand as he jerked himself to the most ecstatic of peaks over his own degradation.

'What a fucking pansy!' Andros sneered, and Daniel found himself nodding in mute agreement.

'Come on, Holly,' Andros went on, getting up. 'That was a laugh, but he makes me feel dirty.'

Holly made as if to protest, but seemed to think better of it and followed Andros from the room, leaving Daniel still kneeling on the floor with Olivia looking down on him. She went to close the door before speaking to him.

'You see, Daniel,' she said, 'you needed that, didn't you?'

Daniel felt far too confused to know what he did or did not need, but nodded his head anyway.

'So there'll be no more peeping, will there?' she demanded.

He shook his head.

'Say it,' she ordered.

'There'll be no more peeping, Mistress, I promise,' he said, hanging his head.

'Good boy,' she answered him, 'and to make sure you stay on the straight and narrow I guarantee to give you at least one good session a weak, in return for your letting me off my rent. Maybe if you're a very good boy I'll even do it topless, or masturbate you myself, but what I say goes, always. Is that understood?'

'Yes, Mistress,' he answered.

'Good,' she said. 'Now stand up and turn to face the wall, with your hands on your head.'

Daniel obeyed, throwing a curious glance back to Olivia. She came close, to run one long fingernail down the length of his spine, before retrieving his discarded underpants and pulling them down over his head to leave him blind. He stayed as he was, listening to the faint creak of springs as she sat down on the bed.

'Stay exactly as you are until I tell you otherwise,' she said 'This is not for you to see.'

'Yes, Mistress,' Daniel promised, and as he caught the soft purr of a zip being pulled down he realised that she was going to masturbate.

A shiver of excitement ran through him, his cock twitching despite his recent orgasm. By the sound of it she'd pulled her shorts down and opened her top, which meant her breasts and pussy were bare with him in the room, an intimacy no woman had ever allowed him, even if he was not permitted to see.

After a while she spoke. 'You know what I'm doing, don't you, Daniel? That's right. I'm playing with myself. I'm touching my breasts now. My nipples are erect now, Daniel. I bet you'd like to see that, wouldn't you?'

'Yes,' Daniel managed.

'Well, you can't,' she replied, her voice now hoarse with pleasure. 'Not now, and not ever unless you're a very, very good boy. That's how it's going to be, Daniel. I'm going to spank you, Daniel, and make you suck other men off, and tie you, and whip you, and make you dress in girls' clothes, but, for you, seeing my body will be the highest privilege, the very highest . . .'

She broke off with a sigh, then gave a little gasp and he realised she was coming. He held his pose, thinking of all the delicious intimacies he could hope for if her served her well, and determined to be the ideal slave for her. Again she gasped, and he had to force himself to stay still, but managed, absolutely still until at last she spoke again.

'Ah, yes, I can see we're going to get along very well, you and I.'

Daniel nodded.

'And no more peeping, ever,' she went on.

'No, Mistress,' he promised.

'Good boy,' she responded. 'You've rather found yourself today, haven't you?'

'Yes, Mistress,' Daniel admitted.

Epilogue

Daniel stood at the kitchen sink, washing dishes. He was dressed in his baby-doll and a pinny, his cock cage and nothing else, the costume Olivia considered appropriate for him to do the housework in. All four girls now knew, and, while Katie reacted with utter disgust and Paige simply didn't understand, both accepted the situation and were more than happy to make use of his services as housemaid. At least, they knew he was Olivia's slave. Only she knew the truth, and by no means all of that. He had dismantled the camera system, terrified of full discovery, but what he was getting more than made up for the loss.

Every week Olivia would call him into her room at some conveniently private moment and put him through his paces. He would be made to strip, if he was not already naked or in his baby-doll. He would be dominated in a variety of ways, licking her boots or serving as a table or footstool, perhaps cleaning her room. He would be spanked, invariably on his bare bottom, maybe given a dose of her hairbrush or even a whipping if she felt it appropriate. When she was satisfied he would be allowed to masturbate, usually with a bag over his head while she did the same. Sometimes she would go topless for him, showing off her glorious breasts while he tugged at his shaft, or even take him in hand herself.

And Holly also used him, and for yet more intimate services. It turned out that Andros felt it unmanly to lick her sex, and so Daniel was made to do it instead. Generally he would be blindfolded and his hands tied behind his back, but that did nothing to reduce his pleasure in the act. Andros knew nothing of the arrangement, but had twice had Daniel suck his cock.

Never had he imagined he could live in such a state of constant sexual ecstasy. He no longer even felt frustrated, despite Olivia's careful control of his cock cage, and even his feelings of guilt and shame were far weaker than they had once been. After all, how could a man who regularly sucked another man's cock feel shame for lesser things?

With the washing-up finished, he was smiling to himself as he went upstairs. His next task was to do the shopping, and while he was obliged to keep his baby-doll knickers on he was otherwise allowed to dress normally. In his bedroom, on the back of the door, were the rules by which he now lived, with his signature at the bottom. Olivia had made them out, outlining in detail how he should behave with suitable respect towards all women and what amounted to worship for her. Rule 3 stated categorically that he was never to view any woman as a sexual object, and as his eyes flicked over it he smiled for the memory of his old life.

Dressed, he collected his shopping lists and some money from Katie, who as usual barely acknowledged his existence. She was now in a full-blown lesbian relationship with Paige, and clearly regarded him as beneath contempt, which only served to fuel his sexual pleasure. Even when he was locked in his room while the four of them played dice it was not so bad, as Olivia or Holly generally used him afterwards.

Outside, the weather was crisp and bright, with the last traces of frost still clinging to the ground in shady spots. Daniel began to whistle as he walked down Myrtle Road, happier than he had been at any time in his life. Holly passed him coming the other way just before he reached the corner, and he greeted her with a respectful inclination of his head. For a while, he found himself walking behind a fashionable young woman in a short leather coat, but he tried to ignore the bob of her well-turned bottom cheeks where they showed beneath the hem, telling himself he no longer needed such mild entertainment.

In the park, the little boating lake was still frozen and two of the cutest little poppets he had seen in a long time were skating, both in tights beneath short skirts which rose as they slid and whirled, displaying white full-cut panties just visible beneath the brown material, a sight too delightful to be ignored. In the supermarket he got a yet more exquisite treat, passing the loo door just as it swung closed to catch a brief but perfect glimpse of an absolute little darling adjusting tight yellow panties around her pink puppy-fat bottom.

The image lingered as he did his shopping, and he imagined how it would feel to ease down those same pretty knickers and lay her beautiful bottom bare, first to spank it, and then to kiss it better, before inserting his erect cock into the tight dirty hole hidden deep in her slit. It was a filthy fantasy, and completely against the rules, but as he was going to be beaten anyway he could indulge it to his heart's content without so much as a trace of guilt.

nexus

The leading publisher of fetish and adult fiction

TELL US WHAT YOU THINK!

Readers' ideas and opinions matter to us so please take a few minutes to fill in the questionnaire below.

1. Sex: Are you male ☐ female ☐ a couple ☐?

2. Age: Under 21 ☐ 21–30 ☐ 31–40 ☐ 41–50 ☐ 51–60 ☐ over 60 ☐

3. Where do you buy your Nexus books from?
☐ A chain book shop. If so, which one(s)?

_____

☐ An independent book shop. If so, which one(s)?

_____

☐ A used book shop/charity shop
☐ Online book store. If so, which one(s)?

_____

4. How did you find out about Nexus books?
☐ Browsing in a book shop
☐ A review in a magazine
☐ Online
☐ Recommendation
☐ Other _____

5. In terms of settings, which do you prefer? (Tick as many as you like.)
☐ Down to earth and as realistic as possible
☐ Historical settings. If so, which period do you prefer?

_____

☐ Fantasy settings – barbarian worlds
☐ Completely escapist/surreal fantasy
☐ Institutional or secret academy

☐ Futuristic/sci fi
☐ Escapist but still believable
☐ Any settings you dislike?

_____

☐ Where would you like to see an adult novel set?

_____

6. In terms of storylines, would you prefer:

☐ Simple stories that concentrate on adult interests?
☐ More plot and character-driven stories with less explicit adult activity?
☐ We value your ideas, so give us your opinion of this book:

_____

_____

_____

7. In terms of your adult interests, what do you like to read about? (Tick as many as you like.)

☐ Traditional corporal punishment (CP)
☐ Modern corporal punishment
☐ Spanking
☐ Restraint/bondage
☐ Rope bondage
☐ Latex/rubber
☐ Leather
☐ Female domination and male submission
☐ Female domination and female submission
☐ Male domination and female submission
☐ Willing captivity
☐ Uniforms
☐ Lingerie/underwear/hosiery/footwear (boots and high heels)
☐ Sex rituals
☐ Vanilla sex
☐ Swinging
☐ Cross-dressing/TV
☐ Enforced feminisation

☐ Others – tell us what you don't see enough of in adult fiction:

_____

_____

_____

8. Would you prefer books with a more specialised approach to your interests, i.e. a novel specifically about uniforms? If so, which subject(s) would you like to read a Nexus novel about?

_____

_____

_____

9. Would you like to read true stories in Nexus books? For instance, the true story of a submissive woman, or a male slave? Tell us which true revelations you would most like to read about:

_____

_____

_____

10. What do you like best about Nexus books?

_____

_____

11. What do you like least about Nexus books?

_____

_____

12. Which are your favourite titles?

_____

_____

13. Who are your favourite authors?

_____

_____

14. Which covers do you prefer? Those featuring:
(Tick as many as you like.)

- ☐ Fetish outfits
- ☐ More nudity
- ☐ Two models
- ☐ Unusual models or settings
- ☐ Classic erotic photography
- ☐ More contemporary images and poses
- ☐ A blank/non-erotic cover
- ☐ What would your ideal cover look like?

_____

15. **Describe your ideal Nexus novel in the space provided:**

_____

_____

_____

_____

16. **Which celebrity would feature in one of your Nexus-style fantasies? We'll post the best suggestions on our website – anonymously!**

_____

THANKS FOR YOUR TIME

Now simply write the title of this book in the space below and cut out the questionnaire pages. Post to: Nexus, Marketing Dept., Thames Wharf Studios, Rainville Rd, London W6 9HA

Book title: _____

NEXUS NEW BOOKS

To be published in August 2007

SWEET AS SIN
Felix Baron

Trixie, a widow, was petite, curvaceous, wealthy and sexually adventurous. Rolf, a widower, was tall, good-looking, even wealthier than Trixie and had been celibate for far too long. His son and Trixie's daughter made a handsome couple. Both relationships seemed to have been made in heaven, except that Rolf lusted after the daughter as much as he did the mother. Penny, he discovered, only looked pure. Beneath her innocent exterior, she was ten times as kinky as her mother. Penny was sweet, all right – *as sweet as sin*.

£6.99   ISBN 978 0 352 34134 1

A TALENT FOR SURRENDER
Madeline Bastinado

Jo Lennox is a woman with a secret. By day she is headmistress of an exclusive private school: by night, a sexual adventurer who loves to dominate and humiliate men. Dan Elliot is a documentary film-maker who uses his looks and charm to persuade his subjects to expose their secrets. When their paths cross, Dan realises how much he has to learn about his own nature and his hidden desires. He becomes her willing pupil, eager to obey and hungry for experience. And Jo assumes the role of his teacher and guide, providing punishment, pleasure and the perverse by initiating him into a world of darkness and extreme submission.

£6.99   ISBN 978 0 352 34135 8

If you would like more information about Nexus titles, please visit our website at www.nexus-books.com, or send a large stamped addressed envelope to:
Nexus, Thames Wharf Studios,
Rainville Road, London W6 9HA

NEXUS BOOKLIST

Information is correct at time of printing. To avoid disappointment, check availability before ordering. Go to www.nexus-books.com.

All books are priced at £6.99 unless another price is given.

NEXUS

☐ ABANDONED ALICE	Adriana Arden	ISBN 978 0 352 33969 0
☐ ALICE IN CHAINS	Adriana Arden	ISBN 978 0 352 33908 9
☐ AQUA DOMINATION	William Doughty	ISBN 978 0 352 34020 7
☐ THE ART OF CORRECTION	Tara Black	ISBN 978 0 352 33895 2
☐ THE ART OF SURRENDER	Madeline Bastinado	ISBN 978 0 352 34013 9
☐ BEASTLY BEHAVIOUR	Aishling Morgan	ISBN 978 0 352 34095 5
☐ BEHIND THE CURTAIN	Primula Bond	ISBN 978 0 352 34111 2
☐ BEING A GIRL	Chloë Thurlow	ISBN 978 0 352 34139 6
☐ BELINDA BARES UP	Yolanda Celbridge	ISBN 978 0 352 33926 3
☐ BENCH-MARKS	Tara Black	ISBN 978 0 352 33797 9
☐ BIDDING TO SIN	Rosita Varón	ISBN 978 0 352 34063 4
☐ BINDING PROMISES	G.C. Scott	ISBN 978 0 352 34014 6
☐ THE BOOK OF PUNISHMENT	Cat Scarlett	ISBN 978 0 352 33975 1
☐ BRUSH STROKES	Penny Birch	ISBN 978 0 352 34072 6
☐ BUTTER WOULDN'T MELT	Penny Birch	ISBN 978 0 352 34120 4
☐ CALLED TO THE WILD	Angel Blake	ISBN 978 0 352 34067 2
☐ CAPTIVES OF CHEYNER CLOSE	Adriana Arden	ISBN 978 0 352 34028 3
☐ CARNAL POSSESSION	Yvonne Strickland	ISBN 978 0 352 34062 7
☐ CITY MAID	Amelia Evangeline	ISBN 978 0 352 34096 2
☐ COLLEGE GIRLS	Cat Scarlett	ISBN 978 0 352 33942 3

NEXUS CLASSIC

□ EMMA ENSLAVED	Hilary James	ISBN 978 0 352 33883 9
□ EMMA'S HUMILIATION	Hilary James	ISBN 978 0 352 33910 2
□ EMMA'S SECRET DOMINATION	Hilary James	ISBN 978 0 352 34000 9
□ EMMA'S SUBMISSION	Hilary James	ISBN 978 0 352 33906 5
□ FAIRGROUND ATTRACTION	Lisette Ashton	ISBN 978 0 352 33927 0
□ IN FOR A PENNY	Penny Birch	ISBN 978 0 352 34083 2
□ THE INSTITUTE	Maria Del Rey	ISBN 978 0 352 33352 0
□ NEW EROTICA 5	Various	ISBN 978 0 352 33956 0
□ THE NEXUS LETTERS	Various	ISBN 978 0 352 33955 3
□ PLAYTHING	Penny Birch	ISBN 978 0 352 33967 6
□ PLEASING THEM	William Doughty	ISBN 978 0 352 34015 3
□ RITES OF OBEDIENCE	Lindsay Gordon	ISBN 978 0 352 34005 4
□ SERVING TIME	Sarah Veitch	ISBN 978 0 352 33509 8
□ THE SUBMISSION GALLERY	Lindsay Gordon	ISBN 978 0 352 34026 9
□ TIE AND TEASE	Penny Birch	ISBN 978 0 352 33987 4
□ TIGHT WHITE COTTON	Penny Birch	ISBN 978 0 352 33970 6

NEXUS CONFESSIONS

| □ NEXUS CONFESSIONS: VOLUME ONE | Ed. Lindsay Gordon | ISBN 978 0 352 34093 1 |

NEXUS ENTHUSIAST

□ BUSTY	Tom King	ISBN 978 0 352 34032 0
□ CUCKOLD	Amber Leigh	ISBN 978 0 352 34140 2
□ DERRIÈRE	Julius Culdrose	ISBN 978 0 352 34024 5
□ ENTHRALLED	Lance Porter	ISBN 978 0 352 34108 2
□ LEG LOVER	L.G. Denier	ISBN 978 0 352 34016 0
□ OVER THE KNEE	Fiona Locke	ISBN 978 0 352 34079 5
□ RUBBER GIRL	William Doughty	ISBN 978 0 352 34087 0
□ THE SECRET SELF	Christina Shelly	ISBN 978 0 352 34069 6
□ UNDER MY MASTER'S WINGS	Lauren Wissot	ISBN 978 0 352 34042 9
□ THE UPSKIRT EXHIBITIONIST	Ray Gordon	ISBN 978 0 352 34122 8

--------- ✂ ----------------------------

Please send me the books I have ticked above.

Name ....

Address ....

....

....

.... Post code ....

Send to: **Virgin Books Cash Sales, Thames Wharf Studios, Rainville Road, London W6 9HA**

US customers: for prices and details of how to order books for delivery by mail, call 888-330-8477.

Please enclose a cheque or postal order, made payable to **Nexus Books Ltd**, to the value of the books you have ordered plus postage and packing costs as follows:

UK and BFPO – £1.00 for the first book, 50p for each subsequent book.

Overseas (including Republic of Ireland) – £2.00 for the first book, £1.00 for each subsequent book.

If you would prefer to pay by VISA, ACCESS/MASTERCARD, AMEX, DINERS CLUB or SWITCH, please write your card number and expiry date here:

....

Please allow up to 28 days for delivery.

Signature ....

Our privacy policy

We will not disclose information you supply us to any other parties. We will not disclose any information which identifies you personally to any person without your express consent.

From time to time we may send out information about Nexus books and special offers. Please tick here if you do *not* wish to receive Nexus information.   ☐

--------- ✂ ----------------------------